THE RETURN

STORY OF KUNTI

THE RETURN

STORY OF KUNTI

NARENDRA KOHLI

Vani Book Company

Vani Book Company

Head Office

4695, 21-A, Daryaganj, New Delhi 110 002, India
Phone +91 11 23273167 **Fax** : +91 11 23275710

Registered Book Stores and Offices

Ashok Rajpath, Patna 800 004, Bihar
Coffee House Campus, Mahatma Gandhi Marg, Allahabad 211 001, Uttar Pradesh
Mahatma Gandhi International Hindi University, Wardha 442 001, Maharashtra
Sultania Road, Motiya Park, Bhopal 462 001, Madhya Pradesh
Goripur Taliya Para, 313, R.B.C. Road 24- Parganas (North) Kolkata 743 166, West Bengal

www.vaniprakashan.in
marketing@vaniprakashan.in
sales@vaniprakashan.in

THE RETURN
Story of Kunti : *Mahasamar-II*
by Narendra Kohli

ISBN : 978-93-88684-72-9
Fiction / Novel

Translation of *Mahasamar* Part II, first published by Vani Prakashan in 1990
by Bhupinder Singh
Edited by Dr. Urvashi Vasishtha

First Edition 2019
Price : ₹ 399
$ 16.99
£ 8

Printed at City Press, Delhi - 110 095 (India)

Vani Prakashan's signature motif is created by Artist Maqbool Fida Husain

1

Evening. Kunti worried about Yudhishthir, pensive indoors while the others played out in the park. "Why don't you run along with your brothers, Yudhishthir? Old man indoors?" she teased him gently.

She was relieved to see that he fired up enough at once to say, "I go out! I go to Achary, I practice all the weapons, I learn everything!"

"But right now you're sitting here alone! Don't you want to play with the others?"

Yudhishthir hung his head. Stole a quick look at her, so world-weary and helpless she was alarmed.

"What is it?" she asked him softly. Kunti would never get used to this – indomitable as she was, almost dismissive of her own distress, her sons' childish miseries, Yudhishthir's silent sorrows, always felt like a fresh wound.

"Nothing important, Ma."

"What's nothing?" Kunti took his face in her hands till he raised his reluctant gaze. "You have to always, always tell the truth, son. Even if it is ugly. No matter whom it hurts. A lie is never the solution; it is an insult. If a pigeon shuts its eyes the cat does not cease to exist."

"I'm not a liar, Ma!"

"I know. If I thought I could not trust my sons I would no longer know what to do with myself!" Kunti smoothed his cheeks and withdrew her hands. "So tell me – what is this nothing that's the matter?"

"I did not say nothing was the matter," Yuddhidhthir persisted, "I said it was nothing important!" Suddenly the dam burst, and her son's woes came tumbling out in a rush. "Suyodhan says the palace park is for his and his brothers' use. His father has been charitable enough to let us stay, but that doesn't mean we can roam about like we own the place… We need to acknowledge our station." He was looking at her earnestly. "You tell me – is that worth repeating? Is it anything important?"

Kunti could not speak. The indignity her child had tried to spare her – at what cost?

`He had taken her hands in his. "When do we move to our own home, Ma?"

"What home, child?" She knew not which home to call her own. Her progenitor's? Her father's? Her husband's? Was no place her's, her own?

Yudhishthir spoke with unwonted vehemence now. "We were better off in Rishi Shring's ashram, where no one ever said anything 'was not ours'. No one said the hut was not ours, the land was not ours, the river was not ours. Why did you bring us to Hastinapur, where nothing is ours?"

Kunti was shaken out of her stupor. Yuddhushthir had no concept of his inheritance whatsoever. He could not fight for a thing he did not realize he was entitled to – he was not the sort even to seize a disputed prize. He must believe in his prerogative, he must.

"This is our home, son. We are not moving out." She was at once authoritative. "Hastinapur belongs to you. You are the crown prince of the Kuru empire. What do you mean, 'our own home'?"

Yudhishthir was silent, his attention remote. Kunti could not fathom what effect her pronouncement had on him at all.

The next moment, "If Hastinapur is ours," he said reasonably, "why don't we make ourselves a new palace? Why do we stay at Suyodhan's? They don't like us here. They are short of space. They must feel terribly inconvenienced, Ma."

Kunti wanted to take this conscientious, high-minded, ardently generous child of hers into her arms and kiss his kingly forehead.

Instead, she straightened her back and said, "This is the royal palace of Hastinapur, where the king dwells, where I resided with your father before we left for tapasya and which you must occupy as heir apparent. The crown prince cannot live elsewhere. The future king cannot abdicate his place of residence."

"I see that, Ma, but King Dhritrashtr lives here. All this fuss for a palace?"

"I am not talking about a palace!" said Kunti. "I'm not tempting you to grab a hunk of stone and mortar, I'm trying to teach you to strive for your right! Your pitrivy is not king, he is warden of the state. Your father was king; you will be king."

All Yudhishthir could think was that none of this mattered in the present. Clearly it was not as though they had nowhere to go, nowhere else to live; what exactly would they be fighting for? But Kunti had not finished. "Does Kripachary discriminate while teaching you? How does he behave?"

What should he say? "Well… No…" Yudhishthir did not seem able to make up his mind. "I don't think he has anything against me." His brow cleared. "But he is nothing like Rishi Shring's acharys, nothing."

"I understand," Kunti said softly. "Go and play outside, son – it is not healthy to sit indoors all day."

Her son obeyed, dragging his feet.

Yudhishthir's exit coincided with the dashing entry of

Bhim, soaked in sweat. He never bored or had enough or tired of physical exertion and play – on the practice ground he was indefatigable and swift and agile as the wind his father. And his capacity for enjoyment was expansive, abundantly generous. Once in Kautuhal Kunti had asked him to stop just as he was racing out. "Bhim, take your brother Nakul for a walk – he has been fretful all day." She thought he would protest, would stamp his feet and refuse. Take a two and half year old brother along! Dragging him down, or back! But Bhim extended his arms toward the crying child and laughed. "Come on, you! Don't be lazy-bones!"

As he turned to go his gaze swept up Sahdev. "You too, little brother, come on," and he lifted his other brother up as well, swinging both of them with such abandon Kunti had to bite her lip to keep from exclaiming, "Put them down!" He, meanwhile, was inviting 'Ajju' to climb up onto his shoulders…

Kunti had learned to not worry about him – stronger, taller than the older Yudhishthir, quick to laughter as he was to rage, he could more than hold his own. But today…

"Does Suyodhan object to your playing in the park?"

"Yes, he does." Bhim was unfazed. "But I dared him to a race. And I ran, Ma, as fast as the wind!"

Kunti could imagine. "Then?"

"Well, Suyodhan has a lot of brothers. He snapped his fingers and the whole lot of them made a sort of chain to try and obstruct me. I ran past them, dragged a couple of them along and banged their heads together. That was enough. They did not chase me any further. No prompting from Suyodhan could encourage them." Bhim laughed his heart out.

"And didn't Suyodhan stop you himself?"

"He has no guts, Ma. He is only capable of prodding his brothers."

"Do you play all alone then?"

"No! I have friends! There's Yuyutsu – and he has several mates. Vikarn joins us sometimes. Even if I don't, though, I can do a lot all by myself."

"Such as?"

"I race with the wind to find out who is faster."

"What is your conclusion?"

"I am swifter, yet the wind is able to hit his destination before me. Amazing!"

"What madness!" Kunti laughed. "But the wind is everywhere at once!"

"Oh!" Bhim exclaimed with his loud mischievous laugh, "then it's pointless to compete with the wind!"

"What other games do you have – alone?"

"If I can't think of anything else, I try to move trees, sway them to shower fruit, uproot them."

"Are you able to uproot them?"

"No! But no tree is able to uproot me either!"

"You tomfool! Where are your roots?"

"Tom fool?" Bhim gasped in mock injury. "I choose a game I will never, ever lose, and you call me Tom fool?"

Kunti could only wish through tears of laughter that Bhim would rub off on Yudhishthir. "Who sets the rules?" she demanded, wiping her eyes.

"Me! Who else?"

"But how can each player play by his own rules?"

"Everyone has their own rules for tying their dhoti…"

"What do you mean, rules for tying their dhoti?" Kunti asked, bewildered.

"Suyodhan and his lot insist the respectable dhoti falls four inches from the ankle. I ask you! I tie mine no less than twenty inches up, and they call me vulgar. I call them fools. No one can run, or race, or play with dhotis about their ankles!" He started. "Oh I was on my way to the park! How did you bewilder me, Ma, with all this charming gossip?" And he raced off.

Kunti was shaken like one of her son's trees, to the core. She had never been able to forget the day they stood at Hastinapur's Vardhaman gate, dusty and sore from travel. Young Suyodhan calling the boys 'dirty,' scorning their appearance. He still called Bhim vulgar – what words did he use for Yudhishthir and Arjun? Nakul and Sahdev were still small. Suyodhan thought himself superior to her boys for the regal luxuries of his Hastinapur upbringing, and disdained the manners and devices of the ashram milieu.

Not that long ago Suyodhan had mocked them with such thuggish incivility, passing 'accidentally' this way with his brothers, friends, and attendants.

Yudhishthir, Bhim, and Arjun served themselves, while Kunti fed Nakul and Sahdev.

"Why! They have no maid or servant," someone said derisively.

"No maid or servant!" Suyodhan exclaimed. "If it hadn't been for my over-merciful father, they would be eating from a pattal apiece. What did they have when they came to Hastinapur? The very shirts on their backs had been sent them from our palace. They were paupers, these foresters."

She'd lost several days' sleep over that comment. Was it Suyodhan's own opinion or was he voicing someone else's? And she was amazed as well. Yudhishthir and his brothers would never dream of thinking, much less speaking, in such terms. Reduced circumstances reduced conveniences not worth, or entitlement to esteem. And how in the world could Suyodhan have assumed his father was king? Why did no one tell him 'his' palace and properties belonged to the Kaurav King Pandu, to his heir Yudhishthir? Could Dhritrashtr and Gandhari be oblivious of all their son said, all he did?

One of Gandhari's maids came looking for Bhim. "Where is that fat boy – Bhim?"

The adjective was offensive. The maid seemed not to care. She did not use an honorific to address Kunti either – did not even preface her demand with a commonplace 'arye' or 'bhadre'. Before the samrat's widow and soon to be queen mother a servant from the royal palace did not fail to pay obeisance in ignorance or out of mortal bravado. Whose will did she do by insulting the sometime queen?

"Oh, hello. Are you looking for a fat child? Or for Bhim?"

"Isn't Bhim fat?" the woman asked impudently.

"No…" Kunti said sweetly, "'powerful' despite his imprudent age, which makes him liable to knock ignorant heads that abuse him off ignorant shoulders than obtrude."

This did not have the desired effect. The maid neither paled nor blushed, and went right on speaking. "I know! No one is safe. People will fall like flies, now you people are here."

"Kindly recollect your self and station," Kunti snapped.

"My station! What stations are left intact in Hastinapur, when vagrants are indulged would-be royals?" She stared at Kunti with palpable distaste. "The next time your fat son touches my Sushasan I will break his head for him. Don't say then that I didn't warn you!"

"You're Sushasan's attendant?"

"I was his breast-giver! My milk is his flesh – I will not stand by to see his blood spilled. Don't bask in any illusions about your own or your little clan's glories!" She turned her back and stalked away.

Kunti's distress redoubled. Had Bhim really attacked Sushasan? She execrated the conduct of Gandhari's sons, but she did not want blood shed among brothers. If arguments escalated to violence the burgeoning enmity between 'them' and 'us' would be fixed, final. And then? Defense would surely fall to Bhim alone – Yudhishthir was no fighter, and the other three were too small. How many of Suyodhan's brothers would her champion son defeat, and how many times succeed? And the adults? What this breast-giver dared today, others would attempt tomorrow, and tomorrow, and tomorrow…

Was this her home? Surrounded by adversaries, without her royal husband to legitimize her position, precariously isolated, ought she to secure her sons' persons or their place, their station? Oh why did Bhim fight?

He didn't. Her son, for all his strength, was anything but combative. He barely acknowledged acrimony – everything was a game, an occasion for mischief and play. Like a gust of wind he danced this way and that, entranced by his own capacities and the promise of the physical world. He was as likely to stoop and caress a weed on his way as to crush it – Kunti had never caught the slightest whiff of sour envy or bitter hatred around him and dreaded the day those parasites would push eager roots through his healthful, wholesome being.

He gusted in again, drenched and deliriously out of breath, laughing. "Guess what? Sushasan's smashed his head open!"

"What?"

"He runs like a vole in the underbrush, Ma, it was bound to happen! Looks neither right nor left, up nor ahead – his forehead smashed right into a tree and bled so much you could barely tell he was weeping buckets too!"

Kunti stared at him incredulously.

His brow furrowed uncertainly. "Why are you looking at me like that? Don't you believe me?"

"You didn't hit him?"

"He was after me!"

"Answer my question! Did you hit Sushasan?"

"Sure! I ran ahead of him, doubled back, turned myself into a tree and lowered my arm invitingly for him to smash his idiot head into."

"Why did his attendant come here to quarrel with me about broken heads, and complain about you?"

"Because she could not possibly go to the tree's mother and complain about it!" Bhim was transparently outraged now. "I don't even care about Sushasan, but I definitely will break Kalika's head one of these days. It's always some absurdity or other with her: we've brought a plague of flies upon the palace, or her precious princes haven't milk to drink since we hog it. Thank God the wind and the sun haven't run short yet, and skimped her little lords." Bhim looked at his mother with uncharacteristic shrewdness. "She picks a fight with someone on a daily basis, Ma. With me, with Bhaiya, with you, today."

Well, the royal palace of Hastinapur was neither overrun with pests since its population had increased by six nor running short of provender – so Kalika was simply a belligerent, ill-tempered woman who picked fights with everyone! Of course Yudhishthir had said nothing – he would protect all and sundry from unpleasantness if he could – kinship meant added care. But in usual circumstances such rancor would not find safe haven in the houses of state. Kalika would ordinarily have been whipped raw and tossed out like a rag doll for such expressions of virulence…

Suddenly Kunti thought of Arjun. Where in the world was he? Yudhishtir was quiet but always around; Bhim was so loud and so visible she would hear of him even when he wasn't. But she was never sure what Arjun was up to…

He was sitting under a tree, staring into the void.

"Don't the other boys play with you, Arjun?"

She had startled him badly. "What? No, I've no wish to play with them, Ma."

"Why?"

"They aren't my friends."

"So be friendly with them!"

"But none of them is worth the trouble!" said Arjun

indelicately. "I don't think any of them is trustworthy – one could never be wholly open with them."

"How does Bhim manage?" demanded Kunti.

"Oh, Madhyam… he can play with anyone; he doesn't distinguish between familiarity and mere acquaintance," said Arjun sagely.

"He fosters familiarity, son! That's how you make friends!"

Arjun shrugged. "I don't need loads of friends like he does, Ma. Just the one will do."

For a moment Kunti didn't know what to say. Who did this odd little child of hers think he was? Passing such categorical judgment on the characters of his fellows! "Very well my lord," she said, "what are you sitting here all by yourself and doing?"

"Practicing!"

"Practicing what?"

"Single-mindedness!"

What? Kunti spoke with difficulty. "And why?"

"So I can hit the bullseye."

"What does practicing single-mindedness have to do with hitting bullseyes?"

"Guruji says that before readying your bow, when you are considering your target, absolutely nothing should divert your attention."

"None of your brothers practice single-mindedness like this!" said Kunti. "Doesn't Guruji instruct them to do it too?"

"He does, but none of them wants to be an archer."

"Why not? They all practice archery, learn how to handle the bow, and how to be accurate."

Arjun looked cross. "Shooting arrows is different from being an archer – I want to be an archer!"

"You don't want to be anything else? A king? A commander or a minister? A warrior or a scholar?"

"No, I only want to be an archer, Ma." There was such yearning and determination in his voice Kunti couldn't help smiling.

"Will you win wars as an archer?"

"I don't know – I can't think about all that. Why, what for. I want to be an archer for the archery. Knowledge is its own reward, Guruji says. Don't pursue it as a means to some other end."

Arjun too was unlike his brothers. Yudhidhthir thought deeply, about everyday affairs, responsibility, action, right conduct, and truth. Arjun did not care about definitions of reality. He wanted to define himself.

He was waiting, politely, for her to either continue or leave him to practice single-mindedness in peace.

She bit her lip. "What I came to ask you was whether Sushasan's maid ever says things to you."

"Sushasan's maid! Oh you mean Kalika! She talks like that with everyone, Ma – it's really useful."

Kunti's turn, again, to be astonished: how was the harpy useful?

"When she starts her nonsense, I practice tuning out extrinsic noise. Exactly what you need to do on the battlefield. Guruji says being able to detach at will is key."

Kunti laughed. "You could find pearls even in pigstys, child; I'm delighted. If everyone wanted to be an archer I imagine there would be no need either for them or for battlefields!" She turned to go. "By all means keep practicing! But don't forget to come in and eat!"

Arjun smiled. "I won't."

Vidur came by in the evening.

Kunti knew in times of distress she could turn to and trust only two persons in Hastinapur: Pitrivy Bhishm, and devar Vidur. Pitrivy was an elder, her all-father, Pitamah; she could not speak to him of the daily grind. For that there was only Vidur. Her equal in age and kindred in thought; if she had not had him to talk to she felt she would have gone mad. She could bear a great deal, conceal a lot, stay silent past human endurance, but this insult had locked itself like venom in her throat; she felt blue with breathlessness.

Vidur heard her out, but said nothing at once; what did he think?

"Bhabhi!" he said at last, "I don't think Dhritrashtr or Gandhari sent her to oppugn you, per se – I wouldn't even have thought they would know she had behaved in this manner… But…"

"What?"

"I am equally convinced they make no effort to hide their disdain for you. You have been thrust on them. They make it evident. And if they did hear that you had been insulted they would not consider it an occasion to take disciplinary action of any kind."

"And why?"

Well they have no interest in your comfort here, in Hastinapur. Certainly no interest in esteeming you."

"Why?" Kunti persisted.

Vidur looked at her. "You don't know?"

"I do! But I need someone to say it!"

"Dhritrashtr benefitted from your departure, and Pandu's."

"I can see that!"

"If your sons leave his own progeny will likewise benefit."

"Yes." Kunti's relief at the acknowledgement was palpable.

Vidur waited for a few moments, then said, "I'm afraid this is only the beginning. I suspect such little inconveniences are symptomatic of … machinations. Intrigue. I think you should be careful of your selves."

Kunti's gaze fixed on his face.

Vidur was dark. A broad forehead, beady eyes, bushy brows, hooked, prominent nose, he was not exactly good looking, by any standard. But he exuded sympathy, so that Kunti had felt an instant affinity with her brother in law. He was transparent, eschewed insinuation and innuendo and said it always as he saw it; Kunti had never known him to exaggerate, or to lie in word or deed. If he said he had heard rumour of intrigue, and was warning her to be cautious, she should listen, believe him, and do so.

"Shakuni's sobriquet for Yudhishthir, Bhim, and Arjun is 'Kontey'. He calls Nakul and Sahdev 'Madrey'. When he is talking about the five together, they are 'Pandavs'."

"So?" Kunti's brow furrowed. "It's the truth."

"Dhritrashtr's and Gandhari's sons are not Dhartarashtrs or Gandhares. They are the Kauravs." Vidur looked at her still face. "Do you understand?"

"Yes. That dastard does not accept my sons are Kaurav dynastic heirs."

"And he wants a schism between the Konteys and the Madreys." Vidur nodded.

Kunti felt her heart sink and limbs weaken: how were her guileless sons to thwart such wickedness? They were better off with the worthies of Rishi Shring's ashram. They would not be princes, but they would not be beset – and neither would she.

"I've been observing for a while that Dhritrashtr seems to encourage Shakuni – such language and snide aspersions…" Vidur was saying – he stopped short at the look on Kunti's face. "Please don't be overly concerned. I brought it up because you should know – but the custodian of Hastinapur's crown is not powerful enough to seize the throne in the teeth of Bhishm's will."

"What does Pitrivy think?"

"If Dhritrashtr is Vichitrviry's son, our five are Pandu's."

Kunti breathed a sigh. "It all depends on Pitrivy."

The woman pranamed to Kunti.

Kunti started.

She had stopped expecting courtesy from Hastinapur palace staff.

"What is it?"

"Maharani Gandhari sends remembrances," said her servant. "If it does not inconvenience devi, would she accompany me to the palace? The maharani awaits us."

Kunti smiled inwardly. For Gandhari to become a maharani, Kunti becomes a devi? But it really was not in the least amusing. To Kalika she did not merit an 'arye'.

"Any particular enterprise?"

"The maharani did not suggest anything to me."

"Please wait outside – I am coming."

Kunti was not concerned with her presentation at the palace, but she did need to collect herself. Gandhari had 'remembered' her! Kunti had never had occasion or opportunity to really know Dhritrashtr's wife: Pandu's behavior following their marriage had left her no leisure to forge friendships or kinships or alliances. Pandu began his martial quest soon after – then they left for the forest – by the time Kunti came back to Hastinapur Gandhari was Maharani, and unapproachable. Kunti had no right to 'remember' her.

Well, since she had called, Kunti ought to go. If not quite on an equal plane, they would meet as kin…

"Let's go." Kunti emerged from within.

Kunti pranamed to Gandhari.

Gandhari smiled.

"Kunti! Do come," she said. "I have been waiting a long time to for you to come and meet me – but you never have. Don't you ever feel like seeing me?"

Kunti could not remain impervious to such a display

of affection. She felt her tensed muscles relax a scintilla. "How could you suppose that, Didi!" she spoke warmly. "I have the house to look to… "

"Why? Don't you have servants?"

Kunti stared at Gandhari. Did she not know? Of course Kunti had no servants – if ever Gandhari directed one of hers that way they might deign to come, but otherwise… But how could she know? Kunti thought pityingly. The maharani had blinded herself after her husband. And was flocked by servants attentive to her every wish… How could she imagine Kunti's life in her two bare rooms? She thought her own circumstances were like those of an impoverished distant relation who visits with wealthy kinfolk and has no hope at all of being understood.

"And the children…" she began.

"More children than I have?" Gandhari said with amusement. Kunti thought she saw anger flash across Gandhari's features, and grief.

But the eyes! We grow so used to deciphering our interlocutors' intentions, feeling, real meaning as they speak – we cease to notice it is the eyes that offer up those revelations. Gandhari's secrets were shrouded behind the cloth that bound her eyes closed.

"No – not more – but I never see any of yours around you… Mine cling to my knees."

"I do not permit it. They are being brought up by nurses, governesses – and of course Kripachary."

Kunti recalled Sushasan's breast-giver. "Oh yes, one of them came to quarrel with me the other day."

Gandhari barely reacted. "Yes, she is troublesome." She swatted the Kalika-Kunti altercation from the perfumed room of her attention as one might a stray, insignificant detail. That Kalika might have hurt Kunti, or offended her… "She can't see beyond Sushasan; quarrels with everyone on his account. She's been cosseted too much herself!"

Kunti looked at her, speechless.

"But children - you have only three…"

"I have five sons," Kunti interrupted.

"Two are Madri's." Gandhari snapped.

"No, devi! Now they are mine." Kunti's voice was involuntarily harsh in its turn. "There can be no distinction."

"I had thought," Gandhari returned in her previous tone, "that since you have returned to Hastinapur you will share my burden. I have heard so much about your capacities – the organization of your household. My own husband has but divine sight. I am blind-folded. Our sons are not yet capable. We are compelled to leave it all to servants. The palace would receive very different care under a member of the family."

"But why should my absence have prevented you from calling on that care?" Kunti asked politely. "Vidur and Paransavi have always been here. They could have assisted you?"

It was as though she had committed a faux pas of the first water. It took Gandhari's half-hidden face a long moment to recover its equanimity. When she spoke her voice was sopping with camaraderie. "How is Vidur a member of our family? How can Paransavi be to me what you are? Shall I remember Maryada the maid as I do my mother in law?"

Kunti refused to be shocked by Gandhari's words. "I was always told that mother Ambika regarded Vidur's mother as her sister. Neither Mahamuni Vyas nor Pitrivya Bhishm made any distinction between the three brothers…"

"Mother Ambika belonged to another age," said Gandhari doggedly, disregarding Kunti's resistance. "They respected neither their own stations nor the family's stature. Who can say why any of them were so enamoured of the lower classes. In Gandhar a slave is a slave." She barely paused for breath. "As for Pitrivy, none of us is his progeny, really, why should he bother to make any distinctions? And

Mahamuni is a sanyasi: all of creation is one to him."

Kunti could not help herself. "They are all the sons of his body – Dhritrashtr, Pandu, Vidur."

"But his mother was a slave, na! If we are faced with one father, it is the mother who matters! Suyodhan and Yuyutsu are not equal. Innumerable women serve the king; there is one queen."

Kunti's good sense was pleading with her to refrain from this ugly debate. She could not. "Aryaputr made no distinction between his brothers. Neither can I."

"Pandu paid for his lack of discrimination," said Gandhari mercilessly. "Vidur is a great proselytizer, isn't he. Barely stirs beyond the bounds of the palace walls himself – but was foremost in egging Pandu on to take refuge in renunciation and the forsaken forest. It was he wouldn't let Pandu rest content in Hastinapur."

Kunti wanted to scream she knew who and what had Pandu running ever away from Hastinapur – but what was the point? Even if Gandhari were not actively trying to antagonize Kunti, this was all her blindness, her disquiet and her self-involvement, saw. She was beyond Kunti, who could not change her mind nor accept this perverted version of reality… She changed the subject. "You were giving me directions, so I might assist you."

Gandhari looked peeved, but did not pursue the first. "I have not seen this of course, but I am told those charged with the upkeep of the palace are either incapable or more interested in keeping up with the king. The grandeur of the palace ought to exceed and showcase not diminish the gravitas of the Kuru empire. I should like the work done in accordance with the wishes and under direction of the Queen. Every servant, overseer, and artist will obey you."

Kunti was instantly transported back to Bhojpur. Not only had Maharaj Kuntibhoj's palace been decked at her desire, every lord attendant had been at her command. That life remained a strange refracted memory of her authentic identity. The same aesthetic attributes Gandhari wanted to use had had her hosting Durvasa… and that wound was still fresh, still sore. He was in Hastinapur, somewhere, that child of her youth and innocence. What would he be like? How old now? …

"What do you say, Kunti?"

Gandhari's words stirred her out of her reverie. "As you wish, Didi. As you wish."

Back at home Kunti was in two minds. She was glad that Gandhari was had recognised her as one of the family. She would have the same rights she enjoyed in Bhojpur. She had not had the right Gandhari bestowed upon her even as King Pandu's consort.

But what was there to be glad about, really? The royal palace was in fact hers; she should have needed no acknowledgement from Gandhari. Gandhari could concede her nothing; she deprived Kunti more or less.

In the evening as she prepared to go see Vidur and Paransavi. Kunti remembered her mother in law Ambalika, who had once consoled her by saying that she may be unable to make her happy but might surely share her sorrows. Kunti now felt that Satyavati, Ambika, and Ambalika's removal to the forest had not been in her interest. Their presence in the palace would have saved her such loneliness, such helplessness! She felt as if every bit of Hastinapur now belonged to Dhiritarashtr and Gandhari. Of course, Pitrivy Bhishm was there, but Kunti would not approach him.

Bhim and Arjun were out playing. Yudhishthir sat browsing a book.

"What are you looking for?" she asked.

"I am trying to find out what truth is."

"What for?" she demanded.

"Truth paves the way for dharm," Yudhishthir replied.

"Why do you need dharm?"

"Achary says that dharm holds up the world. The absence of dharm debases it. Man is born not to destroy creation but to uphold it."

Kunti felt as though the weight on her heart had lightened suddenly. "That is very, very good," she said to Yudhishthir affectionately. "You do that – you find dharm and uphold it. Pitrivya, Mahamuni Vyas, your kaka Vidur – they all uphold dharm in their own ways. I don't know much about civilizational dharm but in my own everyday way I try to uphold it too… Ok, I'm going to visit Vidur kaka now – shall I leave Nakul and Sahdev with you or take them along?"

Yudhishthir immediately straightened and shut his book. "I want to see Vidur kaka!"

"Come along then!"

Vidur lived with his family in a separate, small unit within the palatial premises.

Nakul and Sahdev joined Vidur's playing children. "Hello!" Paransavi came to greet them. "Come on in! Oh is Yuvraj here too today?"

"Yuvraj!" Kunti couldn't keep the bitterness entirely out of her voice. Paransavi and Vidur sat down with her. "Gandhari called me to the palace today," she began.

"Oh yes the palace is abuzz with your visit."

"It is?" asked Kunti in astonishment. "Was my visit that important?"

"The algebra of significance in royal households is a weird incomprehensible thing." Vidur was smiling. "When a servant is murdered in his bed or one of their majesties' subjects is knifed no one cares – but you approaching the person of the Queen? All Hastinapur is in a tizzy."

"I don't know about Hastinapur, but yes, even I can attest to the mathematics." Paransavi turned to Kunti. "What do you think, Bhabhi, are you revelling in a superfluity of significance or have you been further impoverished?"

"Yudhishthir," said Vidur, "would you like to visit the library? I'm sure there are a few new books there you'll find interesting... We are going to be boring for a bit – I'll come join you too!"

To Kunti's relief, Yudhishthir stood up with alacrity. "I really couldn't say," she said to Pransavi.

Paransavi's response was biting. "What do you say to this calculation... Gandhari added to something, by handing you the keys to the palace. But by calling out all the servants to inform them she had replaced their extremely capable matron with Kunti devi she sabotaged whatever position she had purported to grant you."

Kunti's heart sank again. She felt tired.

"Don't take these things to heart, Bhabhi," said Vidur quietly. "It's just petty palace politics. I'm going to see if Yudhishthir found those books."

"Kaka!" Yudhishthir asked Vidur, "People older than you – you respect them?"

"Yes I do. Age and experience deserve all consideration."

"Do we have the right to... think about the actions of those older than us? Disagree with them?"

"Of course! If we don't critique the actions of age how will we teach the young?" His tone was grave. "Those who instruct the young in adharm lack foresight – they don't recognize that its only denouement is death. If the young wish to live at all they must dissent against the follies of the old."

"It isn't discourteous? Insolent?"

Vidur spoke slowly, carefully. "Between the dignity of age and the dignity of truth, or of ethical conduct? Choose conduct!" He examined Yudhishthir's anxious face. "Life is greater than the comforts of courtesy, son."

2

When Bhishm heard the news, all his discipline fled. He had not felt this agitated in a long, long time. He wanted to haul Dhritrashtr bodily off the throne, snatch the crown off his head and say, "Wretch! You are supremely unfit to occupy the seat of Kuru kings. You haven't the least concept of governance. Stewardship of justice? You couldn't do it if you tried – you don't know the meaning of the word. All you can hope to secure is your own sorry skin. A creature like you doesn't belong here – where Bharat and Nahush, Yayati and Shantanu sat."

He did not feel an ounce of sympathy for the sightless steward. Bhishm had reared this man from infancy – for what? So he might sit in power and dispense outrage? The faculty of sight was denied him – was the faculty of thought denied him as well? And if the fool found his own brain wanting could he not do those who might think for him the courtesy of consultation? Vidur, his mob of ministers, Bhishm himself, the intellectuals Hastinapur prided itself on, rishis and acharys... Could he not check his raging whims long enough to ask if something were right, what its consequences might be? A man who couldn't think straight when it came to his nearest and dearest, his own brother's family...

Bhishm emerged into the sunlight. The carriage stood ready. He climbed in without a word. The reins flashed and the horses moved. As they cantered down the main road

Bhishm's charioteer called back, "Where to, Ary?"

"Take me to the palace."

The character of the Kurukul was changing apace. To seize rather than to sacrifice, regard status over maturity, wisdom, rectitude... Bhishm resigned power, his position, and those who assumed it assumed too that they deserved it. He fostered this family with renunciation; Dhritrashtr would raze it through sheer rapacity. He simply refused to comprehend that creation itself foundered without dharm to sustain it – the bare fact that a king's just stewardship was an act of self-preservation, that conservation of dharm begot the fruitful world, the ordered state, the sound citizen, was beyond him. Simply, that if he did not institute ethical conduct, who in Hastinapur would? And if no one did, how long could Hastinapur remain his, or remain Hastinapur?

In the throne room Bhishm's rage rolled itself back, waves receding after a turbulent high tide.

The Kuru samrat sat on his throne, being fanned with the tail feathers of giant birds. Ministers and commanders stood in huddles before him. Bhishm was subtly directed to wait his turn.

Dhritrashtr was no wayward child his elder might lambast for bad behavior. The Maharaj of Hastinapur could not be berated in open court. He could not be censured; Bhishm could, as an advisor, draw the king's attention to a possible miscarriage of justice, a misapplication of some point in law... He might perhaps make a suggestion.

Bhishm sat, and waited. The ministers and commanders left, one by one. They were alone.

"Rajan! You removed Kunti and her sons from the palace and sent them to live in that ruin... simply because Kunti did not treat Gandhari's wish as command?"

Dhritrashtr blinked his lightless eyes. "Yes, they've been allotted a separate mansion."

"The reason?"

"They found their former residence inadequate, and we too were short of space. Suyodhan needed the room those people had annexed," he continued shamelessly, "and then, you know the royal palace is for the use of the king and his family…" He fixed his eyes approximately on Bhishm's face. "Pitrivy had to ride all the way over just to ask me this…"

"This is wrong, Dhritrashtr."

Dhritrashtr's ebullience was not punctured. "Either you make up your mind once and for all who rules Hastinapur, or stop interfering in the administrative affairs of the kingdom."

Bhishm was silent. It was not Dhritrashtr but the king who spoke today. Before the king a man is a subject or an alien – not pitamah, not kulvridh, not kin. Dhritrashtr had graduated from arbitration to adjudication.

He pressed his advantage. "The king has the right to make independent decisions; and no one is entitled to question their validity."

Dhritrashtr was not schooling Bhishm in what was due a king; he was delineating the bounds of Pitamah's prerogative. Just as Chitrangad and Vichitraviry had resented his claim as advisor, the restrictions he placed on their otherwise untrammeled desires, Dhritrastr demanded the freedom of an absolute monarch. No ruler did appreciate interference… And truly, if King Dhritrashtr chose to do this thing, and yes, Bhishm did think it unjust, so what? What could he really do? Dhritrashtr did not admit either to the stewardship of a king, nor his own double stewardship: he had no intention of vacating the throne for Yudhishthir. Pandu's son would be king when Dhritrashtr's term was over – no sooner – and till then the royal family was Gandhari and her progeny.

Bhishm stood up and turned away. He left Dhritrashtr's palace and headed straight for for the waiting carriage. It was only after some time that he remembered to ask the charioteer where they were heading.

"Home, Ary."

"No! Take me to Kunti's new residence." Her new residence! The words were offensive.

As they approached the place Bhishm surveyed it again. It was not a palace. It was not a mansion. It was, at best, an old house in a state of atrocious disrepair. When Bhishm was a child he vaguely remembered an old ex-minister had occupied it. It had been shut up and forgotten after he died. Bats and mice and snakes had probably lived and bred and died here, generation after generation of them. And why not – it was certainly not fit for human habitation. Dhritrashtr's lowliest servants lived better.

Kunti greeted him with reverence. She invited him in, carefully seated him in the cleanest and most comfortable chair at her disposal.

"How are you, Daughter?"

"By your grace, Father, well!"

"Where are the children?"

"Oh, probably tumbling about around here somewhere!"

"Are they well?"

"Yes, by the grace of God!"

Bhishm wanted to say I am so unhappy you have been evicted from the palace, I want to find you a really good place to live – but ought he to admit that by the grace of King Dhritrashtr he is no longer entitled to make administrative decisions – in the kingdom or in the Kurukul? Should he say as so many old men must, that Dhritrashtr would not listen to him, would not obey him, or he, Bhishm, would surely make excellent arrangements for Kunti and her sons?

A sudden shock ran through his somnolent grief. Bhishm! Kunti returned to Hastinapur because she believed this is her home. She believed the people of Hastinapur are her people. If you indulge your self-pity before her, regurgitate your helplessness to relieve your feelings, she will sense the precariousness not only of her current abode but of her position; she will not fail to see that she is amidst those on the one hand who do not wish to further her wellbeing and those on the other hand who cannot. Does Bhishm wish to be the precipitator of her own ill will toward the king? Does he wish to sow the seeds of discord that divide this family? Bhishm raised Dhritrashtr and Pandu, he has watched over their sons. Shall he goad his sons against each other? Shall he admit that he himself would if he could – but Dhritrashtr prevents him? Does he want to divide them, into two opposing factions…?

But he could not help himself. "This house is not fit for you to live in, Kunti."

"Well, there aren't any other options," said Kunti with smiling self-possession. "But please do not worry yourself. My children and I are accustomed to ashram cottages. This is decidedly better. And I am not really as concerned about my sons' physical comforts: I want them to learn! Their development – physical, mental, and moral – I do seek. And they must be able to live amicably in Hastinapur."

"Doesn't Krip treat them well?" Bhishm asked.

"No, no, it's not that," said Kunti. "Just – my wish."

"You are really not worried, being here?"

"There are a few discomforts, yes, but nothing that can't be fixed. I have my sons with me," Kunti made no attempt to conceal her pride and affection. "A little labour, and this place will be eminently habitable."

Bhim came in like a hurricane and shot out a vexing question. "Ma, Hastinapur! Whose is it?" His posture betrayed unbridled belligerence. He did not want curiosity satisfied – he wanted a just verdict. Contradictory emotions warred in Kunti: she was proud, as always, of her son's strength and self-confidence; her heart ached that he should be outraged to the point of its full expression. Yudhishthir was always asking questions – but he always 'wanted to know' to understand. Arjun looked, and listened, and arrived at his own conclusions – when he could not he waited, and looked and listened. Bhim – always had the answer. He asked questions when he had the answers, had no doubt, and wished for an acknowledgment. Demanded acknowledgement. No bad thing, where and who he was. And yet, Kunti would give anything to save him the vexation, the painful agitation.

"Why don't you answer?" Bhim advanced the way he might toward a tree he wished to try and uproot.

"Where are your manners?" Kunti said sharply. "Pranam Pitamah at once!"

Bhim turned and touched Bhishm's feet. "I wish you triumph, son," said Bhishm benignly. "Do the Kurukul proud."

"Tell me!" Bhim turned right back to Kunti.

"She laughed. "And what shall I tell you? Is Hastinapur a toy? That you and Arjun can squabble over?"

Her son looked instantly abashed. Kunti had never met anyone this capable of absolute reversals of feeling – but she was happy to see this too – Bhim did not hang rigidly on to his questions, to his beliefs; they were fluid, open to reconsideration and amendment..."You'll storm in here tomorrow asking me whom the sky and the river belong to..."

But her words had a startling effect – Bhim was furious again. "Then why does Suyodhan say it is his? He says his father owns this place and we are his dependents!"

Kunti's precarious self-posession wobbled. What now?

In truth, though, she was unbearably weary. She wanted to say, let him talk, he is a nonsensical fool, let him utter his inanities. But Bhishm was here, for once. "What else does Suyodhan say?"

"He says that just as he drove us from the palace of Hastinapur and dumped us in this ruin, he will..."

"What ruin?" interrupted Kunti. "This is the most ancient and revered part of the royal palace!"

"Suyodhan says," repeated Bhim.

"He will...?"

"He will have us expelled from Hastinapur the moment he assumes kingship!"

Kunti felt a satisfying shock race through her veins. This was no meaningless quarrel, these were not meaningless words. This was a declaration of policy, of political intent.

"Why would Suyodhan say such a thing?" she asked Bhim irritably. "What had you yourself been saying?"

"I?" Bhim stepped back.

"Why does Suyodhan persist in talking such rubbish at you? If you piously mind your own affairs, are you saying he comes witlessly over and accosts you for the express purpose of disgorging nonsense?"

"He is not witless, he is insane! He plays with us, loses, weeps, and then proceeds shamelessly to threaten us with hideous punishments!"

"Oh, was that it? You defeated him in a game?"

"That's nothing," said Bhim, torn between impatience at the digression, and childish, delighted pride. "I do that every day. He can't run, he can't wrestle, he can't even swim like I can... But whom does Hastinapur belong to?" Bhim insisted.

"Hastinapur belongs to Bhishm pitamah," said Yudhishthir's voice, uncharacteristically buoyant. "What are you going to do about it?" He came into the room and touched Bhishm's feet.

Bhim did not laugh – he was uncharacteristically grave. "That's all right. What belongs to Pitamah belongs to us too, but whatever is Suyodhan's is not ours."

Yudhishthir could say nothing: Bhim was right. It was precisely that simple. Bhishm's pity was mingled with relief: they did feel him theirs. "Every city belongs to its citizens, my sons; the king and queen are named sovereign simply because they are responsible for the wellbeing of their subjects. Much as parents are sovereigns in the home. The moment a parent begins to use a child to further other interests, or a ruler her or his subject, all sovereignty ends."

But Bhim was not interested. He was satisfied that Hastinapur did not belong to Suyodhan. The boys left together, and Bhishm stood up. "Don't worry about the children's education. I will make sure their potential is not wasted – I'll speak with Kripachary too. And I am going to send over a chariot and charioteer – use them." He left without looking at her again, or waiting for her reply.

Kunti revelled in her solitude.

At first she was able to sidestep that terrible question – think of her home, her self, look around her. But as the silence got deeper and the presences faded, her thoughts, like a housefly obstinately hovering over a wound, plagued its echo in her mind: to whom does Hastinapur belong?

She had asked herself that too, as she waited at Vardhaman Gate for entry into the city. She did enter – not as mistress but as an unsolicited guest who could not be turned away.

For Queen Gandhari she was an impoverished dependent… Why, why, why? Why was King Pandu's consort not the Queen? Why was the progenitor of Crown Prince Yudhishthir not Queen Mother?

Kunti would get easily hurt, then. She often thought of leaving Hastinapur and retiring to a distant place where there would be no Kaurav dynasty, no royal palace, nor refugee status. But how could she leave this place? Would it solve anything? Fulfill the purpose that had made her leave Rishi Shring's ashram?

It was different now. Kunti was different. No longer distracted by trifles, toughened by each blow. Escape was not now, if it had ever been, an answer. If Kunti could not counterattack, she would at least offer resistance. She would make efforts to secure her self and her children. Either she dismiss Suyodhan's statements, Kalika's behavior, Gandhari's and Dhritrashtr's double-dealing as petty domestic play – else she take the whole as declaration of war. The question of succession would hinge on the establishment of right, of who could prove entitlement to the crown. Through use of force, a test of strength. But not hers. She must wait till her sons could claim their right, and if necessary, retrieve it by force. She knew by bitter experience that violence was essential to statecraft. Those who ventured power must face it, and commit it.

Dhirtarashtr would never care for his brother's sons – Bhishm was sure now. In all likelihood he was seeing his own son's decline in the Pandavs' rise. He had always been a jealous boy. He had never resigned to his disability. And now Shakuni too was deeply enmeshed in the politics of Hastinapur. Dhritrashtr was dreaming of his progeny ruling the kingdom, and conflict was inevitable... Bhishm could not stop worrying about the fatherless boys.

He directed his chariot toward Krip's academy.

Krip's teaching must be at fault, Bhishm ruminated on the way; there should have been no question of distinctions being made, between the sons of Dhritrashtr and those of Pandu. Academies, ashrams, and hermitages dissolve all discrimination. Was this academy encouraging it? Why should Suyodhan pronounce his father was the lord, the owner of Hastinapur? Why could Krip not have succeeded in inculcating morality and courtesy in him?

Krip greeted him with surprise. Why did Bhishm pitamah deign to visit?

"Nothing in particular, just a general discussion about the boys I have left in your charge... They are raw, clay. You shape them and bake them. You know their kind; I only see the shape you give them. You alone know whether the heat will leave them unbaked, or burn them up."

"Of course!" Kripachary was flattered. "You are that rare kshatriy, Pitamah, who possesses all the qualities of a teacher… I have indeed examined the kind of clay these boys are made of. They are true kshatriys! Yudhishthir is perhaps more contemplative than a kshatriy ought to be, and comparatively tender, but Bhim, Arjun, Suyodhan, Sushasan and the other princes are strong. They will make true warriors. I see the best warriors in the making here… Adhirath's son Vasushen Karn, though a charioteer's son, is endowed with all the attributes of a kshatriy too. He has the potential to equal any of our princes in the art of war. But I will not train him to equal the princes."

Bhishm frowned. "You must not bother about your pupils' castes! Or their families! A teacher's duty is to bring out the best in his disciples, regardless of whom he teaches."

"You are right, of course, Ary!" said Kripachary. "But wise is he who would turn wood to coal, not let it flare up and consume the forest."

Bhishm chose to ignore this comment. He wanted to know what skills Krip was teaching the boys. Use of the mace and sword, archery and wrestling, Krip recited. The handling and care of weapons, strategies of battle.

"Are you instructing them in theology, logic, and politics?" Bhishm demanded.

"They have brahmin teachers for those subjects."

Sports? asked Bhishm.

"Yes, Ary! They take daily exercise. They run, they swim, they practice team sports."

"Whatever they do, I want it to create closer bonds – I want them to love one another, and learn to sacrifice for others. Let them be selfless and forbearing. Let them be good humans before good warriors. Let them respect noble qualities in others. Let them venerate the venerable. Let them protect the weak and defend their subjects. Let the Kurus never be stigmatized on their account."

"Of course, Ary!" Krip bowed. "Don't worry – they shall."

Bhishm returned, he thought, with a fresh understanding of Kripachary. The Kuru family had brought Krip and his sister Kripi up so he felt indebted to the royal family, which accounted for his… sincerity towards that household. But was he qualified to teach – by aptitude or otherwise? Though a barhmin himself his attitude toward the more ascetic ones was significant: Krip traded in arms; did he ever contemplate in solitude the essence of statecraft? Did he try to understand what the moral duty of a kshatriy was, and what human qualities bore developing? Did he ever transcend the present for a moment? Did he think about the long history of humanity and its eternal future?

Bhishm did not think so. Kripachary did not deserve his position, and the Kuru princes deserved better.

Kripachary sat baffled: why was Bhishm here? What did he mean by what he had said? Did Bhishm really want the princes to grow up sages?

He readied his chariot and appeared before King Dhritrashtr, who was in conference with Shakuni and Kanik.

Kripachary was given a patient audience. "What is your opinion, Achary?"

"My view is that kshatriy and arms are synonymous. If a kshatriy won't train for war, what else will he do?"

Shakuni spoke up, with immense conviviality. "I don't think Ary Bhishm said anything injudicious, Achary! The princes must indeed know where to use arms, and when. They must uphold justice and protect their own rights. For which, you are right, they must certainly become indomitable warriors."

Kanik looked amused. "I think it imperative to remember that there are two types of people in this world. Those who dread destruction and those who don't. That is, the incapable and those capable of causing it at will. The princes should fear neither death nor destruction. A man averse to conflict will, sooner or later, forfeit his rights. Our princes should be warriors people flee from and before at all costs. The essence of a kshatriy life is hunger..."

This was precisely what Dhritrashtr had been waiting to hear. "He who has abandoned desire can certainly never be a kshatriy exemplar. Don't let Pitrivy distract you; I want to see my sons grow into brave kshatriys – not impotents..."

On his way back Kripachary mulled over the situation: Bhishm spoke of an ideal education; Dhritrashtr would have his sons reared as combative kshatriys hungry for whatever they could seize. What ought Kripachary to do? He was the king's servant. He must do his master's bidding. He was no sage, no mystic mentor. He was in the king's employ; his first duty was to honour the king's command. His livelihood and position in Hastinapur were subject, after all, to Dhritrashtr's pleasure, Dhritrashtr's mercy. He could not afford the ire of the king. But Bhishm...

It was a special day at the gurukul.

Though sports had always been essential to Kripachary's curriculum, Bhishm had inspired him to include several for sheer recreational value. If Bhishm wanted to see harmony in teams, Kripachary was not going to object.

Kripachary had invited the entire royal family, clearly stipulating that this was not a tournament or an exhibition; it was practice. There was no question of losing or winning. Participation was all.

Dhritrashtr did not deign to attend: such an exercise was meaningless to him, both because he could not see, and because the king could spare no time for play.

Bhishm had ceremoniously registered his attendance. He was very pleased he had been able to realign the princes' education even a little: toward the development of individual abilities rather than the gratification of egos.

The games began.

Bhishm noted with approval that Krip had divided the boys up into teams so Pandu's and Dhritrashtr's sons would not be able to face off. Bhim and Suyodhan were one team, Arjun and Sushasan were another, and Nakul and Sahdev represented different teams. Would the boys side with their teams or favour their own even if it meant a loss to their side in the games? Would Bhim let his team lose in order to facilitate Suyodhan's defeat or play his best even if that meant victory for Suyodhan?

But everyone on the field acted in good conscience. Bhishm was glad his presentiments seemed unfounded. Perhaps his fear was disproportionate, and the rivalry between cousins was just that – childhood rivalry…

Kripachary announced the final event. A marathon, to determine the best runner. All students, big and small, youngest to oldest, assembled at the starting post without distinction. They would run together, and drop out when their strength failed. The last one still running would be declared champion. It was the only part of the day that offered a reward – individual recognition.

As the race progressed, Bhishm was drawn into a philosophical allegory: was this not analogous to life? An individual is born, he is surrounded by compatriots. Slowly but surely, compelled by a variety of circumstances, they drop off. He finds himself alone at the end. Perhaps accomplishment was inseparable from loneliness, he thought with some bitterness. The accomplished woman or man realizes that when there were people around to partake of success and largesse, s/he had none. They desert him through his struggles, and by the time there is leisure and joy to share, there is no one left.

Or is the ambitious man necessarily self-engrossed and selfish? Disdainful of his fellows, justifying his neglect of others as single-mindedness and devotion to his vocation, only waking to the significance of camaraderie when he has lost it? "But you already know no one drops voluntarily out of company, Bhishm, and those who continue to do because they must!" his inner voice interrupted. "Fate ceaselessly consumes the universe. Your own parents, your brothers and their children, your family – neither did they desert you nor you them. What happened was inevitable, fated…"

Barely five or six runners remained through the last leg of the marathon. Suyodhon was in the lead; Bhim lagged behind. It might be the last round.

Bhim accelerated. Perhaps he had let others run ahead so he could conserve his energy for the decisive lap. Well, life was greater than any one round, thought Bhishm – any single, short-lived achievement.

Bhim left all the runners behind; he was abreast Suyodhon. Then he was ahead, and Suyodhan was visibly struggling.

Suddenly Suyodhan leapt forward, and collided with Bhim. Bhim turned his head slightly to look at him, but kept running. Bhishm's heart raced with them – if Bhim fell at this speed the impact would break a couple of bones if it did no other damage. They were neck and neck again. One minute, two. Suyodhon's veins were visible on his forehead; he was gasping. He stumbled. Threw out his arm as he fell and tripped Bhim's pounding legs. They went down together.

Bhishm was instantly on his feet and racing across the grounds toward them. But long before he got there, Bhim had stood up and was cursing Suyodhon vociferously. His face, knees, and palms were bleeding freely, but he was shouting that he could go on running, should he go on running? Suyodhan lay on the ground, his face hidden in his arms.

"You don't have to run any further," said Krip with a pat on Bhim's back as Bhishm examined his wounds and felt along the limbs to make sure nothing was broken. It wasn't. "You've been declared the best runner."

Bhishm turned toward Suyodhan. No. Toward Duryodhan. He was distantly aware of a furious storm raging within him – the commander he still was should drag this miscreant by the heel to a dungeon and throw him in with the rats, have him whipped publicly for such an outrage of honour and human decency. The pitamah was screaming inwardly at the double loss just barely prevented by fate – if Bhim had broken his head they would be mourning both him and his killer, Kuru scions both, and the disgrace would have finished what was left of the dynasty. Even now, this atrocious act had plunged another knife of discord between the Pandavs and Dhartrashtrs, had diminished Dhritrashtr's eldest son in full view of the world. And what it had done or meant for his character…

Duryodhan was sitting up. His features were drenched and contorted with agony, and rage. "Bhim tripped me!" he howled. "I was winning, and he felled me! Punish him! I want him punished!" Bhishm closed his eyes briefly; disgust and shame and pity overwhelmed him. He had to get out of this place, and he had to take this child with him.

"Duryodhan!" said Bhishm aloud. Duryodhan, as well as Bhim and Krip, were shocked into silence. "Come with me." He turned and walked away. Duryodhan hesitated for a moment, then stood up and followed Pitamah to his chariot.

"Get in," said Bhishm.

Duryodhan's expression of uncertainty flickered – anger again, and intractable spite. "Where are we going?"

"Home."

"Yours or mine?"

Bhishm stared at him. Duryodhan got into the carriage.

They rode in silence for a while. Duryodhan's emotions oscillated wildly, between ear-ringing fury and shattering fear – what was Pitamah going to do? Take him to the palace? Whip him? But the thought made him sneer – Pitamah wouldn't dare. He was like Kalika that way. All he ever managed was 'wait till your father hears about…' And Father wouldn't even glance toward Pitamah. He would ask Duryodhan if he was hurt, blandly say that everyone must be fair, and no one ought to indulge in unprovoked violence, and brush his hands off the affair… That cheating savage Bhim would of course not be subjected to even this, however – he had been declared the best runner! How? Duryodhan had been right there with him! Right to the end! But what was Pitamah going to do?…

Bhishm tried to understand what he himself felt – what should he do? He may wish to mete out punishment, but that was Dhritrashtr's prerogative, or Krip's. And in all honesty Duryodhan's behavior – the state of mind it betrayed – disturbed Bhishm. He felt the boy was teetering on the edge of a precipice. Injudicious force would tumble him into irredeemable destruction. There were acts no human being could return from.

"What are we doing, Son?"

"What?" Duryodhan looked at him with apprehension.

"Right now, what activity are we engaged in?"

"I don't understand what you want me to say," said Duryodhan, belligerence creeping into his voice again. "I don't understand your question."

"We are moving, toward a destination. We are on a journey. How we get there is immaterial in the end. Whether we walk, or ride an elephant, or sit in a chariot, as long as we keep moving, even at a crawl, we will get there. Sooner or later, we will get there… But if we stop moving and start obstructing others moving towards the same destination, though we might delay them, we will most certainly never arrive ourselves." Bhishm tried to decipher the effect of his words on Duryodhan, but the boy was uncharacteristically blank.

"Why all this to me?" he asked with habitual intransigence. It had just occurred to him that he never succeeded in any plan to deal with Bhim precisely because of people like Achary and Pitamah. They were always there, there was never any time alone, a few hours with no one watching his every move or checking up on the oaf. And the answer was around him this instant: a journey! They needed to go away somewhere quiet and secluded – all the 'brothers' – and enjoy some serious 'recreation'... But what would the pretext be, and where would they go?

"Because I want you to understand that to be the best at anything you need to enhance your own abilities. By obstructing Bhim, you may prevent him from winning one race, but you will never become the best yourself. Even more importantly – we each of us have a course we must traverse. It is the nature of the universe. Each beast or being must walk her or his path. Each object is made, and moves through its cycle, and is destroyed. What do you think would happen to a planet that decided to abandon its own course to obstruct that of another? It would collide and be smashed to dust itself, and irredeemably wreck the balance of the system... Nothing would be gained, and everything lost. Do you understand?"

Pramankoti! thought Duryodhan. Everyone loved water sports – no one more so than Bhim. And none of the adults would be in the least concerned about them: the place was an oasis, and every one of the Kurus born by the Ganges could swim like a fish. "Yes!" he said aloud.

3

Once out of Ganga, Bhim sat down on the sandy shore and wondered whether to call it quits or take a break and go for it again. He could never get enough of the water. More so because Ganga, river of gods, showed off her most spectacular form at Pramankoti, pristine and glorious. Bhim was for once profoundly grateful to Duryodhan, for planning an excursion to this serene place.

He popped up as though Bhim had thought him into being.

"Come on and sit, Dharamavatar, righteousness personified!" said Bhim. He knew the sarcasm would offend Duryodhan, who would make off in a huff at once.

But to his amazement Duryodhan did not appear in the least offended, nor did he leave. He smiled, and sat down next to Bhim.

"I'm exhausted," he said.

Bhim was speechless for a moment. Duryodhan was sitting next to him and attempting small talk! But then, he had been markedly friendlier to all five of them since that sports day. Bhim had wondered before whether this excursion was an apology of sorts – whether his own actions during the race had shocked Duryodhan…

"You get tired?" he teased. "I'd begun to think you're completely indefatigable – or at least believe you are."

"I'm no Bhim!" Duryodhan laughed – but the laughter was strained. "I have neither your strength nor your stamina!"

The subtle discrepancy between his fawning words and his manner repelled Bhim. Duryodhan stank of deceit.

And yet Bhim could not simply walk away. The situation was too surreal.

"What have you got to eat, my friend? I'm starving," said Duryodhan. Bhim wanted to ask him whether he was high. Friend? But he was suddenly aware of his own hunger. He was astonished at himself – when had he last eaten?

He laughed. "You really are a friend, Duryodhan! Swimming always does make one hungrier than anything – I don't know how I haven't headed straight for food! Actually this should be common practice: a person emerges from the water and is presented with platters of laddoos; arrives at the finish line at the end of a race and finds women waiting with sweets, so it seems as though he has been running toward them all along…"

This time Duryodhan laughed with unfeigned delight. "Oh excellent! I ask you for something to eat, and you take the opportunity to fault my arrangements!"

"I wasn't faulting anything!" said Bhim quickly. He had no wish to alienate Duryodhan if he was inclined to friendship – however late. "I was just fantasizing."

"In that case, do have a taste!" Duryodhan clapped, and ordered the jack-in-the-box attendant to bring a box of laddoos.

"Don't tell the others!" said Duryodhan. "Or we won't get a sniff of them again." He picked a laddoo and practically fed it to Bhim. "To unfailing friendship."

Bhim ate the laddoo, as well as several more. Duryodhan continued to chatter and hand him laddoos, till Bhim thought he would fall asleep right there on the bank. He was so, so tired… He didn't even think he could eat in this state.

He stood up. "I'm going to go sleep in my tent for a while," he told Duryodhan. "The great and the good always do have only two passions: food and sleep. But you had better make sure there's food left over when I wake – or all your arrangements will have amounted to nothing!"

"Not at all," Duryodhan assured him. "I made sure food was set aside specifically for you on this trip – neither does anyone need it more than you do, nor does anyone enjoy it as you do. No one is entitled to food like you are…"

Bhim could barely respond. He was aware that Duryodhan was pleased with him for some reason – and he did want to know what the reason was – but he felt he was going to sink into the ground if he did not find his bed at once.

"Shall I walk you to your pavilion?" Duryodhan sounded a little anxious. Was Bhim's exhaustion that evident?

"No, I'll manage."

He did, barely. He was asleep before his head touched the pillow.

When the chariot race was over, Yudhishthir realized he had not seen his brothers for quite a while. His mother would never have permitted her brood out of sight for this long.

He left his carriage with his charioteer Chirantan and walked to the stables.

Of course Nakul was there. He was practicing mounted swordfighting on a racehorse.

Yudhishthir yelled at him not to venture too far into the forestand join them in time for food. "Where's Sahdev?" he asked, as Nakul's steed careened about.

Also swordfighting, in the grounds.

"Why aren't you with him?"

"I can't practice with him," said Nakul irritably. "He's always distracted! Half the time his eyes are on some star or planet he can see in the daylight, or the wind smells of something strange, or he's just forgotten what we're doing and is staring into space!"

Yudhishthir did find Sahdev in the grounds. He was surrounded, swordsmen attacking him from every direction. Excellent practice in self-defence, thought Yudhishthir, and moved on.

Arjun was on his chariot. The bridle was in his mouth, he held bow and arrow in his hands, and was shooting moving targets. He wouldn't have noticed even if his brother had passed right by him. For Bhim was conspicuously missing.

Worry for Bhim was never far, for Yudhishthir. In any case Bhim was quick to anger. He rarely started fights but never backed down from one. And then there was Duryodhan. And Dushasan, and Shakuni, and Karn. They took every opportunity to provoke Bhim – and Yudhishthir was always afraid one day things would get out of hand. He was starting to feel uneasy now.

Yudhishthir spotted Vikarn and enquired about his friend.

"I just saw him – he was on his way to bed! He said swimming had exhausted him and he was retiring to the pavilion for a while."

Yudhishthir headed for Bhim's tent. Bhim was tired? The word wasn't in his vocabulary.

To his amazement, though, Bhim was indeed dead to the world.

"Bhim!"

No response. Yudhishtir touched his shoulder and called loudly, "Bhim!"

No response. Yudhishthir shook him hard. "Bhim!"

Bhim stirred and mumbled.

"Are you alright?"

"Yes, yes, I'm fine. Just a little tired."

That word again! Yudhishthir was at a loss. Usually Bhim leapt out of bed and stood up, as though lying still for an instant once he was awake was a waste of time.

"Get up," said Yudhishthir. "Come and eat."

"I'm not hungry."

Yudhishthir was alarmed. "What do you mean you're not hungry? If you sleep through the meal you won't get anything to eat till the next one – you'll be bouncing off walls with hunger!" Though at this moment Bhim did not look like he would bounce anywhere ever again. "You have to eat," said Yudhishthir with finality. "Get up."

Bhim dragged himself off the bed and followed Yudhishthir lethargically to the mess, muttering that he should be allowed to sleep. He forced a few bites down, and stood up. "I am going back to bed. I really need to sleep."

Yudhishthir watched him go with consternation.

When the meal was over everyone returned to their activities. "Shall I stay with Madhyam?" asked Arjun. Yudhishthir made a decision. "No. Go practice. Just in case he actually is just tired, we should let him sleep. If he's not well by evening we'll consult the physician."

Duryodhan approached Bhim's pavilion on tip-toe. He had a number of his hangers-on and brothers with him. He gestured them to stop and stole into the tent. Bhim lay there, unconscious. Duryodhan said his name once, then louder. There was no response. Duryodhan touched his shoulder, then shook it. No response. Duryodhan shook Bhim vigorously. No response.

Duryodhan's face was ecstatic. He looked back through the door and gestured his friends in.

"Completely out of it, like a corpse," Duryodhan whispered. "Tie him up well, but only with the water vines. Don't use rope, so even if his body floats ashore people conclude he was entwined accidentally. Shouldn't look like he was tied up…"

His assistants – accomplices – had everything they needed to hand. They tied him up and knocked him about to check that the knots would hold. They turned to Duryodhan.

"Done?"

They nodded.

"The probability of his waking is nearly nil, but just in case he does, you're sure he won't be able to untie himself?"

"No Maharaj. This is a man – even an elephant wouldn't be able to free himself from our bonds."

"Pick him up," said Duryodhan quietly. "Carry him to where the river is deep and where poisonous snakes abound… We have to allow him no chance to escape or survive."

"Your will be done Maharaj!"

They left.

Duryodhan returned to the sports grounds – but he could not stay still. Till he knew Bhim had sunk to the riverbed, and had not gotten free, he could not rest. He jumped onto his chariot and set off across Pramankoti. This way and that, crisscrossing the paths along the river – his attention was fixed on the bank.

Dushasan. Duryodhan stopped the chariot.

"It's done, Bhaiya."

"No problems?"

"None. I submerged him myself."

"You saw the snakes?"

"Yes."

"The river wasn't disturbed too much? He sank?"

"I stood on him till he sank."

"No one saw anything?"

"Who would see? Everyone is in the grounds."

Duryodhan wanted to laugh aloud, but he maintained a kingly gravity. "When I am enthroned, I will immediately appoint you crown prince," he said grandly. Dushasan did laugh, all the way back to the grounds.

At dusk, Yudhishthir went looking for Bhim again: was he still sleeping? Not that he never would – Bhim was as fond of sleep as he was of food. He could sleep for hours and hours at a stretch… But was he unwell?

But Bhim was not in his pavilion. Had he woken and gone out on his own? And where?

He was not in the wrestling pits or the mace yard. Yudhishthir searched along the riverbank and enquired after Bhim of the swimmers and others there. No one had seen Bhim.

Yudhishthir met Arjun, Nakul, and Sahdev again, but not him.

"You look worried," Duryodhan called across the lawn. "What's the matter?"

"Have you seen Bhim?"

"Why would I want to? No doubt he's engaged in one or other sport like everyone else. It's not as though Fatty is capable of sitting still."

"I've looked everywhere – I can't find him."

"Arre, he must be chasing tail in the forest then. With his appetite who wouldn't be. He'll appear in a bit with a dead deer, roast and eat it, hooves and all."

Talking to Duryodhan was useless. He was probably drunk anyway. Rumour was, he'd been sousing himself regularly these past few months. Yudhishthir turned to go.

"Arre Dharmraj!" Duryodhan shouted from behind him, "Maybe he returned to Hastinapur."

"Without telling anyone? Why would he do that?"

"Must be missing his mother." Duryodhan's gang guffawed.

Yudhishthir was too disturbed by Bhim's disappearance to contemplate a response. It wasn't rational to expect better from Duryodhan anyway: he had always been incorrigible, and had only gotten worse as he grew older. He'd gathered goons around himself, and led his younger brothers into like viciousness. They all did as they liked, said whatever came into their increasingly violent heads, and beat up anyone they felt like beating up, whenever they felt like it. Bhim was the only one who ever really confronted them or paid them back in kind… But where was he?

Yudhishthir wanted to pack his brothers up and return to Hastinapur at once, just to check if his brother had for some inexplicable reason gone home. On the other hand, what if Bhim had in fact wandered into the forest in that weird somnolent state and gone to sleep there? Or worse? There were predators in that forest as well as deer…

Arjun offered to search Pramankoti again – but Yudhishthir said no. "Will I go looking for you, next?"

As twilight spread its tentacles, the camp was dismantled and they prepared to travel back to Hastinapur.

The chariots were readied and the camping equipment and other wares were loaded onto the wagons. Some four or five of them rode each chariot. Duryodhan was raving drunk. He shouted and sang, and pricked his gang to do the same. Dushasan and Karn were trying to control him.

Yudhishthir, along with Arjun, Nakul, and Sahdev rode the chariot with Chirantan. There was a whole caravan of such carriages charting their route.

Suddenly, driven by some drunken whim, Duryodhan challenged Yudhishthir to a chariot race. Chirantan looked at Yudhishthir.

"No."

"Why not?" Duryodhan shouted. "No guts?"

Chirantan shifted in his seat. "We've practiced quite enough for one day," said Yudhishthir quietly.

Duryodhan laughed and raced off. "Shall I bring him to heel, my prince?" asked Chirantan. "It will take me two minutes."

"I have no doubt," said Yudhishthir wearily. "But he's a drunken fool – why should we dignify his idiocy?"

Kunti received them at the door. "Welcome home!" And the next instant, "Where's Bhim?"

"He's not here?" exclaimed Yudhishthir. But he already knew Bhim would never have made off like that – would not have returned to Hastinapur without his brothers. What possessed him to give credence to Duryodhan's throwaway words?

"Where is Bhim?" Kunti asked again.

"Let's go inside," said Yudhishthir.

"I asked you a question. Answer me!"

"Please, Ma, come inside the house." Yudhishthir held his mother's shoulders and guided her in.

Kunti's face had gone white; her knees buckled. What had happened?

Yudhishthir told her slowly, gently.

Kunti sat like a statue. The turning of the world seemed to be slowing; it was still. She could not feel her limbs. She felt a flash, and tears leapt into her eyes. "Of course, something like this was bound to happen. We are cursed – I am cursed."

"Don't be sure of the worst, Ma!" He took her in his arms. "Bhim is not a child, who may have lost his way. He went somewhere. He'll be back. When he does not find us in Pramankoti, he will come back home. Where else is there to go?"

Yudhishthir did not believe the words his tongue formed. He'd known something was very wrong when he saw Bhim sleeping in the middle of the day. But where in the world did he go?

Kunti watched her sons for a while. Then she asked quietly, "When did you see him last?"

"At lunch," said Yudhishthir.

"Did he eat well?"

"No. He hardly ate. He was weak, slow, sleepy, kept saying he wasn't hungry. I know he was ill. I knew it then," answered Yudhishthir.

"I can imagine nothing but evil. He was absolutely well

when he left. What happened between here and there, that he could neither play nor eat? Could Suyodhan have done something?"

"Yes," said Yudhishthir very softly. "I can't help suspecting him either. But I don't want to believe Suyodhan has crossed that bridge – that he has arrived at such a pass of malevolence."

"Ma!" Arjun grasped Kunti shoulder. "If anything has happened to Madhyam, if anyone has harmed him, I swear I will riddle them with holes."

"Unless we have certain evidence of an actual mishap, we must not lose hope." Yudhishthir seemed to quell Arjun's declaration.

Kunti looked at her Arjun's bright face, at his assured form. He had grown. Her son the warrior, the renowned archer! He betrayed neither worry nor fear.

Nakul and Sahdev sat on the ground facing her, lending unspoken strength, consolation. Her sons were no longer under her protection; they were her protectors. They felt her anguish more than they felt their own.

She dried her eyes and rose with renewed resolve. "Come on! We are not going to sit idly and play at dejection. We have to look for Bhim. He's mischievous – he's not a fool. He did not wander away, or leave Pramankoti on his own. He is in danger."

"You are right," said Yudhishthir, "but where to look? We searched Pramankoti end to end – I scanned every bush and building twice. And taking Bhim anywhere forcibly is not a task for two or even four strong men. He has to have left of his own accord."

"In that state?" Sahdev asked. "He barely made it to his pavilion, of his own accord." They all looked at him: he was right

The silence stung like a wild thing.

"You should not have left him alone," said Kunti.

"Yudhishthir, go call Vidur kaka. Let us discuss this with him. He may see something we don't." She considered for a moment. "You can't go looking for Bhim at once anyway, in the dark. And son," she said to Yudhishthir, "don't go anywhere unarmed. And don't go alone. Take Arjun with you. Arjun, take your bow and arrows, and fire them if you so much as suspect danger."

"You think someone attacked him?" asked Yudhishthir.

"I can't think! Go! Don't spend a moment more than you need to outdoors just at present – I will be in agony till you come."

"Come, Arjun!" Yudhishthir left with his brother.

"Nakul, Sahdev, stay, please," Kunti said to the other two as they moved to go as well.

"Shouldn't we go with Jyeshth?" asked Nakul?

"No! I cannot afford to send all my sons out at once."

Vidur was there in no time. As soon as she heard Yudhishthir and Arjun's voices Kunti opened the door. Vidur waited to shut the door and spoke softly.

"This is terrible, Bhabhi."

"What do you think happened to Bhim?"

"It's too early to say anything. We must anticipate his safe return in any case. That he went somewhere himself, and will be back shortly. Or if he's in trouble, he will find his own way out."

"I have said nothing to anyone, Vidur," said Kunti. "I have kept my sense silent and secret, but it has been abundantly clear from the start that our return was not welcomed by my dear Jeth and Jethani. Suyodhan and Sushasan insult us at the slightest pretext. They would concede us no rights. None of us, except Bhim, have ever resisted. I am afraid Suyodhan may wish him dead, may plan to kill him."

"That is unfortunately not unlikely! I have had this in

my mind ever since I heard Suyodhon was organising water sports in Pramankoti."

"Why, Kaka?" Yudhishthir asked desperately.

"Son, Suyodhan has, to say the least, never been cordial with you. Why should he suddenly develop such a feeling of affection for his cousins that he should make such elaborate arrangements for a joint excursion? When a recent antagonist approaches kindly, I am always suspicious. Pramankoti was renovated with such pomp to lure you there. I don't believe he took such pains just to have fraternal fun with you all. Bhim's disappearance is vindication of my doubts, until they are proved unjustified."

Kunti was outraged. "Is Hastinapur an anarchist state? Will someone ask that Suyodhan – no! Duryodhan! – what he has done with Bhim? Or is his person to be elevated above above laws, above ethical frames, above the moral codes of the land?"

Vidur seemed to get calmer as Kunti's temper rose. He spoke with still solicitude. "I sympathise fully with your anguish, Bhabhi, but I am less interested in Suyodhan's…"

"Duryodhan's!"

"Duryodhan's punishement than I am in keeping these four safe. If Duryodhan has harmed one of your sons he can also harm a second, and a third… Anarchy is self-perpetuating. It is folly to imagine institutional recourse is possible under Dhritrashtr's rule – the monarchy is the first institution in this state, and it is corrupt. You would not even be approaching Dhritrashtr for justice; you would be approaching Duryodhan and his goons for mercy. Does that strike you as a viable option?"

Kunti's face was bloodless. "Should we… do you think we should tell Pitrivy?" she stammered.

"Pitrivy will not stay silent. He will race straight to the palace and shake Dhritrashtr and Duryodhan till their teeth rattle," said Vidur. "And then? He has no power to sentence

Duryodhan, to death, to jail, to banishment. Duryodhan may cower for an instant, but his rage will rise redoubled, and direct itself squarely at Pandu's sons and their mother. He has the resources of the Kuru dynasty at his command. How will we defend ourselves?"

No one could say a word.

"But we must defend ourselves," Vidur continued in a stronger voice. "At least till you are all able to do it alone, till you have attained majority at the gurukul – you must do it together. The first step is to disregard Bhim's absence – express no doubt of Duryodhan's sincerity and integrity, and no anxiety on your brother's account."

"But we will not be able to keep Pitrivy in ignorance – and why could we want to?" Kunti asked. "He will feel very hurt when he finds out… And how could he not… He will feel we othered him, that we disdained his protection… Shall I even be able to protect myself and my sons without his help?"

Vidur looked down at his hands for a moment. "The sky is very mighty, Bhabhi," he said finally, as though speaking to himself. "It shields the earth from the void and protects its fruitfulness. But the sky cannot protect the earth from the beating of the sun, or from the pelting rain." Vidur looked up at Kunti. "I regard Pitrivy as I do the sky."

"I had braced myself for all kinds of slights, insults, neglect, and benighted indiscretion." Kunti turned away. "I did not anticipate murder."

She passed a sleepless night.

One half of her was absolutely sure Duryodhan had had her Bhim killed. The other rejected the possibility altogether. She would never believe Bhim was dead till she saw his very corpse before her. But the salient fact remained that if Bhim was in trouble, Kunti must try and help him. Sitting indolent would mean consolidating the catastrophe; it might push Bhim further towards death… It was unbearable. The next thought was more unbearable still: whom would she send to search and support her son? She could not press the army of Hastinapur into action! Yudhishthir? Arjun? Nakul? Sahdev? The four of them together? Not one of them could outface Duryodhan's treachery. They were likelier to end up in worse trouble than Bhim.

What to do? Put her other sons into peril to save Bhim, or look to their security and abandon Bhim? What a horrific choice. She warred with herself so vehemently she almost missed the sounds outside her door. Footfalls, a careful knock. Kunti was paralysed. Bhim's voice came muffled through the wood. "Ma!" She pressed her ear to the door. There was no other sound. She returned to bed, returned to the door, returned to bed again. Kunti's ears rang all night with flutterings, murmurs, creaks, taps, the muted sound of steel on steel, and low inarticulate cries.

At sunrise she observed her heavy-lidded sons closely: had they been kept awake too, with the noises through the night? "We are not going to school today," announced Nakul.

"Why not?"

"We have to find Madhyam."

"Where will you search for him?"

"In Pramankoti! Perhaps he went to the forest to hunt, perhaps he wandered away and fell asleep somewhere we didn't think of, perhaps he got left behind somehow…"

Kunti was briefly tempted to slap her wayward child. Was she going to have to go through this, now, in addition to heartsickness about Bhim? Was it going to be this, every day? But he had dark circles under his eyes, Sahdev's lips were chapped and bitten, a groove had been furrowed into Arjun's brow, and Yudhishtir looked suddenly pale and thin. Their mother stepped forward and pulled Nakul into her arms. "I know you're worried, dearest, but where will you look for him?"

"We can't sit still," said Yudhishthir, "and just accept that he's gone for good. We can't and we mustn't!"

"But where will you look?"

Yudhishthir looked away. He said, very quietly, "Perhaps we'll find him sunk in the river, or dragged by an animal into the underbrush…"

"Yudhishthir!" Kunti sobbed.

"We have to face the facts, whatever they may be. We have to be prepared for anything, or we will certainly never find him…" He stepped forward this time and hugged her, his chin resting gently on her head. "I don't want to think about it, I don't want it to be true! But if it is, we have to know…" He said with assurance, "The truth does not cease to be if we close our eyes to it – it is not possible to live in the blind dark."

When did he grow so articulate and so wise? He did not grow – he sensed that a grown presence speaking the unpleasant truth was necessary, and he stepped into that role… He had been preparing for it all his short life… Had Kunti failed to face facts, to accept them? Had she been unwise? He was right – if Bhim was gone she must accept it. But was he gone? That tall, broad, vital force of a child, booming, blustering, whipping through the world in some kind of perpetual ecstatic dance – how could he be gone? She would not let him go so easily.

"Go, son! But take your weapons, and don't go alone – take Arjun and Chirantan with you…"

"We're going too," said Sahdev with unwonted finality.

"No, no, you must stay home and protect me!" said Kunti, extending her hands take one each of Sahdev's and Nakul's. They looked mutinous and miserable, but did not refuse.

Yudhishthir hugged them too. "You're right, Ma, we ought to have thought of your protection… But I don't think Duryodhan will harm you – you pose no threat to him…"

For the first time since the moment she laid eyes on them last night, Kunti smiled. "Don't worry about me – I worry about you."

"Then let Sahdev and Nakul come with us! They will hate not going to look for Madhyam."

Chirantan appeared at the door and pranamed her. "Are they princes ready, Queen Mother?"

"Yes! But they won't go to school today – they are going back to Pramankoti to search for Bhim."

"Good! I kept thinking all night that we ought to have immediately launched a thorough search for Madhyam. No matter what state we might find him in…"

Chirantan looked away, lowering his eyes as though regretting his words.

"You are right," Kunti said forcefully, "we must find him. No matter what. I am entrusting these boys to you, Chirantan! Chariot them carefully and bring them back safe and sound. Don't venture into any kind of hazardous territory. Beware of enemies – expect them always." Suddenly she started. "All night… Could you not sleep either?"

"Who could have slept, Queen Mother? There was such a commotion in our basti through the night. Even the children didn't sleep."

"Why?" Yudhishthir asked at once. "What happened in your basti?"

"Yuvraj! Duryodhan's cook – Chakraval. He lived in our basti. It seems he never returned from Pramankoti either. His wife waited and waited, asked everyone, but no one seemed to know anything. So she went to see Suyodhan. She couldn't meet him, but his brothers bullied her back. Rumour is, they thrashed her too. Whether or no, no one slept last night." Chirantan waited, but none of his audience said anything at all. Kunti looked alarmed, Yudhishthir worried, and Arjun more serious than usual.

"Well, let's go," said Yudhishthir finally.

"No," said Kunti. "Wait. I've changed my mind."

"What happened?" Her sons looked at her in surprise.

"I've changed my mind. None of you is going out to look for Bhim – none of you is going out today." She turned to Chirantan. "Go home, Chirantan. The princes are not going anywhere. And you should go home too, at once." All six of them stood still, looking at each other blankly.

A corpse lay in the middle of the Hastinapur highway.

A small group of people lingered nearby, curious and afraid.

Yuyutsu halted his chariot at the sight of the crowd. He pulled the reins to guide the horses toward the dead man. He leapt from the carriage and bent down to turn the corpse over. He recognized Yudhishthir's charioteer.

Yuyutsu smiled grimly: he'd known it was only a matter of time…

He addressed the crowd. "This is Chirantan charioteer. Go tell his folk in the coachmen's colony to collect the body and arrange for the final rites."

No one came forward. Their fear as well as their anger was palpable.

"Will you tell them?" No one spoke. All eyes but the dead man's stared at Yuyutsu.

As soon as he turned his back and climbed his chariot a voice shouted from behind him, "How long will this atrocity continue, Prince?"

He turned the carriage again and approached the crowd. But it was anonymous, all alike. "Do you wish to say something to me?"

"Nothing, Prince, nothing." Several members of the crowd shook their heads.

Yuyutsu was trying to think. What was this? They no longer dared to ask a simple question? Then, suddenly something flashed through his mind. He understood. He pulled the reins harder and sped towards the charioteers' colony.

Around midday Yuyutsu charioted into the Pandavs' residential premises. The grounds were silent – no one appeared outside. He knocked on the door. There was a pause. Kunti opened the door.

Yuyutsu pranamed.

"Oh, come in, Son! What brings you here?" She was kind, but her voice was suspicious, and her manner slightly strained.

"Don't worry, Kaki! I really am like one of your sons," said Yuyutsu. "Have none of you ventured out today?"

"No! Is anything wrong?"

"Have you had any news about Bhim?" he asked. She led him in and Yuyutsu sat down. The Pandavs surrounded him.

"No," said Yudhishthir. "Have you?"

"Not exactly," said Yuyutsu. "But I do have some information. I've been piecing it together."

"What information?"

"Bhim disappeared in Pramankoti. Chakraval who cooked all the food there did not return home. And your charioteer Chirantan who lived there has been killed."

"Chirantan was killed?" Kunti and her sons looked horrified. "Who told you?"

"I saw his corpse on the main road. No one there told me anything. But people I trust have since told me Suyodhan beat him to death himself. They are so terrified, they won't even name Suyodhan."

"But why did Duryodhan kill him?"

Yuyutsu was amused to hear that name slide out of Arjun's mouth – Duryodhan! Indeed, he was Duryodhan.

"He found out that Chakraval laced some food with poison at Duryodhan's behest..." Yuyutsu smiled again, at the ease with which he himself was able to rename Suyodhan... "and that Duryodhan fed them to Bhim."

"Well then it's clear what happened," said Arjun. "Madhyam was poisoned. The cook who laced the food with poison disappeared, and Chirantan who learned all this was killed so it wouldn't come out."

"Duryodhan is not afraid of the truth being known," said Yuyutsu, "or he wouldn't have murdered Chirantan like that in a public place."

"So what is it?"

"This was a warning, to you."

"But is it true?" asked Kunti. "That Duryodhan poisoned Bhim? Or are you guessing?"

"It is true, Kaki."

Kunti surveyed Yuyutsu carefully. "I'm going to ask you a question, Son. Don't take it ill, and tell me the truth."

"Ask, Kaki."

"Why are you giving us this information so readily? Duryodhan is your brother too!"

Yuyutsu smiled. "Duryodhan is my brother, but Maharani Gandhari is not my mother. My mother is not kshatriy; she is a prostitute, and she is not the king's consort."

"So?"

"So it is not essential for me to approve of Duryodhan's misdeeds. I cannot become his accomplice for gain. He can give me nothing."

"Why? If he becomes the king will you not be Crown Prince?" asked Kunti. "You are his elder brother."

"Yes I am. But Maharani Gandhari's second son Dushasan will be the crown prince, not the whore son Yuyutsu."

Kunti was silent. Yuyutsu had called Sushansan

Dushasan. But her heart recoiled with fear nonetheless – if Yuyutsu was impelled by envy of Duryodhan…

"And, Kaki!" said Yuyutsu with another of his irrepressible smiles, "Even if I stood to gain something, I would not support a clearly abominable act."

"Granted you are not given to greed," said Yudhishthir, "but have you no fear either?"

"I am Dhritrashtr's son – I need not fear." Yuyutsu laughed. "In any case I do commit perfidy, demanding the right to speak the truth and support what is just in Hastinapur. Well! I will beg your leave now. Take care, be careful!"

4

Bhishm was delighted the boys had gone to Pramankoti as a single group. He had been receiving sporadic news of the sons of Dhritrashtr and Pandu making two different groups and harbouring some sort of animosity, which had sorely distressed him. Individual fights were part of growing up together. But fights between brothers divided into opposing camps, the sons of Dhritrashtr and those of Pandu, were ominous: it smacked of war. So he was thrilled to hear about the joint venture. But he was disappointed they had not come and told him about it themselves, or come and seen him after. Their fathers would never have failed to extend him that courtesy – he was their pitamah... Whether Kripachary had failed to train them in etiquette or this new generation was uninterested in learning it, Bhishm decided on a philosophical approach – to take the initiative and go meet them instead.

Bhishm made the palace his first stop.

"How are you, my sons?"

"Very happy, Pitamah!" Duryodhan responded, indeed looking happier than Bhishm had seen him in a long time. "Pramankoti is such a beautiful place; one can never get enough of it! Have you ever been there?"

"I have! Over the years I have been to the remotest places in this kingdom – Parmankoti is both magnificent and relatively near. How could you imagine I might not have seen it?"

"Only on account of your age, Pitamah."

"Yes, I have grown old! But I was young too, once." Bhishm laughed. "Did you gain anything from going there?"

"It was all gain, Pitamah!" exclaimed Duryodhan.

"What gain? Did you win some huge amount gambling?" Bhishm had always been suspicious of Duryodhan's inclination towards games of chance.

"No, Pitamah!" Duryodhan protested, a trifle resentfully. "We raced, we played water sports, we had survival contests, sword fights, mace fights, and wrestling competitions. Everything! It felt like I was experiencing a truly kshatriy space for the first time. One needs fire to be tempered."

Bhishm raised his eyebrows.

"Any quarrels?"

"Not even an altercation, Pitamah."

"Not even between you and Bhim?"

"No!" Duryodhan exclaimed. We are always so unjustly blamed. This time we were positively amiable."

"I am glad – keep it up. Amicability between the two of you bodes well for the Kurus."

As Bhishm prepared to leave, Vikarn spoke up. "There was a mishap too, Pitamah."

"What?"

"You keep quiet!" said Dushasan immediately, savagely.

Bhishm turned to him in real anger, but spoke quietly. "What do you mean by not letting him speak? Tell, Vikarn."

"Our cook Chakraval has not returned from Parmankoti, Pitamah! He has probably got lost there."

"Not lost!" objected Duryodhan. "His parents in law live nearby. He must have gone to them."

"Without informing anyone?"

"Don't say another word!" interrupted Dushasan again.

"Sushasan, you are presuming to intimidate your

brother, in your pitamah's presence." Bhishm's countenance was stern this time. "It's indecent behaviour, to say the least. I have come here specifically to see you all, and hear about your excursion. You have no business to interject in a conversation I might have with Vikarn – you have no right in any case to sit on your brothers. Tell, Vikarn. What happened with Chakraval?"

"Chakraval disappeared without a word," said Vikarn with evident relief. "Bhaiya Suyodhan is least bothered, but. Chakraval's wife came late at night looking for him. Sushasan neither received her warmly nor tried to search for him! Pitamah, are we not responsible to people we employ?"

"Of course we are!" Bhishm cried warmly. "You have done the right thing in disclosing this to me. I will do what needs to be done at once. If he is in any danger, he has to be helped out. If he has left voluntarily without notice, he deserves punishment."

Bhishm said his goodbyes and left. He was not worried about Chakraval, per se, but he was worried about Duryodhan and Dushasan, their impudence! How dare they defy his presence and harangue or threaten Vikarn!

He was greeted by Yudhishthir at the entrance to Kunti's desolate little house. He looked hollowed out and exhausted, completely absent his usual equanimity.

"What's the matter?" asked Bhim. "What's happened?"

"Bhim has not come home from Pramankoti, Pitamah."

"What?" Duryodhan and his brothers had not even mentioned him! Warning bells clamoured in Bhishm's ears.

"What do you mean by not having coming to me at once, Kunti?" he demanded of her, responding prefunctorily to her pranam. "I'm sure you are convinced – as I am – that Bhim has made off willfully and will be back in a day or so, but you ought at least to have come and told me, or sent one of the boys to do so!" He glanced at Arjun, Nakul, and Sahdev. They too looked drawn and anxious. "But even if he doesn't come back, you are not to dispatch these boys to search for him! I will do that, at least! In fact it might be best to send them away while we perform a thorough search." He looked at Kunti with some puzzlement. "These boys are, of course, your sons first, but they are also my grandsons. I do love them, and worry about them," he said.

"I know that!" Kunti was apologetic. "But I did not know what to think, or to do… I could not make up my mind whether worry was justified. Otherwise I would have informed you immediately, Pitrivy."

"Another time tell me first and deal with your dilemma afterwards." He tried to smile. "The greatest tragedy of old age is not the slackening of limbs but of bonds, you know. Let me worry about Bhim. I will look for him."

As he settled in his chariot, Kunti suddenly delivered another blow. "Pitamah, Chirantan is dead."

Bhishm did not want to say for the third time today, 'What?' He was silent for a moment. "How did it happen?"

"People say he was murdered, beaten to death on the highway."

Bhishm struggled to stay calm. "When did this happen?"

"The day after the boys' return."

He digested this. "Thank you for telling me. I will need to investigate immediately." A feeling of helplessness trickled through Bhishm – why had no one told him this either? What was going on in Hastinapur? Would he be the last to know? "It is the state's business to protect every one of her subjects. It is the king's duty to find and punish his killer; that much at least he must do."

And he sped away to Chirantan's house.

He emerged from the artisans' basti utterly incensed. Bhishm had to confront Dhritrashtr.

"Regards to Pitrivy from this blind Dhritrashtr!" The king rose and made an attempt to welcome Bhishm. He had been enjoying some kind of intimate tete a tete Bhishm had no leisure to decipher.

"May God give you prudence, Dhritrashtr! An individual may choose to be blind, but the king can't afford it, surely. He needs a thousand eyes."

"You sound annoyed, Pitrivy. Did I blunder into a crime?"

"No crime, Rajan! But you have been negligent. I should not have needed to come here." Suddenly, Bhishm found his rage cool and harden into absolute composure. "Are you not aware that charioteer Chirantan was murdered on Hastinapur's main road in full public view?"

Dhritrashtr was relieved. It took but a moment for him to resume speaking normally. "No! Nobody informed me."

"Does the king sit waiting for someone to approach him with information about crimes committed on the high streets through his kingdom? Is he not in fact obliged to ensure none are? And if a crime is committed, is he not obliged to make sure he receives report of them immediately, the perpetrator is apprehended, and justice is done?"

"That's exactly right Pitrivy!" said Dhritrashtr with a straight, knowledgeable and grave-looking face.

"Why were you not informed, then?" Bhishm demanded.

"Must have been someone's carelessness. I will see to it at once."

"It was your own of course, my king. Allow me to inform you further – Duryodhan killed Chirantan."

Dhritrashtr didn't miss a beat. "What evidence do you have, for making this barbarous statement?" he demanded.

"My testimony is not enough? Very well, I can produce any number of eyewitnesses – how many would you like to hear from?"

Dhritrashtr sat still for a moment, blinking vacantly. All at once he beat his forehead with his fist. Again and again. He threw himself down on the floor and began banging his head against it. He was screaming, "Kill me, kill my sons! Kill them one by one! I am blind, I am helpless. Can't do anything. Can't say anything. Take my sons' life for that of an accursed soot, a coachman! Annihilate the Kuru dynasty…" His courtesans and comfort women tried to restrain him, but he banged on. "Nobody wants me happy. They can't stand my sons' happiness… Oh, leave me," he grumbled, finally drawing to a halt and lumbering back to sit on his heels. "I will die here and now. If my son's life is not even equal to a charioteer's, what shall I do with this kingdom, or this life! Let the charioteers live, let the princes die. Why should this kingdom need any princes?"

Bhishm did not move a muscle. He stood precisely as he had as he entered the pleasure room, relaxed now and calm for the first time today, cool and unmoved, watching Dhritrashtr's histrionics. The absurd behaviour of the king meant… nothing. What was it meant to prove? That the king was not, could not be, responsible for his subjects' safety? That the king and the princes were above law, because they were highly strung and volatile? Bhishm felt nothing. Not even disappointment. True, no good could be expected from King Dhritrashtr. He was blinded by perverse love for his sons and would never acknowledge their mistakes. From this day forth the Kuru kingdom would no longer be recognised as the cradle of virtue. No one would stay: no wealthy noblemen, no competent professionals or artisans, no erudite scholars, no artists, no merchants. If the public lynching of Chirantan went unpunished and ignored, Hastinapur was finished.

Yet the king would do nothing. The onus was on Bhishm again.

As he turned and walked back through the palace halls toward his waiting chariot Bhishm felt that faintness again, that helpless sense of defeat and misery. Once, he would have single-handedly fortified and buttressed the tottering governance of his beloved city. He would have spoken to the right people, strengthened the resolve of others, made war and peace through his skill at arms and sheer force of will... perhaps. But did he intend a coup, now? Did he intend to finally break his vow, seize power, and prosecute his grandson? The fact was implacable: Bhishm was not King. And yet, he was or purported to be a righteous man. He was a kshatriy and a renowned warrior. He could clearly see that injustice was being done. A strong and powerful man had killed a weak and powerless one. Was it not Bhishm's duty to protect the weak from the powerful and punish the guilty? When his mentor Parshuram had heard Amba's appeal for justice, he had sacrificed all love for his most exceptional pupil and placed his own life in grave jeopardy to try and ensure she received it. So how could he – a senior Kuru if not King, Bhishm pitamah – fail to bring Chirantan's killer to justice, at any cost, personal or otherwise? He tried to imagine it – and could not. What he imagined instead was his sad and impotent future, trudging through the twilight of his clan... "You are Bhishm, my son," said the musical voice of his mother Ganga. "You are not Parshuram, you are not Dhritrashtr, you are not even Shantanu. Your dharm is not merely the dharm of a kshatriy, it is the dharm of the man who took a terrible vow. You swore to forfeit your royal prerogative; you were Devavratt; you are Bhishm. You are Bhishm...

No, he could not take it upon himself to transform either Dhritrashtr or Duryodhan; he could not turn the tide of the Kurukul. He had lived, he lived now, this unnaturally long life on sufferance; it was his vow that lived. But this was no longer his time. If Hastinapur desired release from the despotism of Dhritrashtr and Duryodhan, they must depose their regent would-be king, and insist on Crown Prince Yudhishthir. Oh when would he grow up!

Bhishm straightened in his carriage seat. He knew what he had to do. Kripachary was a wholly inadequate Guru for a king… In fact Bhishm needed to appoint a better preceptor not only for Yudhishthir but the other princes as well. But, he recalled with a horrified start, where was that ridiculous boy Bhim?

Bhim found the darkness slowly receding. Or maybe he was passing from the world of darkness into the world of light. Had he been sleeping and was now awake? He opened his eyes slowly and realized that he was in moving water, but he was not swimming – how could he anyway, when his limbs, his whole body, were firmly tied?

He tried to look around and saw two strangers swimming by his side, carrying him along with a grip on either arm.

He wondered how he ended up like this. Who did this to him and why? He couldn't bear being restricted anymore. He applied his enormous strength and snapped the bonds holding him. He started swimming independently. The men moved aside and accompanied him to the bank where, to his utter astonishment and dismay, he saw their attitude shift. They were not here to help him. At the shore they were joined by others who were waiting for them.

Apparently oblivious to the strangers, Bhim sat down on the ground. He was unusually fatigued.

He tried to remember. He was at Pramankoti for water sports, and was offered laddoos by Duryodhan, which shot him into a torpor, and he trudged down to his pavilion and slept. But this water?

He looked up. It was nearly dusk. Soon it would be dark. What was this place? Where were his brothers and all the other people of Hastinapur?

Bhim got up.

A crowd had gathered around him. They spoke an alien tongue, but their excitement was evident.

Bhim was not scared of them or their clearly hostile intentions. From the few words of their tongue intelligible to him he concluded they belonged to a Nag tribe.

A man tried to tie Bhim by his wrists but Bhim pushed him away. The push was enough to topple the man over; he was just saved by his companions. They decided to take Bhim on as a united force, together. They soon realized it was a mistake. Bhim shrugged them off impatiently.

They changed their strategy and formed a wide circle round him, evidently waiting for reinforcements.

Bhim did not wish to offend them. He wanted to tell them who he was and seek their help getting home. How far was Pramankoti, how had he reached there, where were the rest of his group from Hastinapur, and how far he was from Hastinapur now?

He also wanted to know the cause of their hostile stance and what they wanted from him.

Presently there was another group, apparently one of some eminent and respectable men, approaching him. They scrutinized Bhim and discussed him amongst themselves for a while. Finally a hoary-headed man approached Bhim. Bhim could not even think of attacking him; he seemed older even than Pitrivy Bhishm.

When he spoke the old man's speech was even more soothing than his appearance. "Do not fear, my son! We are not your enemies," he said. "We are not here to harm you. Our youngsters are just scared of you."

"Why?" Bhim asked. The man had spoken his language.

The old man laughed and answered, "They say you were dead and your kinsmen had tied you up firmly and had thrown you in the water. They saw several venomous snakes wrapped round your body. The snakes must have bitten you but the men did not remove the serpents assuming that the creatures could possibly do no harm to a dead body. But shortly they saw your body stirring and signs of life appeared in you. They took it as a demonic omen. Still, they could not kill their curiosity. Even as they were carrying your body it came to life! They decided to keep you tied up so you would do them no harm, but then on shore you flattened several of them!"

Bhim would have laughed at this construction, but he was genuinely anxious. The old man said he'd been deliberately tied up and thrown into the river so he would never show up; the snake bites did not kill him because their poison countered the poison already in his body – he had been poisoned before being drowned. The snake venom acted as an antidote.

The old man offered to help remove whatever traces of venom were left in Bhim's body, but first, he said, "Tell me who you are."

Bhim told him. The revelation exhilarated the old man beyond measure. "So you are Kunti's – Pritha's – son?" he exclaimed. "I am Aryakanag – your maternal grandfather's maternal grandfather! My daughter Marisha's son was your maternal grandfather Shurasen! Once Marisha left this place, I never saw her again. I am now practically cut off from them all. I see no one, I just hear about them. I heard about Marisha's granddaughter being reared at Kuntibhoj's palace. I heard about Pritha's marriage with Pandu – and about your father's demise. I could just listen, I could not do anything. I grieve often but I will not weep today. I must celebrate you coming to my home."

He introduced Bhim to the king of the Nags – Vasuki – and to the others assembled there. "Bhim will stay with me," he declared.

It was unreal. Like a fairy tale, where there were no laws and where all odds turned in his favour. He had survived all these carefully engineered mishaps and his captors had turned out to be his own kin.

Sporadic worry about his mother and brothers surfaced to bother him but Aryakanag would not allow Bhim a single moment to either contemplate recent happenings or lapse into uneasiness.

Bhim accompanied Aryak to his home, which was actually an entire village of cottages – every couple had an exclusive cottage to themselves. It was a community; all things belonged to the community as a whole.

Aryak seated the freshly bathed Bhim on a raised platform beneath a peepal tree, drew several circles around him along with some figures which appeared unintelligible to Bhim. He recited some old hymns and showered flowers and other fragrant objects on him. Once the rituals were over, the old man offered Bhim a potion from a large pot to drink.

"A medicine?"

"Yes!" Aryak said. "But we call it 'ras'. It's a panacea, my son! The essence of life."

The drink was delicious. Bhim drank several pitchers and fell asleep again. The old man covered him with a cozy blanket and shooed off the noisy children.

In the morning Bhim was wakened by sounds of people engaged in various chores.

His initial disorientation soon gave way to a recollection of events leading up to the exotic potion. He recalled his separation from his mother and brothers and was acutely pained by thought of their frantic search for him.

"My mother and brothers must be looking for me very anxiously," he said to Aryak as he approached. "I must go home now."

The elder reluctantly gave in to Bhim's eagerness. "I will not keep Kunti anxious long." Aryak advised Bhim to stay on his guard. "My grandsons will see you off to where they found you… But my son, be sure to find out those who tried to kill you. Beware them. If it weren't for the snake bites you would be dead. Why do you live amidst your enemies?"

"They are our brothers. I do not know why they are our enemies…"

"Rivalry among kin bodes ill for the whole clan, my son!" said Aryak. "Beware them."

Bhim approached and greeted Bhishm courteously, who eyed him with love and anger in equal measure. "Where have you been?"

Bhim wondered whether his anger was real.

"We were all suffering pangs of deathly anxiety here! Have you been asleep till now?"

Bhim was in a fix: Shall I spill the beans? Tell him this was Duryodhan's doing? Let Pitamah know how and why he had been sleeping? That Duryodhan wanted him asleep forever? He was on the brink of an outburst, but caught sight of Yudhishthir's and Kunti's faces, forbidding him silently. He resented it more than he could say, but stayed silent.

"All crave slumber," Bhishm was saying. "But there is a limit. All of us sleep, but we do not sleep to the point of getting left behind on out of town excursions!"

This was past endurance. "I was not asleep, Pitamah!"

Kunti was terrified lest Bhim utter the truth. What a ridiculous situation – she had always been afraid they would utter untruths, had always taught them to always speak the unadorned truth, and now she was preventing them from doing so! What did she expect from her young sons!

On the other hand they were not children of a recluse in a hermitage. They were princes and had been brought up in a ruthless, unlawful and all-devouring political environment, where the mere mention of truth or suggestion of justice could be fatal. They must be instructed in both ethics and diplomacy. They must be taught how to uphold the truth, but also how to protect themselves. Secrecy at certain moments of crisis was necessary in royal families; it was part of appropriate royal conduct. A prince's life could not be starkly public like that of a sage's son. Had not Kunti kept the fact of her own illicit pregnancy and son a secret?

"Then where were you?" asked Bhishm in exasperation. He was beginning to feel truly offended by what he considered Bhim's defiance, as well as his repeated glances at Kunti and Yudhishthir.

"Why do you keep on looking at your mother? Will she protect you? Is she older than your pitamah?" But he was weary too. "I am not against hunting either – it is a favorite avocation with kshatriy princes. But you ought to have left at least some information! Or did you think the elders of this family are so stone-hearted they would feel nothing? You don't realize how concerned we all were till you got back. While you roamed about hunting, our hearts bled like wounded deer."

"I did not go hunting," mumbled Bhim mutinously.

"Where have you been then, why don't you tell me?" Bhishm cried. "Were you in the water?"

Yes!

Bhim immediately bowed his head as if in guilt and said, "Yes, Pitamah! I swam too far out in Ganga."

Bhishm calmed down immediately. He wanted to embrace the guilt-stricken Bhim and tell him, "It is not your fault. Ganga is like that. She drifts your heart away and your body just follows… I too used to swim miles and miles and miles in Ganga."

But he restrained himself: he had no intention of encouraging Bhim into doing this again. Bhishm's father Shantanu too had loved Ganga…

"Excess in nothing is good," said Bhishm, simulating

anger. "Learn discipline and know your limits. If you behave like that on the battlefield you won't know where either your troops or you yourself are."

Bhishm looked down at Bhim, who already seemed oblivious of what was going on. Or maybe he simply did not agree with Bhishm… He glanced at Kunti thinking he would exchange a look of agreement with her at least but there too he discerned unspoken resistance… In Kunti, who knew above all else the virtue of forbearance, and who was always pliable, always willing to abide by decisions made by those who were older, more learned, more experienced? He looked at Yudhishthir: no agreement there either. The younger boys too looked frightened.

What was wrong with these people? Like deep water in a pitcher concealed behind an impenetrable cover! Wherefore this secrecy and reticence? Even Dhritrashtr who beat his head against the floor at least declared what he wanted. Duryodhan at least asserted that he did not recognise Pitamah's rights… It was strange, this position as Pitamah of the Kurus. Bhishm had responsibilities but no rights. He could not advise the children, nor admonish them. If Kunti wouldn't recognise his right, he had no power to assert it to her children.….

"Bhim will not participate in any such sports till he has learned forbearance; I don't want this type of thing to ever happen again."

There was no reaction, even from the usually unrestrained Bhim. A thread seemed to bind the six of them together, and leave him out. Bhishm decided to leave. They followed him to his chariot, bowed their heads and touched his feet in reverence. Somehow the realization that is was not they who had made an outsider of him – that they were the outsiders – did nothing to alleviate the ache in his heart. It only intensified.

Recalling the events of the past few hours, Bhishm's

attention paused at the punishment he had handed out to Bhim. In self-reproach his inner voice asked him why he had not seen fit to punish the killer of Chirantan instead. He had not so much as admonished Duryodhan. But he was so prompt in pronouncing punishment for Bhim's harmless little misdemeanour! Why? Did he too exercise power and authority only on the vulnerable? Was it because Bhim was fatherless and his mother had schooled him in love for Bhishm?

At home he called his cook and asked, "What are we eating tonight?"

The cook was pleasantly surprised – Bhishm had never once evinced interest in what she cooked for him every day.

"Were you wanting any particular dish, Ary?" the cook asked.

"Cook something nice, something delicious. Both meat and something sweet at the end. And cook a lot!" said Bhishm with an affectionate, remembering smile. "My grandsons will dine with me today."

"Suyodhan and his brothers?"

"No! Yudhishthir and his brothers."

"But they are just five. Why a lot?"

"Oh, you know that fat boy Bhim! He is a glutton, can't eat enough.." Bhishm said it with such love the cook smiled too. "I want him to eat to his fill. He hasn't dined with me for too long. Have they no right over their pitamah's rations!"

5

Dron's hands fell short of knocking at the latch. Kripi frowned – he was not the one to dwell in dilemma long. Nobody had the wherewithal to obstruct his path. His resolution would knock any hurdles off his path out the way as an elephant crushes grass.

"Why do you hesitate, Ary?" Kripi asked softly.

"It is late," Dron said. "They must be sleeping. Is it appropriate to disturb them?"

Had he made the wrong decision, coming to Krip, his wife's brother and the Kaurav achary? Why would he risk his post and prestige for Dron? Why should anyone else for that matter? And, there was no likelihood that both Krip and Dron would serve the same king and Dron would consent to be Krip's subordinate. And if Krip lost his position to Dron, would Krip not harbor ill-will?

Kripi knocked with authority.

Dron protested: "You make such a racket in the dead of night. Other people might wake up and find out that there's a visitor at Kripachary's. By tomorrow morning Hastinapur will know Dron, friend of Panchal, the sworn enemy of Hastinapur, is in town; and the Kauravs will put me in shackles!"

"That won't happen," said Kripi dismissively. "I was brought up here in Hastinapur. I know the Kauravs well. If they know Kripachary's sister has come to see him, they will at worst think nothing of it."

She knocked again.

Dron resented his wife Kripi's tenacity. How daring could stupidity be! The dangers that he could see before him, Kripi could not even imagine. The generally taciturn and bashful Kripi felt absolutely secure among her relatives.

The knock was answered by a scrupulous celibate.

Kripi said, "Inform your Achary that his sister is at the door with her husband and son."

The initiate rushed back to inform the guruji.

Dron examined Kripachary's residence. How magnificent! Not at all inferior to a palace-block. What did he, Dron, gain from all that penance and meditation? Only humiliation and contempt, privation and discomfort, whereas Kripachary was enjoying the full benefits of whatever meagre knowledge he had! The greatest master of archery lay like a block of gold in the dust whereas the brass in the royal crown glittered.... Dronchary now wanted to find out which was in fact preferable, being gold or being a crown!

Kripachary was delighted by their unexpected arrival. He greeted them very warmly and insisted they eat at once, but Kripi declined. "We ate on the way. We could not keep Ashwatthama hungry too long."

"Only after the morning bath shall we take anything now," said Dron.

Despite sleeping late Dron was up at his usual hour.

Krip too had his routine but gave thought to Kripi and Dron. Kripi behaved as she always did, but Dron appeared tense and wary.

Dron waited for an opportune moment and said, "Krip, I would like my stay at Hastinapur to be secret for a while. As you are aware, the Kurus and the Panchalas are traditionally rivals. My father and I, we have both been on the side of the Panchalas. If the Kurus come to know an ally of the Panchalas has found his way into Hastinapur in the dead of night, there will be trouble. I know they would probably not attempt to kill a brahmin but they would at least want me expelled from their kingdom, which I cannot afford at present."

Dron's doubts baffled Krip, and frightened him not a little – Krip always credited the generous and forthright Bhishm for his stay at Hastinapur and trusted him implicitly… But if Dron really was there with some evil design against the royal family, even Bhishm would not be able to defend Kripachary.

Krip felt a frisson of tension course through his body. He realized how reckless he had he been to get Kripi married to Dron. The factors dictating his decision were reasonable enough – the orphan siblings were brought up at the royal palace. They had no ties with ascetics after all those years. Kripi had no ashram of his own and no contact with the other brahmins. Moreover, sages, hermits, recluses and forest-dwelling brahmins were beginning to give more weightage to caste and clan and no longer saw children as a sacred gift. Children of indiscreet lust were being denied recognition in society. Krip wanted to settle Kripi quickly, and Dron's disregard for social constructs was no minor point in his favour.

With Kripi's family around him Krip felt all the more vindicated – the sense of a burgeoning clan was a new kind of bliss.

In fact, if it weren't for Dron himself, Krip would have no reservations about telling anyone his sister was visiting with family – the pride of saying this, the joy of having inquisitive neighbours and friends drop by… The idea that he might lose his home for sheltering Dron was a double irritant.

Krip was not accustomed to dwelling like an anchorite in an ashram or a meditation hub. His earliest memories were those of the Hastinapur palace. He could not afford to lose this city's refuge. Bhishm was all right but now it was Dhritrashtr, or rather Suyodhan through Dhritrashtr, who held the reins, and the young prince was unbridled in his despotism. Neither Dhritrashtr nor Suyodhan were dependable, or hesitant in faithlessness. If they suspected any resistance from or in the form of Dron, their wrath would fall heavy on Krip. This was not Dasarath's or Ram's council where the command of the household mentor-sage Vashisth would be law even to the king. Krip was 'achary' but for Dhritrashtr and Suyodhan he was a mere employee.

Dron's abrupt exit offered Kripi and Krip to speak uninterruptedly.

"You must be surprised to see us here unannounced!" said Kripi brightly.

"It is a pleasure to have you," Krip said. "This is the first time since your marriage you've come here."

"Well, my husband isn't like the most of men. I haven't been able to vist my maika – my household isn't exactly normal…"

"Surely normalcy is overrated."

"I don't know. Surely it has its place. The achary has no time for it at all," said Kripi. "He thinks an individual has but one home. He abhors the common feminine practice of maintaining two homes – maternal and married. A married woman should have nothing to do with her parents, he believes."

"Which means he loves you a lot," Krip said.

"Does it? When he is with me he is also thinking of his bow; when he is at archery I am forgotten. Is that the case with all men?" asked Kripi.

"All intellectuals are like that, yes," said Krip. "I think they want a wife so that they can serve knowledge; they don't want knowledge to be able to serve their wife."

"Yes but other intellectuals have no difficulty acquiring

basic necessities. My son Ashwatthama has never tasted milk except from my breast…"

"The Achary does not feel the need to keep a cow?"

"He never paid attention to the question! He taught King Drupad's sons, but it never occurred to him to receive a cow in return! He devoted time to acquiring more and more knowledge and serving sages at different ashrams… While my son Ashvatthama and I became more and more impoverished."

"You never urged him to acquire an appreciation of necessities?"

"He convinced me instead – that a brahmin must be self-content. He should not desire wealth."

"Shall I try to make him understand?" Krip offered.

"No!" Kripi said forcefully. "Not now – life has done it already."

Ashwatthama returned home one day, agitated because his friends mocked him for not having tasted milk. Kripi was at her wits' end. Then a solution seemed to present itself: she mixed rice flour and water, and gave it to Ashwatthama to drink. Her son was so delighted he immediately went back to his friends and boasted to him that his mother had 'made' him milk.

"I never imagined you could be in such straits," said Krip. "Otherwise I would at least have sent you a few cows."

"How could you, Bhaiya. I neither invited you to our home, nor visited. How could you have imagined the talented Achary Dron was a pauper! I will never understand the pride of the intellectual who says he will ask for nothing – others must give as they gain. Who in this wide world gives as they gain? Besides, men who serve Saraswati cannot expect Laxmi to serve or favour them."

"Ashwatthama's friends added to their bullying and their mockery of the boy who drank tree milk – whatever that means – they were merciless in any case. Achary Dron found our son and brought him home without a word. He sat like a stone statue in our compound till darkness fell – his visage like thunder, pressaging disaster… When he came inside, he came to me, and all he would say was, I have made up my mind. My son will drink only cows' milk from now on. No matter what…!' I was scared. His speech sounded… there was something diabolical about it, Bhaiya!"

Krip listened in silence and Kripi continued without pause, as though she found incredible relief in finally speaking of all this with someone, needed badly to have done so months or years ago and had been suffering the silence as much as she suffered in it.

"Things were never the same for him again, after that night. He told me that he was atoning for his sin. When I asked, 'What sin', for I had never seen him commit one, ascetic that he has ever been, he said, 'The fact of sin announces itself. My family is hungry and impoverished – isn't it the consequence of my sin? I have insulted Laxmi. The talent I have – I squandered it. Isn't it a sin to have distributed what I had for free? Is it not clear that Laxmi is punishing me for it? I will not commit this sin any more.'

"You have suffered a lot… If only you had sent me a message," said Kripachary with quiet agony.

"I had no means to do so," Kripi confessed. "There was never anyone coming this way. Meanwhile, I was afraid my husband was going insane. I could not decide whether he hated himself or the world more… What a house for my son to be growing in! A mother worried to skin and bone and a father… One evening he returned home suddenly jubilant. I asked him what had happened and he told me Bhargav Parshuram had declared he would distribute all his wealth to brahmins. Achary Dron was convinced that this was the way out – neither beggary nor sale; what he received would be a gift.

But, as it happened, he returned empty-handed from

Parshuram's ashram at Mahendragiri. Well, he did receive some rare gems of learning – secrets of arms and their wielding that Parshuram disdained to teach kshatriy – but no money or material valuables."

"But Parshuram taught Bhishm! He was a kshatriy's mentor then!" Krip exclaimed.

"Of course! Perhaps it was after observing Bhishm's conduct with the princess Amba that he made a resolution not to teach the fickle and cruel warrior caste," said Kripi.

"In any case Dron returned, and his sense of content fell and kept falling, at home. When he leaned his proud, venerable head against my shoulders and uttered in utter desperation, 'Kripi! I know not if my life has any substance,' my heart broke to pieces."

"Don't think like this, Kripi!" Kripachary's said encouragingly, "Your husband is the most renowned student of archery in this side of the Himalaya. Your son will be a great archer too. And this too shall pass."

"I am afraid his contempt for the world which has spurned him and his hatred for the social order will spell disaster for the world and for the order," said Kripi. "I urged him to establish an academy after he returned from Mahendragiri, where we could teach together. But he says he will not live the life of an ordinary man…"

"Achary is right!" said Krip. "But why should you worry?"

"I do not know. He is terrified now that he is in Hastinapur. He is terrified of being ordinary… I do not know what he wants, or what will happen!"

"Why should he be afraid?" Kripachary asked. "How does friendship or hostility between the kings affect scholars, acharys, and gurus?"

"When I suggested we stop here, he said in Hastinapur politics is fear, and life is politics, nothing more, and nothing else, nothing more for anyone… Hastinapur is the burial ground of sublime principles. One must compromise with degeneration in Hastinapur, every day."

"Then why did he come anyway?"

"We went to Panchal," Kripi told him. "Achary Dron decided to approach King Drupad for a competence – he and Drupad were in school together, and the very best of friends. Drupad promised him aid through life… Achary Dron said, 'I cannot penalize my son for being a sage's son. I must provide him the essentials of a comfortable life. I must go to Drupad.' So we went. The journey was harrowing. We were half-starved by the time we arrived – we had to cross Ganga to knock on the doors of the city, and the boatman refused to take us at first. It was only later, after another terrible night – Ashwatthama falling ill with cold and hunger, we too sick with both – that a boat consented to take us for free."

"Did you see Drupad, then?" Krip asked, not sure what he wanted to hear.

"Barely!" said Kripi. "We were not permitted to, at first. Achary wanted to leave, when the guard like the boatman denied he had heard of Dron. But I insisted we would stay, and wait, and try… We sent word – it was all we could do – that Achary Dron begged an audience with King Drupad. We waited through another terrible night, in the cold. But yes, he called for us the next day.

"And?" asked Krip impatiently.

"He refused to recognise his childhood friend. King Drupad said that he was glad to see the renowned Achary Dron in his court, and that he must stay and avail of its hospitality, but it was not possible for the king and the sage to describe their relation as friendship. Friendship is a relation between equals…"

Krip sighed with Kripi – but it was only partly in sympathy. He was relieved too – that Dron had arrived here under the cloud of a Panchal insult – not Panchal favour.

"Achary Dron stormed out of Drupad's palace," said Kripi, "vowing revenge. He walked on heedless as Ashwatthama suffered, as I suffered – I stopped him when we got to the riverbank and once again it was Ashwatthama's plight that gave him pause. He settled us, brought us fruit and water – he was tender, and I nearly wept with the joy of it… 'Let us go back home, to my home, where no king will torture us,' I said.

He nearly said, no. He opened his mouth in anger, to say no. Then he stopped, as though a new thought had struck him. 'Yes,' he said, 'we shall go to Hastinapur.'"

"What made him say yes?" asked Krip. "Can you guess?"

"I don't need to! He told me!" exclaimed Kripi. "We are here because the Kauravs hate Panchal. 'Yes, we shall go to Hastinapur. Not only is Hastinapur the wealthiest and most magnificent of the kingdoms of the north – where an achary might after all find favour,' he said, 'but your brothers masters hate the man I called my friend. I will go there, and see what I can find with the enemy of my enemy…'"

Krip looked horrified, and his sister laughed. "Yes, that was how I reacted too. The sage, the disinterested seeker of knowledge, the scholar most celebrated for asceticism, seeks revenge… Do with that what you will…"

They were both silent. Then Krip spoke.

"Never mind, Bahin!" Kripachary said. "We can only live the life we are given, and only with the materials we are granted. What he wants, what he's after, only he knows. I shall try to get him a respectable post here, because I want to keep you near, now. I want to keep Ashwatthama near. Your son will not go without milk again… Let me see what I can do. I do not think it will be difficult to convince Dhritrashtr that Dron is my friend and not a friend of the Panchalraj…"

6

Dron continued to insist upon secrecy. He wandered around Hastinapur as a bhikshu, a mendicant, and observed students, schools and gurukuls. He watched the princes. They were instructed in scripture, something that passed for strategy and philosophy, and were trained in arms. The instruction was mediocre, the training woefully inadequate. Dron felt a measure of satisfaction – there was certainly room for a man of his calibre here – but he was also afraid. Hastinapur swam in intrigue.

One day when he returned to Krip's home Kripi told him some people from the court had been there.

"Why should I care about politicians in your brother's house?" he asked her.

"Bhaiya called them to meet with you!"

"I have already told Krip, I do not want anyone to know I am here! Not yet!"

Kripi sighed, and wondered whether she might have been married to a kshatriy like Bhishm if she and her brother had not been accorded the dubious distinction of brahminism as orphans in the palace… She wondered if Bhishm would agree to become their patron if she approached him directly… Hers and her son's and her husband's… Despite Drupad, despite Dron…

Krip went to bed thinking about responsibility. He had felt responsible for Kripi, so he got her married. He felt his responsibility to her ended with her marriage.

Dron had not exactly fulfilled his responsibility to her and to Ashwatthama – but he had felt a conflict between this domestic, family responsibility and his responsibility to learning, to his craft, to knowledge as a sacred vocation and as a mistress. Bhishm had abdicated responsibility as king, but responsibility for the Kurukul clung to him like a burr. Krip was never entirely sure what it was Bhishm closed his fist around so desperately, as though it were sand... Was it freedom from care, or in fact care itself? Did not Bhishm choose to care, choose to be responsible – try to care and to be responsible even when the objects of his care and responsibility resisted it?...

But Krip was certain of one thing – he himself would not ignore his sister. He would not let her be drifted away from him. He would do anything for her progress and prosperity, and those of her husband and son...anything!

But Dronchary's decision to keep his presence in Hastinapur a secret handicapped Krip. What did Dron's secrecy mean? Was he up to some mischief that could aggravate the crisis for his wife?

It happened very quickly.

Dron had been hanging about the Kaurav training grounds for some time, looking for an opportune moment to attract the princes' attention. Their gulli fell into a well, and the Pandavs and Dhartrashtrs got into a heated argument about how to get it out, and who would enter the well.

Dron stepped out of the bushes.

"A brahmin!" they noticed, pranamed him respectfully and awaited his pleasure.

Dron asked them why they did not get their gulli out of the well, why they stood about arguing.

"We cannot," said Arjun. The well is deep, its sides are slippery and the risk is too great."

"You don't have to enter the well to get something out

of it…" Dron plucked blades of glass from the ground. He spoke a few words over them, and they went down like darts. One after another he flung them at the gulli, one dart in the gulli, one in the dart stuck into the gulli, another in the dart stuck into the one stuck into the gulli, till there was a spiky branch peeking out over the lip of the well. He plucked it out and handed it to the boys.

"How extraordinary!" Arjun exclaimed again. "The gulli is barely scratched! If I had shot an arrow into it, it would have shattered!" He turned to the mendicant and folded his hands. "Please, wise one, can you teach me? Can you teach us how to do this?"

"I would have loved to," said Dron, "but I am afraid I am no longer a teacher. I am in search of a living."

"Could you please at least tell us who you are?" asked Yudhishthir.

"Tell your pitamah what happened here," said Dron. "He will know me."

"Call Dron!" said Bhishm almost before he crossed Krip's threshold.

"What?"

"You did not tell me your sister and her husband were visiting!"

"Achary Dron has been insisting on secrecy."

"What for?"

"Nothing sinister, Ary," said Dron, entering the room quietly. "Just the precaution of a defenceless brahmin."

"In that case, why did you enter an enemy's territory at all?"

"If friends behave like foes, one must turn somewhere, anywhere, else."

"Bearing a grudge into untroubled waters?"

"Oh Hastinapur is hardly untroubled waters," said Dron with a mirthless smile, "But in any case I assure you I bear no grudges, and no hostility in any direction. Grudges are the prerogative of kings. The Kauravs resent that I taught the Panchalas? Here I am, now. Looking for a livelihood." Dron said.

"Teach the Kaurav princes, then, and your livelihood will be taken care of."

"I must have a gurukul," said Dron blandly.

"Dhritrashtr and Gandhari do not wish for their sons to live anywhere but at the palace."

"Education must have its autonomy, as must the prospective preceptor of the Crown. I cannot teach in any other way."

Bhishm laughed. "Very well. I am sure the Kauravs have too much respect for Saraswati – and for war – to let you drift out of their lives. You will have your gurukul."

"Dhritrashtr will honour your word? You are not the king."

Bhishm shrugged. "Yes," he said simply. He stood to leave, then spoke to Krip. "Come to my house with your sister, Kripachary, as soon as you feel able. I should also very much like to meet Ashwatthama..."

Krip bowed, and showed him to the door. Kripi, Ashwatthama, Ashwatthama, Kripi, Kripi, Ashwatthama...

Dron barely heard him leave. He had had such a powerful vision, so physically real, that it shook him. His foot on Drupad's chest, as the king's broken body lay inert on the ground – a felled tiger and its triumphant hunter..."

Vidur touched Bhishm's feet reverentially.

"After so long!" Bhishm exclaimed. "How are you?"

"Well, by your grace. Just confined to the web of the household you arranged for me."

"We can none of us escape that web, Vidur – it isn't the matter of it that confines and binds us, but our attachment to that matter… Look at me – I am no householder like you, but I too live in a like web of attachment…"

"No Pitrivy! Your household is not an attachment; it is penance, for you. And it is generosity – if you had abandoned us there would be no Kuru clan left," said Vidur.

Bhishm smiled. "I asked Krishn Dvaipanya – your Vyas – why I did not seem able to leave off rearing Kurus though I sired none of my own. He asked me a very important question. Did I rear the children?" Bhishm looked away, into the distance. "I did not. I felt I had reared them, I am known for having reared them. But they were reared by creation, which brought them into the world. Which took Chitrangad, and Vichitraviry, and Pandu, out of the world as it had brought them into it. I played the part creation allotted me, no more or less. If it had been up to me… What do you think I could really do, if these children today were marked by creation for death?"

Vidur was silent.

"This large household was not given to me, a single man, so I would nurture it. It was given to me so I would thrive, nurtured by it. I am not necessary to them; they are indispensable to me…"

"You are generous, Pitrivy," said Vidur, when Bhishm looked at him again. "You are being generous with Dron."

"Yes! Just our luck, Vidur, that a war strategist like him happens to be here, and is inclined to stay! Whenever I thought about whom I would like to have teach our children I thought of two men – Sandipani and Dron. I never expected to have either!"

Vidur said slowly, "If the reports I hear are true, Dron is here because he and Drupad had a falling out. What brought him here is resentment, and possibly an active desire for revenge…"

"Of course."

"Will it not warp our princes' education?"

"The object of Dron's vengeance is not our ally. And he is a master of military science. We must exploit his exemplary expertise in shaping excellent warriors."

"Excuse me, Pitrivy," said Vidur with a smile, only very slightly strained. "Can a teacher consumed by individual desire rather than by what is universal justice or truth, one who has, philosophically speaking, contracted himself rather than expanding his consciousness, teach a king to rule? Should not our chosen achary be capable of the magnanimity of the sky, open and indiscriminate and bountiful as the earth, be preoccupied with the function of humankind on earth and as a unit of the creation you were just speaking of?"

"Yes he should!" Bhishm laughed. "But you are speaking like a sage, not like a statesman. Posterity will curse me if I let this man slip through our fingers. He will train the mighty everywhere he goes. Let him train them here."

"Pitrivy!" Vidur tried again. "Will we tell our children they must not thirst after blood while the man who teaches them to kill dreams of death with every blow he teaches them to strike?"

Bhishm did not laugh again. "You are right," he said, very softly. "But I will not allow Dron to return to Panchal, Vidur."

"Matul, were you trying to flatter my father when you called him the greatest expert in arms across Aryavart?" asked Ashwatthama. Krip was helping him practice.

"I never indulge in false praise – as you should know by now. Hold that arm up straight! And why would I bother to flatter him, anyway?" Kripachary said.

"To appease him. He said he is now a great achary, and that he is building his own training center where he will turn the kshatriy princes into invincible warriors who will topple mighty empires. He said in a few years no king will be throned without his say-so… We will live in a great mansion beside Ganga. He said our days of distress are over."

"You doubt that?" asked Kripachary.

"No."

"My son! Your father is afraid of no one. If he wills it, he can demolish all the armies in this world without any support."

Kripi approached her brother in the evening when no one was around.

"Bhaiya," she said. "Ashvatthama told me what transpired between you and him this morning. Do you really think Achary is not afraid of Drupad?

"Why, did you put that thought into his mind?"

"Of course not. But I know it is true. Achary Dron was afraid, in his court. Fearful angry men frighten me. Do they not frighten you?"

"What he has gained is incalculable. You will not want for anything. Ashvatthama has a secure future awaiting him."

"I understand all that, Bhaiya," said Kripi. "But it has cost you a great deal. I fear my brother may have to pay for my husband's prosperity."

"Don't be silly," said Krip affectionately. "This is exactly how you behaved as a child. My future is Ashvatthama. All the losses of my life are redeemed, now you are here."

7

A gurukul on the banks of Ganga, a home adjacent, an army, and the numerous practice grounds. Two curricula, for kshatriy princes, and for common folk. Dron prepared to address the Kauravs.

Perhaps it was a divine provision that only by wholly hazarding one's present could future victory be contemplated and prepared for. He would be feared as the undisputed supreme military commander of Aryavart. He would then make royal dynasties dance to his tune. He would be an island in a sea of scorn. He hated not only Drupad but, like Bhagwan Parshuram, all these kshatriys – he had built himself a nest of vipers with his eyes wide open. When he was done with them they would be cannibals; they would be so violent they would not pause even before total annihilation.

"Who are you?" demanded Achary Dron.

"Karn," said the boy. "I am the son of the king's charioteer."

"Not a Kaurav prince?" Dron asked.

"No."

"What are you doing here? Why don't you go to your class?"

"Gurudev!" Karn looked straight into Dron's eyes. "Learning is the dessert of those with the calibre to wield it. Saraswati is carried by a swan, not a crow."

"Princes are imparted training so that they become

warriors and protect their states. Training sons of charioteers in warfare is in the interest of neither the princes nor the states. Go to your own class."

"I want to be a warrior, not a charioteer."

"A soldier is also a warrior, Karn!" the guru said. "You may become a soldier, but you cannot become a commander. You are not the descendant of kshatriy warriors."

"Gurudev," said Karn, helplessly, but Dron had turned away.

Only Duryodhan's eyes followed Karn as he left, head bowed and shoulders slumped. Achary Dron was talking about perseverance. He was promising them they would be great warriors – Duryodhan already knew he and his brothers would be mighty… Achary Dron was known best as an archer – no doubt Arjun was pleased he had replaced Kripachary – but Duryodhan was only interested in his mace…

"Do you vow to apply yourselves, and to do my will in this place, and as long as you accept me as your guru?"

What? Why! Kripachary would never have said such a thing!

How could they promise such a thing, cowardly Yudhishthir was saying… Suppose he could not accomplish it after promising it! There was no sin greater than making false promises to one's guru!

What a fake little saint, thought Duryodhan contemptuously…

"Such calculations are misplaced, my son, in devotion!"

Arjun. "Gurudev! I pledge to accomplish everything you require! No matter the cost and the means!"

"Bless you, my son. May you be ever known as the greatest archer in the world."

"On yonder banyan tree is the wooden image of a bird some ten arms above the ground. You have to shoot at its right eye. Take aim. What do you see?"

"I see the bird, the branch she sits on, the tree, the

forest around the tree," said Yudhishthir.

"Lower your bow. Return to your place."

"Duryodhan! Come forward!"

"My name is Suyodhan, Gurudev!"

"Suyodhan is one who fights fairly; Duryodhan fights fiercely." Guru Dron said, "Do you fight fairly or fiercely?"

"Fiercely!"

"Of course. There is a wooden bird on the top of that ashvatth tree. You have to aim at its left eye."

Duryodhan trained his bow and before the guruji could command him, he shot an arrow.

"Your arrow has wandered off into the trees Yudhishthir saw. Go and retrieve it. Leave your bow here. You will not need it again till you have learned patience and respect for the rules by which you are sworn to live."

Duryodhan lumbered off. His brothers heard him crashing through the trees.

Bhim. "I see the bird. I see you. I see my brothers."

"Lower your bow."

It was Dushasan's turn. He was neither curious nor impudent. But, "The bird is badly made, Gurudev. It looks deformed. Its eye is barely visible. The branch it sits on is crooked. There are things crawling up the tree trunk…"

Dron asked him to step back hurriedly, and made a mental note to have the physican exmine his eyes.

Dushasan revolted. He said, "Let someone shoot an arrow at least, Gurudev. Otherwise, what are we doing?"

"Kripachary has clearly spoiled you all," said Dron coolly. "Obey."

"Arjun!" The syllables were music on his tongue, in his ears.

Arjun pranamed to Guru Dron and waited.

"Train your bow, my son," said Dron. "Tell me what you see!"

"The bird's eye, Gurudev!"

"What does it look like?"

"It is a black dot, Gurudev!"

"Can't you see me, or your brothers, or the forest?"

"No, Gurudev!"

"Don't you see the leaves of the tree?"

"No, Gurudev!"

"You can't see the bird's wings, its body?"

"No, Gurudev!"

"You don't see the white, the veins of the eye?"

"No, Gurudev!"

"Only the pupil?"

"Yes, Gurudev!"

"Shoot the arrow."

The bird toppled, an arrow piercing the pupil of its left eye…

"What is it, Karn?" Duryodhan found him in a corner of the yudhshala. "The achary expelled you from class in the morning and you disappeared for the whole day!"

"The achary did not expel me from class; he pointed me towards mine." Karn was dispassionate. "He told me and everyone else in that room in very clear terms that our classes are separate, yours and mine. He does not approve of my offensive presence into your class. I have this life, this intellect, this military skill so I can serve kshatriy princes as a charioteer on a battlefield, or die an anonymous, fameless death as a soldier in their wars…"

"Your warped perceptions always aggravate things for me and add to my worries," said Duryodhan peevishly. "Earlier only the Pandavs were our rivals, now Guru Dron has also joined them. Our adversaries are getting stronger and our strength is being steadily depleted…"

"You all belong in the same class! You kshatriys and brahmins!"

"Drop it!" said Duryodhan, irritated beyond endurance. "So what if an achary segregates us into different classes in a gurukul? Once I assume power I will overturn all rules in my favour! Achary is nothing without state support!" He stood up and began pacing. "Why don't you understand? Till now only Bhim was tormenting us, now that weakling Arjun is also growing wings. Who knows what all Achary will teach him? We will have to find a solution for him too!"

"If you ask me to I will finish him today, and end all your worries."

Duryodhan knew Karn had always perceived Arjun as his sole rival; he never regarded Bhim as his match. But Duryodhan had to deal not just with those two but with all five of them.

"Yes! If ever such a chance presents itself neither of us should drag our feet. And if there is a duel don't stop short of killing him. But for now…"

"For now what? If I were incompetent or lacked talent I would admit inferiority. But they are shutting their eyes to me as though I don't exist."

"Kripachary was never like that. I was convinced Arjun would never attain to your skill or be able to beat you as an archer. But, Achary Dron…!" Suddenly he stopped moving, his eyes wide. "I have a plan. Come with me!"

"Guruputr," Duryodhan called out.

Ashwatthama was surprised at this address. No one ever called him that!

"I am Duryodhan, Guruputr, and this is my friend Karn. We are here to extend you our hands in friendship." And he offered Ashvatthama his gold necklace as a token.

The gold seemed to sweep Ashvatthama right off his feet. Even his mother had never owned gold.

"Very precious, is it?" Ashvatthama could not take his eyes off the gold.

"Very!" said Karn. "Only the crown prince of Hastinapur can wear it."

"Could it purchase a cow?" Ashvatthama asked a bit anxiously.

"This necklace could buy you several cowsheds," replied Karn, surprised.

"Then I will do that!"

"No, my friend!" Duryodhan said, a bit alarmed. "You will not do that. This is for you to wear. You will not have any dearth of milk products here. I will request my father to send you five score herds of cow tomorrow."

"Five scores! Are you kidding?"

"Why should the crown prince be kidding?" Karn asked. He felt as though he had walked into a farce.

"Leave it! Let's go swim!" said Duryodhan.

"Guruputr!"said Duryodhan, as they swam – Karn was pumping away at a distance – "My sincere wish is that when I become king after my father, you should become the patriarch Achary, after your father."

Ashvatthama agreed. "That's an excellent idea. I will not live a hermit's life and leave my children starving."

"An achary, however, must be an expert," Duryodhan continued. "He should be the best in his field. Do you think you will be, despite the blessing your father bestowed upon Arjun?"

"But my father has only blessed Arjun!" Ashvatthama said at once. "It was no boon. If I am competent, I will be better than Arjun."

"Is it not possible for Gurudev to teach Karn as well? I can assure you that Karn is decidedly competent," offered Duryodhan, gesturing to where he was battling the current head on.

"My father will not teach the sootputr," said Ashwatthama with some disdain. And he would never go back on his word. But," he continued with a struggle, "I will teach Karn all that my father teaches me."

"Yes! That will surely work!"

"Are you going to make Arjun a better archer than me?"

"Who said such a thing to you?" asked Dron.

"You blessed him to be the world's best archer."

"Oh! My son, I blessed him among my pupils. You are not my pupil but my son. The son inherits the father sum entire; the disciple gets only what the master gives."

Ashvatthama was not quite convinced.

"Matul," he asked Krip, "Whom does my father love more – Arjun or me?"

"Why do you ask?"

"I am his only son. Even Dhritsdyumn was his pupil – sons do not come and go; they are not replaceable – that is what I believe – but I must know."

Krip answered slowly, carefully. "As far as I know, Achary Dron will do anything for you, Ashwatthama – but he will not expend himself raising another Dron. The sea gives of itself wholly to the clouds – but it is not a river that pours itself into the sea. The sea remains the sea..." Ashwatthama looked even more puzzled, and a bit hurt. "I am not suggesting your father does not love you! He loves you unconditionally and absolutely – as Dron's son. He will train Arjun up as the best archer in the world, because Arjun will be useful to him. He will teach you more than any of the others, because you are his son. He might not train you the way he trains Arjun, for you are not a weapon. And he will not teach you what he wishes only Dron to know. But why should this bother you? Attain your own goals around Dron's ambitions, as I do!"

"Have you attained your goals, Matul?"

Krip smiled and caressed Ashwatthama's hair. "Yes."

8

"Vasu, what is it?" asked Radha, "Are you too tired today?"

"Not physically, Ma," Karn replied, "but yes, my mind seems to be tired."

"Is it a girl?"

What should he say to her? Karn had never known his mother as anything but the busy architect of a limited domesticity. Politics, ideology, even the fraught relations of a masculine schoolhouse – how would he explain them to her? Perhaps he should tell her, Ma, that Achary Dron is a queer kind of gardener. He sows one plant in fertile soil, fertilizes it with mountains of manure, irrigates it thrice a day, erects a barbed fence around it. The other plant, as vital, as healthful, as fruitful, he uproots and tosses on the dust pile – or alright – replants on rocky ground and does everything to dwarf it. Why should the outraged would-be dwarf accept this fate when it has been deliberately denied opportunity to flourish? Why should the plant accept the superiority of that adjacent tree? And how was this just or fair?

"Vasu! What it is, my son?"

Karn looked up at Radha. "I think I have outgrown Hastinapur."

"What nonsense!" Radha laughed. "Are you Ganga or the sun that Hastinapur has already palled?"

Karn laughed. "Yes! Your Vasu is like Ganga and the sun, both! I will live up to my name and make the earth tremble from the twang of my bow!" Radha raised her eyebrows. "Do teachers regularly measure out knowledge in accordance with varn and caste, dole out what they will find useful in their students and withhold the rest?"

His mother's anxious face cleared and hardened. So that was it. "No, my son. Good teachers are Ganga themselves – one acquires as much or as little knowledge as they can, without obstruction or reservation."

"But Hastinapur does not have those kinds of teachers. They are like the wells exhausted even by a few extra buckets. These gurus decide which buckets to fill and which ones to send back empty," Karn said in utter desperation. "My growth is being stunted, a barbed fence has hemmed me in and locked me out!"

Karn slipped into a soliloquy: "Such ambitions I entertained! Such dreams I cherished! I resolved to scale the Himalayas, to touch the sun like an eagle soaring on its mighty wings and… and they've relegated me to a dung hill, to accept the flight of the chicken as my portion."

Radha stroked his hair and said gently: "An eagle's flight cannot be confined to a tiny hamlet; it crosses oceans and mountains and covers thousands of miles to find its destination, its prey, its mate."

Karn looked up at his innocent mother – did she know what she had just said? What she had suggested? The eagle takes not flights of fancy but of wings… And knowledge is not the monopoly or patrimony of any one person, any one place, any one school or kingdom…

"Thank you!!" Karn hugged Radha, his heart light and racing. "You have saved me, again!"

Sleep eluded him that night. He needed another guru.
But who?
Sandipani?
Parshuram?

Sandipani, like Dron, enrolled only kshatriy princes. The royal caste would not let any other other receive advanced training in arms. And the gurus would not ignore the regal will because of their livelihoods and power depended on Kings and courtiers.

Parshuram, on the other hand… Parshuram hated kshatriys. There had been two exceptions Karn knew of: Ram, son of Dasrath, and Devavratt, son of Shantanu. But Dron received what he did from Parshuram precisely because Parshuram donated all this stock of arms and his knowledge to brahmins like him rather than allowing them to fall into kshatriy hands… Karn wondered briefly why or how Dron was so set on training kshatriy warriors when his guru had hated them so… But it did not matter. Parshuram taught only those who were not kshatriys. That was enough. It had to be.

He stared angrily up at the ceiling, where in a few hours Surya would be.

"If I was born casteless and classless why was I also not born sans aspiration? Why could I not rest content? Why…" But, spoke a warm voice in his ear, it was not bare aspiration I gave you, Son. Competence is a much greater and a much rarer boon than caste or class – man made idiocies, artificial devices to impose order on the world… Competence is a gift…

Karn leapt out of bed, gratitude and joy radiating from within him, outward. He would go to Parshuram. He would be a soot, a slave, a nothing – whatever Parshuram wished him to be. He would come back from Mahendragiri, and then, then he would be Karn.

9

Kanik approached Dhritrashtr, "for guidance and advice."

"You are my eyes!" said Dhritrashtr extravagantly. "People are kind enough to call me foresighted – they never appreciate that what I know I know because of you and those like you, seeing everything, understanding everything on my behalf…"

"Crown Prince Duryodhan…"

"Nothing could sound sweeter to the king's ears!"

Pitrivy Bhishm was trying to rustle up support for Yudhishthir, getting people impatient for a coronation… Dhritrashtr wanted to enter this phrase of Kanik's to the official vocabulary of the court. But he could not say more – especially not to Kanik. "What is it?" he asked instead.

Kanik was there about a necklace – Duryodhan had given it to Guruputr Ashwatthama.

"So what? I'm surprised Duryodhan has not been giving Ashwatthama something every day. As he ought."

"Rajan! That necklace is not an ordinary ornament. It is the priciest thing from the treasury and meant to be worn by the crown prince on the occasion of his consecration. Crown Prince Duryodhan has been wearing it early, well and good, but now he's given it away…"

"He is well within his rights," snapped Dhritrashtr. "He is the crown prince."

"Maharaj, it is state property, your property! It's our moral duty to preserve it!"

"Kanik! Crown Prince Duryodhan is my son and the lord of this kingdom! Even if he parcels out all the land and rivers I will not object. And you must also accept his actions as his right."

"Maharaj!" Kanika said in a different tone, "of course. This information has been conveyed to you not because anyone objects or can but because we thought you would wish to know all about the prince's generous impulses. So we may make sure, he does not in fact hand over kingshps or get duped by someone more cunning than he is."

"Alert security. Keep an eye on my son and protect him." Kanik bowed out. "As you wish, Maharaj.

When Dhritrashtr summoned Duryodhan his messenger returned to say that Achary Dron did not permit students to make unscheduled visits home.

Dhritrashtr went to Gandhari.

"What is it? Are you well" she asked anxiously.

"I am very well, only exhausted!" Dhritrashtr said unhappily.

"What exhausts you?" Gandhari smiled. She was familiar with Dhritrashtr's exhaustions – especially those accompanied with that particular pout. "It's a tedious business, occupying the throne of a great empire, Your Majesty!"

"I am the king, but Pitrivy's orders are obeyed here and apparently Dron's at the riverbank! What does my kingship amount to?"

"It's normal for gurukuls to require students' attendance at all times, and consistently. And even the Gandhararaj had to comply with Pitrivy's order to send his daughter to Hastinapur…" Gandhari restrained her bitterness in time. "Though as far as I understand it, Achary Dron is trying to establish himself as a new power-centre in Hastinapur. He leans on Pitrivy because it is convenient at present, but his independence can only be a good thing for you and for our sons."

Dhritrashtr told her about the Duryodhan-Ashvatthama episode.

"I think Duryodhan is being kind to the guru's son to attract Dron too," said Gandhari. "He propped Karn up against Arjun, but Dron has undercut that play. He needs a new approach, and Ashwatthama is it. Rajan, you need to concentrate on curtailing Pitrivy's reach and clout – Dron's will take care of itself – and will never threaten us the way Bhishm's does in any case."

Someone knocked at the chamber door.

"What is it?"

Radha. Her son Vasushen Karn was missing. "He slept at home last night," she said, tears running down her cheeks. "But he was not there in the morning."

Gandhari smiled in her general direction. "Don't you worry, Radha! I would wager all your Karn has gone to look for a new guru. He will return safe and sound, and much more competent than before."

10

Achary Dron had the students, regardless of age or varn, run together every day. Arjun kept an eye out for Nakul and Sahdev, small and valiant in the back. His glance caught repeatedly on Guruputr Ashwatthama. He was small too, but fast. He wove in and out of the other runners like it was a game, exhausted himself and fell behind.

It was a different story at the water-gathering. All pupils had to fetch water from the Guru's residence for the academy proper – everyone seemed to disperse, taking time off to chat, stroll about before collecting their pitchers, pick fruit and rest while trudging back. The exercise was meant to inculcate self-reliance and responsibility – remind the scholar–soldiers in training that work was done to facilitate their worship of Saraswati; nothing appeared spontaneously. But everyone enjoyed it as a recreational activity. The longer they took to do it, the more free time they had.

Everyone except Ashwatthama. Arjun, of course, was unbearably anxious about his beloved Guruji waiting, and raced to pitcher, filled it and raced back to Achary Dron. He found, though, that invariably, Ashwatthama was there first.

One day he arrived huffing to see Guruputr release an arrow that shot through the air to fell three targets at once. Arjun nearly tripped himself. It was as if the arrow did not even travel in a straight line, it was as though it lost no momentum at all when it hit, it was as though the arrow had three lives to live from the start... It was beautiful, marvelous!

Achary caught sight of him. Asked him to revise his lesson from the previous day.

What? Arjun had to shake himself to quiet his indignation – he wanted to learn what Ashwatthama just had! But the guru's ashram is not a marketplace, where wares are equally available. The guru's knowledge is a tree: the better you nurture it, the more fruit it yields. And you cannot pick unripe fruit for sustenance. You have to be there when the fruit is ready, before it falls away, and in its season...

Other arrived, and the Achary began the day's lesson. It was not what Ashwatthama had learned.

Did Achary mean to teach them timeliness? If so, would he not tell his pupils they were missing something if they were late? Did he not believe his students were worthy of some knowledge? What had Arjun left undone, what competence did he not have?... He wanted to speak with Bhim and Yudhishthir about it, but it might sound like a complaint – and Arjun had no wish to complain about Dron Achary. If he extended his hands to beg for knowledge and the guru closed his fist...the guru could not be blamed. The fault could only lie in him, the initiate... Woe to the aspirant who could not do so much.

And wasn't Arjun making too much of the guru withholding one mantr? Yudhishtir and Bhim would never obsess about it thus. Yudhishthir's life was a perennial pursuit of truth and righteousness – mere skillfulness did not carry much weight For Bhim, the only weapon that mattered or counted was the mace. Bhim would certainly ridicule Arjun.

Arjun decided to keep the matter to himself. He resolved to be the first to present himself before the guru the next morning. He would honour all that the guru chose to teach him.

The next morning, as Arjun finished his physical training, his eyes involuntarily went looking for Ashvatthama. Perhaps the thought came to his mind that the Achary would start the mantra only upon Ashvatthama's arrival. Yet he tried to scuttle such thoughts for it meant disregarding the Guru, and the disregard destroyed the learning. If Ashvatthama, who was as swift as Arjun, could approach the Achary before everyone else, why couldn't Arjun? He must learn the art from him.

Following the exercise, Arjun noted, Ashvatthama was the first to rush to where pitchers were kept for fetching water. No one else seemed in any haste except him.

Arjun ran with the others, looking involuntarily for Ashwatthama. Dronachary would not begin without him… But that was not important! Ashwatthama was swift; Arjun must learn to be, too. He raced again, all the way to the pitcher.

The Achary's wife handed a pitcher to Ashvatthama, who sprinted to fill it.

Arjun followed, but was baffled. "How are you, Arjun?" said Kripi devi warmly.

She asked him about his doings at practice, asked him about his mother and brothers, asked him about his favourite foods, told him about her own day. Arjun was torn between gratitude at being spoken to in this manner, at the affection in her voice, and wild impatience to be gone. "Ok, hurry up and look for your pitcher," said Kripi devi finally, "or you shall be late." She went indoors, leaving Arjun staring around the scores of vessels that all looked nearly alike. His energy seemed to leave him. It took him so long to find his vessel the others were already trickling in to find theirs. At the practice ground, Ashwatthama was delightedly returning an arrow to his quiver.

"Repeat the lesson from yesterday," said Dronachary to Arjun, and Arjun did not have the energy to quash the horrible thought – that Guruji and Gurudevi and Guruputr had delayed his coming.

"But why should the gurudev act that way?" asked Yudhishthir, when the five of them were alone in the evening.

"Simple!" said Bhim "Ashvatthama is his son."

"But no true teacher would discriminate between his son and his pupils," Sahdev said.

Bhim scoffed. "The worst thing about idealism is that it blinds you people."

"In that case, answer this," said Nakul. "The Achary can teach Ashvatthama whenever and whatever he wants."

"No," said Arjun miserably. "Achary cannot spare any private moments exclusively for Ashvatthama. We are around the practice ground all day, and advanced archery cannot be taught or learned in one's backyard at night."

"Well, that part is true," said Yudhishthir. "Also that it is clear Achary has an exclusive syllabus for his son. It seems to me very simple: we are in his gurkul, we are his pupils, he is our perceptor. His word and wish is law. Leave the mantr alone, Arjun, and focus on your own work rather than holding grudges because someone else is doing something else and you want that too."

The speech irritated Bhim no end. "This is a publicly funded institution. Dronachary cannot use it for private tuitions without at the very least getting public sanction for them."

"Oh drop it, Madhyam," said Arjun wearily, getting up to leave. "Jyeshth is right. We are not talking about land and ownership, we are talking about knowledge. It is Gurudev's to give, where and when he chooses…"

But he did not feel in the least philosophical. Why is Achary not willing to teach me? The thought ran circles round his mind. He had failed to win over his guru wholly. His devotion was not absolute, his efforts were lackadaisical. He should practice, focus on his work. Arjun wandered to the riverbank and plopped himself down. He dragged a few pebbles over and began chucking them into the water. He felt as though that miraculous arrow of Ashwatthama's had smashed through three trees only to come bury itself in him.

But why three, why not thirty? Arjun was sure the potency of that mantr could be enhanced to cut through as many, and even many more, targets again. Suppose it were applied on the battle ground! Companies of soldiers would be cut down. Hours passed, and Arjun became aware of hunger.

Sure enough, it was mealtime at the mess cottage, and Bhim was complementing Shardul, the cook.

"Come, Arjun! Eat," he said, interrupting himself despite his full-bodied occupation. "Hey, Shardul! Serve Arjun his food, otherwise he will eat up my share and you will complain that I consume more than my portion." Bhim ate anything and everything, but he was also a gourmande. He knew all the ingredients, the methods of preparation, what went with what, who cooked what, and what the provenance of the food was. The cook in any household or home they visited was Bhim's dear compatriot.

The food was served. Arjun ate half-heartedly.

"Invert the cause and effect little brother, and look beyond the usual trajectory," Bhim said, eyeing his plate. "Where there is food, there is usually a consumer. You'll sit there lazing over the plate and then blame me for diligently working through mine and starting another close at hand…"

A sudden gust blew out the lamp.

Arjun had an excuse to avoid eating.

"Why do you need light to eat?" Bhim demanded. "Your hand knows where the food is, and it knows where your mouth is, so what's the problem? Hasn't your hand practiced picking a morsel and inserting it into your mouth enough to be able to do it in the dark?"

Arjun sat up. Practice! It was all a matter of practice. In the dark, by sound alone, and yes, several targets with the same arrow – practice, practice!

Arjun hand moved as though it were raising his bow, picking an arrow, notching an arrow, letting go. Picking an arrow, notching an arrow, letting go. Picking an arrow, notching the arrow, letting go… Peace descended in his mind.

Meal over, Arjun got up, took his bow and arrow and turned to go.

"Whither?" Bhim demanded. "It's bed time!"

"I am going for a meal," laughed Arjun, and slipped outdoors. For a moment he thought of Yudhishthir. He had grown acutely anxious since the Pramankoti misadventure.

He told Bhim: "If Yudhishthir comes this way for a round, tell him not to worry. I am going to practice target-shooting."

Achary Dron woke well before his accustomed hour. Why?

A familiar, subdued sound resonated at regular intervals. A bow twanging. But it was dark! Who was there at this unearthly hour, training a bow?

Dron got off his bed and out, without his slippers. He did not wish to alert whoever it was. He heard the arrows strike too, now.

Dron walked in that direction of the archer.

He could now see the bowman by starlight, intensely engrossed and unaware of his presence. He recognised Arjun.

"What are you doing?"

Arjun started out of his trance, though he did not look like he had been caught. He looked happy to see Guruji.

"I am practicing archery, Gurudev!" Arjun said, "I am working out how to hit more than one target with a single arrow. To aim in the dark by sound!"

Dron detected a slight note of complaint. Arjun had realized Ashwatthama was learning things he was not.

"How will you do that?"

"Practice, Gurudev!"

There was, however, no opposition or bitterness in his tone. Only fervour and longing. This child would repay Drupad on his Guru's behalf. What had Dron been doing? What did he mean by not arming the warrior before marching him into the battlefield? Dron was certainly never going to dispatch Ashvatthama to engage with his nemesis!

"How long have you been here?" he asked.

"Since the evening meal."

"You have not slept at all?"

"Why waste life in sleep, Gurudev."

"But sleep is essential for life, son."

After a pause, Arjun said in a low voice, "Life without expertise in archery is of no use to me, Gurudev. Every man can sleep; hardly a handful are fortunate enough to become accomplished archers."

"How long will you practise?"

"Until I have perfected the mantr, Gurudev!" said Arjun with decision.

"No," said Dron, laying his hand on Arjun's head for a moment. "Go to bed. I will teach you how to hit multiple targets tomorrow…"

11

A few days later the boys returned from a hunting expedition. This was the one recreational activity that seemed designed for Arjun. Those who preferred chariots, those who preferred the mace or sword or even the javelin could only enjoy the hunt as much as they enjoyed violence. They went out to escape the rigours of the classroom or practice ground, and they went to appease their bloodlust. But the archers practiced. So Dron was surprised to see him dragging his feet, looking unhappy again. "Well," he asked his students, "how was the day?"

They hunted small animals, cooked their meat over a fire, enjoyed themselves thoroughly. "But a very strange thing happened, Gurudev," said Yudhishthir – designated storyteller.

"Baghera strayed after a while. He'd been barking and frightening the animals away, so we weren't displeased about it – but then he stopped. We were just about to fan out and look for him when he trotted back, his mouth filled with a quiverfull of arrows!"

"Is he dead?" asked Dron, aghast.

"No! He wasn't hurt! No blood at all!" It was just like your pulling the gulli out of the well, without shattering it," said Arjun.

The Achary frowned, looking between the brothers. "Were the arrowheads iron?"

"No arrowheads but the arrows were sharp. Had any

ordinary archer used them, Baghera would at least have been in severe pain."

"Did you not try to look for the archer?" he asked.

Yudhishthir smiled. "We might have turned back, but would Arjun have agreed to it? We went and searched for him. He was a starving Bhil. His body was covered in layers of grime. His hair had matted into locks. His clothes were in tatters. But he was so engrossed he was oblivious even to us till we called out to him."

"Did you not ask him who he was and who his guru is?"

"We asked, Gurudev," Yudhishthir said. "He was Eklavya, the son of Hiranyadhanu, the Bhil chief. And he said he was Achary Dron's pupil!"

"What?" Dron's mind raced. Who was Eklavya? When did he teach a Bhil... He remembered! An eager, small boy, quite talented, who begged Dron to let him learn with Hastinapur students. But Dron had refused – Aryan knowledge was not given to tribals and indigenous folk. In the first instance, they might organise their own armies and threaten the empire's ascendancy. But even if they did not, even if the only consequence were greater trade and possible assimilation across communities, indigenous social mores were non-hierarchical. Caste differentiation would be diluted, prescriptions and practices become more fluid, and the ordering of villages, towns, cities, change to the detriment of those in power now, to the destabilization of the status quo. There could be no Bhil master archers.

"Did he receive knowledge from me, in my ashram?" asked Dron.

"We did not ask..."

"Right. You may retire," said Dron. "Tomorrow will be another long day. Arjun, wait. I want to speak with you."

When others had left, Dron asked Arjun: "What is it?"

Arjun said: "I am trying to confront my failure, my lack of self–control."

"How have you failed?"

Arjun seemed to struggle to find the words. Stayed quiet for some time as if searching for an answer to his guru's question. Then he said softly: "I felt a complaint rise within me against my guru. Eklavya is a great archer. My guru is his. I want to be the greatest archer in the world.... And it angers me that my faith in my guru is not stronger!"

Arjun was not criticizing him. He was criticizing himself for not having complete faith in his guru.

Dron felt renewed affection for his student.He reassured Arjun, and dismissed him. "Tomorrow you must take me to this student of mine. I would like to see for myself what kind and quality he is..."

Why is this Eklavya crediting Dron as his guru? And how good is he, really? If Eklavya declares Dron taught him, nobody will believe Dron's denial... What skill is he going to be remembered as imparting? He felt Eklavya was avenging himself somehow. His declaration would certainly provoke both Bhishm and Dhitarashtr, both for having taught a Bhil, and for having taught anyone other than students approved by Hastinapur. This was not a private ashram. Dron wondered whether Eklavya might be Drupad's stooge.... Else why should he be lingering around in the forests of Hastinapur rather than going back to his father.

Dron imagined Bhishm and Dhritarashtr banishing him from Hastinapur in anger, forcing him to wander wretched a defenceless again, with Kripi and Ashwatthama, while Drupad laughed.

Arjun led the achary to Eklavya's clearing.

The achary looked around to discover somewhat about Eklavya and his life before he appeared. There was no village or human settlement near. Apparently he dwelt among the wild beasts as a thorough forester. He had cleared a small plot; his little hut faced the practice ground. He had various targets marked out purposefully. There seemed no dearth of arrows. In the middle of the ground, Eklavya had erected a crude statue.

This was no yudhshala. It looked vaguely like an ascetic artist's studio. So Eklavya was not an academic in any sense of the word; he was practising humbug. For a moment, Dron's mind shivered. If it was not a humbug, it was a marvelous act of self-mortification. It was hard penance that did no good but to shoot arrows with a bow better; Eklavya would have won more recognition and achieved more power through penance directed at a divine authority.

Yudhishthir's description was accurate to a T. He was clad in tatters, full of dirt, and his hair had matted into locks. But he was practicing with full concentration. His face was calm and satisfied. It was a state of supreme bliss. Dron came and stood beside him. His attention was diverted. For a moment his eyes were dazed, and then he recognized his guru. He bent down to pay obeisance to Dron and exclaimed: "Gurudev, you?"

In spite of all the warnings in his mind, Dron could not stay detached. He said, "I never accepted you as my student, Eklavya."

"It is not always the guru who decides," said Eklavya said respectfully, folding his hands. "It is possible for a pupil to choose and honour his guru."

"But I never taught you anything!"

"Yet everything I have learned, I have learned from you"

"When?"

"Every moment. Every day."

"How?"

Eklavya moved to the center of the practice ground and stood before the statue. Dron walked up behind him. He realized he was looking at a figure of himself.

"You are always near me, Gurudev," Eklavya said. "You came to me. I follow your directions in everything. When you ask, I pick up my bow, when you ask, I fix the bowstring, when you ask I take aim and shoot. It is you who tell me what technique to use. You correct me when I am wrong and encourage me to go on. Sometimes you criticize me, sometimes you bless me. You have given me everything. If ever you deny me something, it was for a grave fault."

Dron's mind was saying that this was neither a conspiracy nor a fraud. Eklavya's devotion and dedication was unique… But how fearful! If he accepted it, Dron's prudence, his calculations, his reputation, would all be finished, fruitless. No! If it was either Dron or Eklavya, Dron must choose the man with greater significance to the world – he must choose Dron.

And Eklavya was brilliant. By himself, he had learned to shoot arrows that would lose neither speed nor direction, but would not pierce, or would hardly piece, their target. Dron had not taught this skill to Ashwatthama, or to Arjun. If Eklavya had mastered it practicing all alone in a clearing, he was dangerous. Dron's heart cleared of affection, and pity. This muddy child had no right to the knowledge of Dron's kin and kind…

"Eklavya!"

"Ary!"

"I am your guru?"

"Of course, Gurudev!"

"You are my pupil?"

"I am, Gurudev!"

"Are you then ready to give me my gurudakshina?"

"Of course, Gurudev!"

Two voices twined around each other in Dron's mind.

Compassion in this moment would be suicidal. It would cost not only you but the entire Aryavart dearly. You don't show compassion to beasts. It is a fool who loves his enemy.

But his sacrifice! If this innocent, credulous, and devoted man committed himself elsewhere tomorrow, he would pour all his knowledge and his skill there. His attributes are not simple, they are stupid. A skilled and stupid man is disastrous. He must be contained.

"What dakshina do you offer?" he asked Eklavya.

"Ask, Gurudev, and it is yours."

"Give me the thumb of your right hand." His eyes would not find Eklavya's face.

Arjun thought Dronachary was testing Eklavya.

But it was too quick. Eklavya did not hesitate. He picked up a sharp, flattened arrow. Severed his thumb and offered it to his guru.

Dron was unmoved, his hands did not tremble, and his faced betrayed no emotion. Arjun was numb.

"May you be forever renowned," said Dron to Eklavya, and walked away. Heading for the ashram, Arjun glanced at Dron, and thought he saw triumph on that powerful face. Something twinged in his mind. Why was this necessary? Arjun examined his own emotions. He was pleased. With Eklavya's thumb intact, no son of the Kuru clan would ever have beaten him as an archer. Clearly Gurudev thought so too. And Eklavya had already defeated Arjun in gurubhakti, in devotion... would Arjun have been able to give that gurudakshina? Eklavya, who might have been renowned as the greatest archer, the greatest warrior, would now be known for this singular act...

"That was cruel," said Yudhishthir.

"Can anyone be ambitious without being cruel?" asked Bhim.

"Righteous men do not ask others to pay the price for their ambition." said Yudhishthir decisively. "What use is ambition for which men have to be so cruel?"

"You are gainsaying Gurudev. Contradicting him..." said Arjun slowly.

"Yes," said Yudhishthir. "May my guru forgive me – but I am neither interested in games of ambition nor in politically motivated wars. Competition should develop one's own self, not destroy others."

Yudhishthir was right.

But Arjun was pleased.

12

Adhirath felt as though his consciousness had left his body and was drifting, like a wisp of cloud on the breeze through exotic worlds. His body was uncomfortable. It seemed to cry out and his soul returned at once, huffing and puffing, to tumble in home. Adhirath woke to his immediate surroundings. It was the dead of night. He was in his own home, sleeping on his own pallet. A recurrent note resonated through his chamber. It was the sound that had pulled him back. Adhirath listened; it took him a moment to recognize it. Someone was beating at his outer door.

He looked at Radha. In bed but not asleep.

"There is someone outside our door."

"I'll go check." She stood up.

The fuddled male in Adhirath took note.

"No, wait! I will check," he said.

"Why don't you rest?" said Radha. "You don't get any in the daytime; a sleepless night will exhaust you."

"That's all very well – but it's too late for anything but trouble. This is Dhristarashtr's Hastinapur – it isn't safe to throw open one's doors in the middle of the night."

Radha followed him to the front door. She was more worried about his health: he was aging fast now, and ailing. Dhritrashtr on the other hand seemed to be gaining in youthfulness what he lost in youth. Incessantly on the move these days. His chariot and charioteer must be prepared at a moment's notice – why he had picked Adhirath, Radha, hadn't the least idea.

"There's no trouble that isn't your sightless sovereign. He fancies an outing and decides at once to get good Adhirath out of his luxuriant bed…" But Radha knew her husband reserved his ire and resentment not for one person, and it was not Dhritrashtr. Karn. His son ought to have been here – was this the moment to disappear without a word? Karn might have asked his friend Duryodhan for help, or have relieved Adhirath occasionally himself. It was past time for him to have enrolled as a charioteer at the palace, taken charge of the household and safeguarded his younger brothers' interests. Karn was not a child anymore; he had the ear of kings and princes…

Adhirath did not reply. Radha did not always need an answer. He approached the door slowly and asked aloud, "Who is it?"

"Pitaji? Open the door!" said a hushed voice.

She had wished to rebuke him a moment ago – had she heard what she wished to hear?

"I shall – but who is it?"

"Don't you recognize my voice? It's your own Vasushen Karn."

Adhirath unbolted the door. "My own would not have crept out and left like a thief in the night!"

Her heart hammered; she did not know whether to take him into her arms or to shake him. He bent down to touch his parents' feet and looked up at them with perfectly unobjectionable conscientiousness. He looked only a little uncertain, perhaps a touch guilty, a trifle unhappy – and utterly delighted to see them.

He spoke not a word.

"Come!" Radha turned into her and Adhirath's room. She sat on the bed and gestured for Karn to sit next to her.

He did, as though he were taking a seat in a stranger's home, at a stranger's pleasure.

Adhirath kept his right hand on the door, afraid of what Karn's stealthy arrival meant and unwilling to come in too far, get too close. He waited for mother or son to speak. Radha simply looked at Karn, and Karn stared at the floor. Adhirath sat on his pallet too. He did not want to be the first to say anything – he was too angry. How did Radha do it? She rebuked her children more thoroughly than he could ever do, and yet they knew it was done in love, and did not feel hurt. He praised them, gentled them, and they felt rebuffed. Adhirath did not want to say something now that would make matters worse, that would lose him his beloved son again.

But Radha and Karn were silent.

"Where were you?" Adhirath heard himself say.

"I was learning archery, in Guru Parshuram's ashram."

"What for?" A miasma of rage and bitterness rose from Adhirath, entered his words like poisoned darts and plunged into his son.

"A dammed stream must overflow into another furrow."

"Water does not need furrows," snapped Adhirath. His anger was not subsiding – Karn showed no signs of regret or remorse; no sense of having been mistaken or misguided troubled him; he had no notion his disappearance may have caused distress or disquiet. He was presenting himself home following an achievement. "Water can accumulate, grow from a puddle to a lake to an ocean into which all rivers flow as though it were an attainment."

Karn looked up at his father with wide eyes. It had been such a marvelously daring feat – living here by the Ganges, to imagine himself its analogue. His father – mere charioteer, he had always felt – had imagined himself an ocean? had always thought it a strange and terrible paradox that this man who earned a living driving horses across distances should be limited, still, and small of ambition. But the ocean, he had never met.

"You are right, Pitaji!" he admitted. "I have always sought a sea – I never dreamed of becoming the ocean. I was always afraid that if I did not race over ground I would be consumed."

Adhirath felt his anger melt away. This extraordinary son of his was so consumed with ambition he could not enjoy his gifts at all – he was perpetually overwhelmed with doubt, with a sense of his own inadequacy. And what was this metaphor? If the earth could soak him up, would the sea emancipate, did he think? And if he was content to lose himself in the ocean, why not to find himself in the verdure? And was there only one path, one course? "Son, existence is not organized into absolutes and opposites. We only ever comprehend as much as our limited understanding permits us to. The truth is neither so limited nor so simple that we be able to categorize it." He paused suddenly to look Karn son again. "You know I wonder whether the earth nests the ocean or the ocean floats the earth? Whether the earth drinks the ocean or the ocean dissolves the earth? Are we earth or water? Tell me, when you imagine yourself a stream and race toward the sea do you never feel the sea your enemy? It will subsume you. And the earth you flee from – it banks you, holds you up…"

"What are you doing?" Radha asked in amazement. "Your son has just returned from a long voyage – is food and rest dispensable? Will you sit here in the middle of the night expounding on his existential attributes?"

"I am not expounding on his existential attributes my love, I am merely pointing out that it is not easy to determine the nature and bounds of kinship! Lose your self here, find yourself in another… Perhaps it is best in this patchwork, involuted life to maintain some kind of individual equilibrium…"

Radha turned to Karn: "Where is this Parshuram's ashram?"

Karn was at a loss. To his knowledge, his mother had never travelled. How to describe the expanse of the world to her?

"East of east, Ma! Walk east, turn a little toward the south, and keep walking till the earth gives way. Above Mahendragiri, at the edge of the ocean," he said.

"So you travelled to the ends of the earth, my son?"

"Who knows where the earth ends," Adhirath muttered to himself.

"You keep quiet!" said Radha, as though she were telling off a thoughtless child. Her husband was silent, as though rebuked by a thoughtless child.

But Karn agreed immediately, eagerly. "Pitaji is right, Ma – no one knows where the earth ends. The ocean begins where earth ends, but earth begins again past the ocean. The earth and the ocean are kin, everywhere."

"That's precisely what I've been trying to explain to you, Son!" Adhirath said enthusiastically. "If the earth gives way to the ocean, the ocean too resolves into earth! Life is very like that: if sorrow gives way to joy here, joy too resolves into sorrow, elsewhere…"

"Was the journey arduous?" demanded Radha.

"I loved travelling," said Karn. "New places, new people. Nothing inevitable. At home every object, occurrence, person is predictable. Nothing changes. Everyday life palls if you are the adventurous sort."

"That's the difference," said Radha regretfully, "To you change is an adventure – for me it's mortal uncertainty. Here where everything is familiar and certain I can act. While travelling everything requires fresh consideration. How long can we walk? Where will we stop? Eat what? Where? When shall we rest? Will rest be possible? Will we travel with people? What will they be like? The very idea of a journey appalls me."

"I know, Ma. There is a quietude about you that abhors physical disruption. But for some people physical exertion is occupational, and accomplishment."

"I'm sure it is. Did you arrive at Parshuram's ashram without too much trouble, then?"

"Yes! I could actually have found my own way – but I ran into a troupe of penitents going the same way. After that it was easy."

"Guru Parshuram must have been delighted , with you as a pupil."

A shadow fell across Karn's face. To Adhirath his failure and shame were at once palpable.

"Did Parshuram not think you meritorious?" he asked.

His son did not respond.

Radha was nonplussed. "But why don't you answer?"

"Because I don't know the answer!" cried Karn with such deeply wounded pride she felt as though she had been struck. "He was very pleased with his student, and to the extent I was his student he was unsparing with his regard... But it was not me he delighted in, moulded with care, commended! It was some brahmin lordling!"

"What do you mean?" asked Adhirath, aghast at his son's sudden fulminations.

"I only found out after I got there," said Karn in a rush. "There is no open-handed and democratic dissemination of knowledge even at the ends of the earth. It was just an accident – a fortunate coincidence that I found out before I introduced myself..." He was pacing to and fro now, barely glancing at his parents, who were deluged in vicarious agony. "Guru Parshuram only accepts brahmins as students of the martial arts. Achary Dron refused to teach me alongside princes; Parshuram does not teach even kshatriys."

"That is a lie." Radha grasped gratefully at the only card in this tumbling house she could lay hands on. "Bhishm was a student of Parshuram."

"I know! But the Parshuram who taught Pitamah Bhishm was this guru's guru's guru! One Parshuram taught Bhishm, his pupil taught Dron and retired to some anonymous place a while ago. The present Parshuram…"

"There are many Parshurams?"

"The principle of the Parshuram academy is referred to as Parshuram, Ma. Each principle adopts a distinct policy, establishes his preferred protocol."

"So where were you all this time," asked Adhirath, "if he would not teach you?"

"He taught me! I sat at the feet of Parshuram and learned the art of combat!" Karn tried to look at his father, but his gaze fell. "…I introduced myself as a brahmin son of the Bhargav clan…"

"You concocted a fiction." Adhirath was winded. "You perjured yourself in a hallowed hall of learning … and defrauded your Guru?"

"How am I at fault?" Karn fired back. "If the truth is worthless in this world will not lies take its place? I am not such a fool that I will speak truths when they will be used against me. Thriving in this world requires a modicum of practicality!"

Adhirath seemed to be looking past him. "Karn tells the truth … as long as it is convenient."

"He forced me into an untruth," said Karn sullenly. "I would never have bothered to fabricate anything if he had been willing to take me on."

"Oh yes, my son, the fault is never yours."

Karn was stung. "I'm well aware you always found my disposition objectionable, but would you please tell me whether each one of us does or does not have the right to an education? What does caste have to do with the endowment of learning? Why can I not acquire knowledge of the martial arts? How am I lacking, inadequate? What is the objective – the justification! – for dividing humans up into castes and categories, labeling some inferior and others superior to their fellows? Why are some people's lives privileged, made easier at any cost, why do benefits accrue to some people while others are denigrated and maligned?"

"I am neither a scholar nor a philosopher, Son. I don't have answers to your questions. But I do wish you would clarify… Are you speaking of social injustice? Or are you frustrated by the limitations placed on your personal advancement?"

"I am protesting social injustice!"

"In that case you ought not to have done this thing. It benefitted no one that you deceived your way into the academy or that you fraudulently accumulated all this knowledge. You ought to have gotten together the sons of charioteers – of all non-brahmins – and petitioned Parshuram to revise his policy. If you were interested in social justice you would speak of social reform. You would speak of educational reform, and you too would eventually conclude that you must make choices to regulate learning, must decide whom you will teach and give access to what branch of knowledge…"

"I don't understand why you always oppose me."

"Neither do I," Radha finally spoke. "Your missing son has returned. Why do you not ask him whether he is well, and welcome him home? Instead of setting up a tribunal through the night in your bedroom?"

"Because it is not for my son's father to coddle his body while his mind atrophies and his soul shrinks! His mother might. Karn's misguided principles and conduct are an active threat, to his physical comfort as well as to his conscience."

"Do you need to secure his soul this instant?" Radha was exasperated past toleration; she could have wept for sheer rage at the concerted adolescence in the room.

"He started it," Adhirath said mutinously. "I just advanced the debate. Besides, he's here today, sitting with us. Tomorrow it'll be Master Duryodhan again, and 'guruputr' Ashwatthama, and the king's royal vassal the prince of Gandhar, Messr Shakuni."

"Wait, Ma, we're not done. I would like to ask my dear Pitaji again whether he really does not think everyone has the right to an education. Whether he is convinced knowledge is the proper purview and rightful inheritance of brahmins and kshatriys."

"Of course everyone has the right to an education." Adhirath spoke with absolute composure. "Every being has the right to grow and better its state – mind, body, and material well being. We all have the right to earn a skilled living. But beyond this we speak of consolidated bodies of knowledge, we speak of research and inquiry, we speak of physical and mental accomplishment. Successive governing authorities have attempted to regulate who learns what based on utility and social good. What good would a man with a mechanical mind do as a healer? Teaching him medicine is a waste, both of his capacities and those of his teacher And the art of war? It must be regulated! Arms should only be handed to those with kshatriy capacities and conscience! One who champions the truth, protects the vulnerable, and wars always and only against persecution and adharm..."

Karn laughed, for the first time since he had entered his parents' home, incredulously. "You're of the opinion kshatriys stand armed and ready to battle injustice and villainy?" His voice shook with anger. "I disagree. They want power, material and political. They want control, and the swords at their sides give it to them. They despise the rest of us, and would crush the life out of us – except that they need us to work for them, to fulfill their corporal needs. It is exploitation, and casteism."

Adhirath looked like he would explode with rage. For a moment he seemed to struggle with himself. Then he spoke, calmly. "I know." Without a hint of distress he said directly to Karn, "I know that most of these weapon-wielding kshatriys are anything but noble. They do not think about dharm, or justice – they are rapacious and increasingly self-interested. They are not about to sacrifice themselves for the greater common good – they are hedonistic, viciously arrogant, and frantic for gain. That is precisely why I believe knowledge ought to be contained within the hands of level-headed, rational, austere-minded, and principled persons. In an amphitheatre the unexceptional player can only lose a game; strategizing bazaar sales an iniquitous master planner can only misuse objects d'art and kitchen utensils. Stand him in the battlefield, arm him with weapons of mass destruction, and the unworthy man will devastate the world…"

"Do you or do you not agree they think us deficient, and wish to devastate us?" Karn argued.

"I do." Adhirath still looked squarely at his son. "I was born to a charioteer. I grew up in a community of charioteers, tailors and ropers, craftsmen and storytellers. But never in all my years have I encountered a son of craftsmen as distressed by that epithet – 'sootputr' – as I have seen you, Vasu. I have no measure for how despicable kshatriys find us – but I witness your repugnance daily, your grievous horror. If it were up to you you would have stripped yourself of our abominable kinship. You find the state obnoxious, the term offensive, so of course you are desperate to be rid of it. You do not even hate the kshatriys. It is your own perceived deficiencies – your ignominy – you wish to avenge. You do not pursue accomplishment at all – you want vengeance. You do not wish to rise – you want to effect a fall…"

Karn had gone cold. He had not thought his father had ever thought about him. What or how his father knew – he was not sure he wanted to find out.

"Pitaji," he said mildly, "What has my wish to learn the art of war got to do with ignominy and vengeance? Arjun wishes to become a great archer – no one asks him what feelings he is motivated by…"

His father lost all semblance of control. "Exactly! I'm so glad you saved me the trouble of bringing him up! All your grand designs and great ambitions are about this fool rivalry – you want to mortify Arjun! Your sacred invocations of Saraswati herself are pathetic, malignant – you want to master a sublime art, for this? To such an end!" He was breathing heavily, almost dizzy – Adhirath calmed himself a shade. "You say these kshatriys disparage us – are you talking about the common kshatriy? The door warden? The foot soldier or the mercenary? Even the petty officer? I ask you, what place have they in the royal household? I chariot the king! But it is not theirs you contrast your own fate with – you compare your life with the lives of princes! Your great misfortune is just this: that you were not born to a king. And why Arjun? Why not Duryodhan? In fact it is Brahmins who impugned you – Dron who threw you out of his gurukul, and Parshuram. Why don't you brave them? Why is all your bile reserved for the Pandavs, and for Arjun? What did he ever do to you?"

His furious gaze bored into his son as though he would pull an answer bodily from his core.

"Forgive me, Father," Karn said with difficulty, "I cannot understand why you, a vassal yourself of Maharaj Dhritrashtr, are such a staunch Pandav ally." His voice grew stronger, more vehement. "I have the right to choose my friends and my enemies. I have grown up under the aegis of Maharaj Dhritrashtr's Hastinapur – it is he I acknowledge as a sovereign and invest with authority. Suyodhan is the crown prince – and he treated me with respect, as his friend. I know I cannot aspire to the position of a kshatriy prince. The Pandavs? Don't! They are paupers of doubtful derivation at best! I cannot defer to them – I cannot stand them!"

"I know." Ashirath spoke gently now. "I know you cannot stand them and their entitlement – but you are wrong, you are wrong. I do not serve Dhritrashtr – I serve the king of Hastinapur. We are the royal household – our loyalty does not lie with individuals but with offices, with functions, with the state. I need you to understand this. Individuals come and go, their policies are inconsistent, the protocols they prefer to institute are at variance with those preferred by their predecessors. It is essential you recognize this. Realize your own role in this complex apparatus, your own dharm. Do not indulge in the petty politics of princes, do not countenance their family feuds. If the earth can soak up your life and leave no trace of you, my son, the sea will do no less. Be who and what you were born to be. You do not know true from false in other people's narratives – you don't know which of two equally alien factions is your familiar. Establish your own selfhood. Be stalwart. Become greater than yourself, as yourself. Don't choke on childish revenge."

When his son spoke he shattered the calm Adhirath's speech had tendrilled into the troubled night. Loudly, harshly, Karn declaimed, "This place destroys all my self-possession, all tranquility and restraint. Forgive me, Father, I cannot, I will not see that fat fool Bhim and that cunning coward Arjun traipse around Hastinapur like they own it and do nothing while they flourish like weeds. I cannot abide by your wishes or your will, I cannot."

"Stop it," said Radha wearily, before Adhirath could

respond. "Talk about something else, or stop. Let me love my son, let me feed him and put him to bed…"

Her husband stood up. "Very well. Feed him, let him rest and restore his tranquility." He turned to look at the two of them from the door. "I do not love you less – I have said what I have said in love. I was trying to tell you what all futures bring… But if any father could do that, no son would suffer, struggling blindly through this inescapable spiraling life."

He left in discontent, and left discontent behind.

Karn stood up too. "I am not hungry, Ma. I should like to try and sleep." And before Radha could say a word, he was gone.

Though he lay long in bed, Karn could not sleep.

He hadn't thought about his parents at all before leaving. It hadn't occurred to him that they might be distressed or disturbed to find him gone. The idea had seemed so bright, so scintillating, that he had acted without pause, on impulse, without considering hows and whithertos. If he had imagined consequences at all they were limited to scenes of his mother clinging to him and weeping, his father forbidding the journey, quarrels inescapable and interminable… "And is that all?" mocked his restless conscience.

Karn stilled. Reluctantly, like a sluggish snake Dron seeped into his mind. Karn had not been afraid of mere tears and squabbles, no. If someone had found out what he planned, if rumour of his humiliation at Dron's hands had spread beyond the border and on, to Mahendragiri – Karn had feared that no Parshuram, no guru, no brahmin, would dare to grant Sootputr Karn a privilege denied by Hastinapur's Dron Achary. He had been afraid of flouting not his parents' will but Dron's, and Hastinapur's.

But he had also not expected anything less that elation at home, upon his reappearance. He was awake now, partly in anticipation of the excitement of his friends to see him tomorrow, partly because he was sorely disappointed. His mother was glad he was back, and that was all – but his father... Was Adhirath so upset by Karn's manner of leaving that he could not enjoy his return? No! Karn knew him. He had never held a grudge in his life. What was it? Fear, again? That Hastinapur would hire no trained warrior to chariot another? Or was he so sure Yudhishthir would be crowned future king and Suyodhan's friend would never be appointed his charioteer? Karn turned onto his side, pitying him. How inhibited and confined his world must be! To suffer such upheaval about so inconsequential an ambition... His life a placid pond, ruffled by the bare whisper of change to come – it did not figure in his estimations of reality at all A charioteer's post was materially significant the mere thought of its privation killed all pleasure. He did not smile once, at his son's homecoming. He had never endured real suffering. He had been happy simply to rejoice in the puny security of serving Hastinapur's royalty.

Karn did not want such security. It would snarl, and suck the life out of him. And why did his father side with the accursed Pandavs, why was Karn's justest critique tortuous to him, are all civil servants bound like this, body and soul? No regard for individuals at all? All loyalty to an empty mantle, all conviction for the letter of incontestable custom and procedure? They defer to he who rules, and eye the potential ruler? Suddenly it occurred to Karn that even if all servants of the state were thus restricted, unable to see beyond their limited scope, Adhirath was wrong. Karn also knew Suyodhan. Yudhishthir would never be king. On the other hand... he had forgotten to ask his father news of the princes, the palace, the gurukul, the king. Got tangled up in that pointless debate. If his father could not recall himself to his son's proximity, Karn had not been able to recollect where he was, either. That was the worst of words...

He must see Suyodhan in the morning. Must get an update from him. If he was going to live in Hastinapur, he must know it. To the uninitiated. Hastinapur was deadly.

Karn bathed in Ganga, made an offering toward Surya and raced to the military seminary. It was essential he meet with Suyodhan… But would he find them, be able to talk? Who knew what the schedule was like these days. Well, it wasn't as though this were Mahendragiri. Parshuram's rules were law; to the determined truant Dron's rules had always seemed flexible. But there they were! Suyodhan and Ashwatthama – proceeding desultorily in the general direction of the gate…"Karn!" Suyodhan yelled at the top of his lungs and lunged toward him. "When did you get back? Why didn't you tell us!"

Karn grinned. "I'm telling you now! I got home in the middle of the night – and have presented myself directly to his highness. I was afraid you might already be practicing and I wouldn't be able to meet you till tonight."

"No! It isn't like that any more," said Suyodhan.

"How do you mean?"

"As far as Achary is concerned our education is complete. We are free to practise as we please – or not. No one is bound to do or not to anything. He'll take questions – requests for help or if someone has a particular curiosity. But he's mostly engaged in his own research and introspection, and we're engaged in… self-assessment." Suyodhan smiled..

"Ah! Why don't you go home then? What's the point of wasting time here?"

Suyodhan laughed. "Because we have leave to remain, not to leave."

"I don't think Pitaji would object if anyone wished to return home," Ashwatthama spoke up. "Prince Duryodhan remains here of his own will."

"Duryodhan! You call him that? You corrupt the name of the crown prince?"

"Oh it's grown on me," smirked the crown prince. "'Suyodhan' battles with lyrical nicety; I plan to devastate. 'Duryodhan' suits me better. Sushasan isn't overeager to rule personably either – 'Dushasan' – a stern and forbidding administration. We have dispensed with chivalry," he said grandly.

"Oh then, mine prince Duryodhan," Karn said with exaggerated courtesy, "why dost thou not return to thy paternal abode?"

"We're not bound to stay, but we will be at home. Either by the pater and materfamilias or by the fragrant bride probably hidden in the palace wings…It's now or never, friend, that we might enjoy a little unrestrain and revelry."

"So this is anarchy before the takeover, is it? Bull standing still under a slack yoke for fear that hurling about might get him yoked elsewhere?"

"Fitting image for dire straits." Duryodhan laughed. "And then there are our resident moronic mucks and mincing misses. Bhim is still harrumphing about with his mace and Arjun has a bow perpetually cocked, arrow permanently glued to his ear…"

Karn could not join in the subsequent merriment. His pleasure of meeting friends after so long evaporated instantly.

"Come," Duryodhan jogged his elbow and nudged Ashwatthama along with his other hand. "Let's go sit by the river. It's been a long time. We have to talk about everything!" He prattled encouragingly all the way to the bank, shepherding the two of them along. "Our Karn must have been at a complete loss for friends in distant lands all this while. He's choking with the weight of his stories and his mountainous woes. He must not have opened his heart or even his mouth once – though it has to be said that Ashwatthama has you beat there" – Duryodhan glanced at Ashwatthama – "Guruputr sticks to one like a burr but I am not even sure I would recognize his voice in a crowded room. At least my impressive baritone will have some accompaniment today."

He pulled them both toward a clean and grassy spot under a shady tree and sat down. "So? Where were you? What were you up to? Why didn't you tell us you were leaving or where for? You disappeared like rain into a river!"

He gestured at the wide expanse of Ganga before them, at its lapping waves beneath. Karn had not recovered his equilibrium entirely, but he could speak with something resembling composure.

"Why is the Achary keeping you here?" he asked. "Is he going to test you?"

"We've had our examinations," Duryodhan answered, mouth twisting into half a smile. "He's waiting for the accolades now. If the reverend guru does not exhibit his pupils' hard-won accomplishments of many years before the royal family and their adoring subjects, how will they rise up as one in awe of his?"

"What do you mean? When there's a war everyone will see who knows and can do how much of what."

"Oh war! What war? Who's about to wait patiently for a war to prove their mettle? Definitely not Archary Dron."

Duryodhan glanced at the Guruputr, but Dron's son was smiling. Karn thought Ashwatthama was stung by this sustained disparagement of his father's proclivities, but Duryodhan did not seem to care overmuch.

"What plans, then, for this great exhibition?"

"You don't know? Oh right, you only returned last night… but have you spoken to no one since then? Arre, they've constructed a kind of amphitheatre outside the city limits. The glamorous and the good all have invitations – the palace, of course, the ministers, select military commanders, all the pillars of our community and their special friends – anyone who is anyone will be there. Achary will present his achievements – us – to the solemn beating of drums, and we will proceed to showcase his talent – by showcasing ours. Everything we've ever learned is part of the performance."

"What have you learned?" Karn heard himself ask. "What has Arjun learned?"

Duryodhan turned to Ashwatthama. "What has Achary taught Arjun, Guruputr?"

"Pretty much everything," said Ashwatthama easily. "How to bring mounted enemies down while grounded – horses, chariots, and elephants. Mounted battle – mounted archery. How to deal with multiple targets at once, offensive and defensive maneuvers and strategies, targeting voice or sound… All the enhancements he knew, I think. Everything a bow can do."

"The brahmastr?" A rushing vacuum seemed to swallow Karn's words. He willed Ashwatthama to shake his head, no.

"Yes," said Ashwatthama, serenely.

Karn felt like he had been turned into a lightning rod – wave upon wave of fire seemed to crash into him. The ends of the earth, his mother had said. Karn had trudged to the ends of the earth – crossed jungles, rivers in full flood, smoking cremation grounds, mountains and chasms – had bathed in his own blood for this one thing, and had failed. Arjun had been gifted the brahmastra. Here, staring forever cross-eyed up at a compassionate sheltering sky, a stone's throw from Kunti's courtyard, Arjun had been handed the weapon gods were afraid to draw. What an accursed fate, what an accursed…

"Ashwatthama, Ashwatthama, Ashwatthama!" Karn ground out through the red haze in his mind, raised his fists and slammed them into the soil.

"Karn?" said Ashvatthama quietly. "All right?"

There was a moment's tense pause before Karn replied. "I'm quite well," He paused again, and asked, carefully, "What were you people doing while Arjun was progressing toward the unthinkable? No one thought of protesting? All in agreement Arjun deserves the brahmastr?" He looked at Ashwatthama. "You have no objection to your father making zero distinction between his only son and one of his many, many, many pupils?"

"Is that all?"Ashvatthama smiled. "No, I have no objection. Pitaji did make a distinction between myself and his pupils. Arjun is Arjun. Don't you know?"

"What does that mean?" Karn slammed his fists into the grass again. "What is there to know, about Arjun?"

Ashwatthama seemed suddenly to be looking beyond the three of them, beyond the river, bank and water, beyond the farthest shore. And as though a lamp had been turned on, within him, or over his forehead, light lay on him like a benediction. His voice carried its own echo when he spoke, enunciating an incontrovertible truth, an article of unshakable faith. "He has no equal. His devotion to his art and to his guru is absolute, an attainment in itself. Pitaji says no teacher could fail to honour it – no teacher would dream of withholding a practice, postulation or principle from him."

Karn screamed. "What is it? What has he ever he done to deserve…? What does he have that cannot be denied?"

Ashwatthama looked at him coolly. "He is steadfast. You have not had the privilege of watching him worship Saraswati."

"You have not had the privilege of watching me do so! Your father turned me out! I climbed Mahendragiri to seek what was handed to you in Hastinapur! You have no idea what all I went through with Parshuram!"

"What happened?" asked Duryodhan at once.

"I was exhausted. I was starving, parched, and threadbare by the time I reached Parshuram's ashram. I could not see him. I was kept waiting for two days, in that state, in that place. I had to get past the comptroller. Do you know what Parshuram said to me, when I finally appeared before him?"

This time, neither Duryodhan nor Ashwatthama said a word.

"What do you want?" asked the guru.

"Knowledge, Gurudev!"

"What kind of knowledge?"

"Archery, Gurudev! The art of the bow!"

"Kshatriy?" He was unforgiving. His eyes blazed, as though he would burn through Karn to get at the truth.

It was this again. Always this. Karn's ears buzzed, he was seeing double, the world seemed to have tunneled and was collapsing into Parshuram. If he is not a kshatriy, he may not learn to draw a bow? Because this handful of wiry, aged men have decreed it shall be so? They shall hoard the world's knowledge in some vast brahminical chest and jangle the keys in front of Karn, beyond his reach, forever? Had he imagined he would step into this presence and it would rise to greet him, clasp him in its arms and say, "My protégé! I have been waiting for one such as you all my years, oh son! You have suffered much for love of Saraswati – but your toil has been your ransom! Come, draw of my bounty and flourish! Henceforth and for always…"? He had not imagined this.

He told the truth. "No. I am not."

"Good. I would have had to disappoint you," said the guru, at his ease.

"Why is that, Gurudev?"

"Only brahmin boys are taught arms at my ashram. You are brahmin?"

A buzzard landed on Karn's head. Truth and lies vanished. The buzzard pierced a hole between his eyes, screamed in his face. Yes! Say yes! Or you will walk all the way back to Hastinapur tonight, with your tail between your legs. Who knows, Sootputr? Who knows you here? Your wretched arrogance will kill for you all that is good and possible in this world – let it go, now! Speak! Say yes! I am brahmin! Body and soul – what lack will he perceive? None!

"Yes. I am brahmin."

"I knew the moment I saw you. Your high colour, the knit of your body… You could not but be brahmin. Gotr?"

For a moment Karn was at a loss. 'brahmin' was easy. What was all this? … The buzzard croaked. But of course! Caste is inherited from one's father. His guru was his father too, of a sort… Karn saw his path clear before him. It was no dishonourable path… He was hurting no one, depriving no one, no one! He sought Saraswati, he wanted to learn. Knowledge is pure, is truth. Truth is the god of gods… "Bhargav!"

The guru was inordinately pleased. "If brahmins are the only beings able to shoulder the burden of truth, my son, it is only the best of them who gravitated toward the martial and the military truths… The art of war is the art of the Bhargavs, it is we who nurtured, pruned, and preserved it, always."

"Father! Why are the kshatriys not the rightful acquisitors of the knowledge of arms? Has not custom favoured them?"

"Yes! And they have dishonoured it! Their martial training is no longer protection for the weak, the safeguard of justice and dharm; it oppresses, is a tool for base intrigue and sadistic savagery. The right to bear arms and to manage human violence rests with those who serve dharm, objectively, and level-headedly. kshatriys do neither. They are at best, erratic. Power does not merely corrupt, it is devolutionary. kshatriys are rabid." He paused in his ruminations and focused his gaze on Karn's face again. "What is your name, and where are you from?"

Would he have to lie, and lie, and lie to sustain his lie? If he mentioned Adhirath or Hastinapur Parshuram would know he had lied, or would hear he had lied, sooner rather than later. He had to reinvent the whole of himself.

"I am Jnanmitr, son of Kashi's Dharmmitr, Guruvar!" Karn said.

"Your father named you well…"

"And this is your dedication!" Ashvatthama's anger and outrage were evident. "Lying to your guru's face to con knowledge out of him? Theft…"

"What was I supposed to do?" Karn snarled. "When door after door is slammed in my face, what am I supposed to do? Tie my hands together and sit quietly on top of them?" He looked at Ashwatthama maliciously. "I am neither lazy nor a mouse, Guruputr! I will snatch the meat from brooding fate and devour it whole."

"Karn the fabulist!" Ashvatthama's voice was venomous in its turn. "And you have the gall to ask, Why Arjun?"

Karn pulled up a heavy clod of grass with his hand and dashed it at the river. "Why don't you answer the forsaken question?"

"Self-surrender! Fidelity! Love!" Ashvatthama shot at him.

"If your father had thought to test my mettle he might have experienced a class of devotion rather different from whatever he has been accustomed to. I served Guru Parshuram better than any son has his father. I slept as he did, I woke when he did. I would have died a thousand deaths to please him. And he loved me. Guru Bhargav, who disdains assistance, took me with him on practice runs to the forest. I worked so hard my guru asked me to be merciful to myself! And one day… Do you know what happened?"

"What?"

Duryodhan said nothing through all this. He lay back, eyes moving from Karn to Ashwatthama and back… He was listening to their debate like a grandfather might listen to children squabbling over pebbles, or sweets.

Guru Bhargav was so enthused by his own innovations in marksmanship that he forgot his age and infirmities. He forgot he had been fasting, and was weak. He continued to practice till his body, suddenly, seemed to give out. Karn had been with him since the previous morning. They had penetrated deep into the woods; the retinue and other pupils had been turned back hours and hours ago. Had Parshuram not loved this particular pupil he would have been alone. As it was, responsibility for his care rested on this sole pupil's shoulders. Karn had been observing for some time that Parshuram had pushed himself beyond endurance. His guru was not the sort to admit to exhaustion, and rest voluntarily. But Karn could neither call for help nor suggest they rest – where in this wet, wild place could suit such a purpose?

Karn worried, and worried the thoughts around his mind. If he asked Parshuram to stop on his. Karn's, own account, perhaps? But this was no moment to appear weak – on whom would Guruji then depend? Besides, he might very well ask Karn to return to the ashram, and never bring him along in future. No, Karn must convince Parshuram he needed rest, and that his pupil was capable and more than willing to keep a lookout while he did.

Suddenly Parshuram's hand shook to draw his bow. "What is happening?" he said aloud. "Why does my hand defy me?"

Karn seized the moment. "You are exhausted, Gurudev.

You have been practicing continuously since morning – you must rest a little."

"Rest before mastering this application?" Parshuram laughed. "I cannot do that, Son. "If we return to the ashram now we will have to begin again tomorrow… And then you will say, tomorrow at this time, rest. Shall I resign myself to learning nothing new? Shall I admit that this Parshuram's sun is setting as we speak?" He was laughing, but something in his laughter pained Karn abominably. He had not graded pain before. The hurt of failure was fleeting in comparison with this – the hurt of having no tomorrow and tomorrow and tomorrow to do better, be better, succeed. The death of hope.

"Not at all, Gurudev!" said Karn robustly. "We all draw our strength from you. You are not losing any of your capacity; you are just fatigued. We needn't return to the ashram. You could easily rest here awhile and resume your venture."

"Here?" Parshuram ran his eyes across the knotty, dense landscape. Karn leaped ahead. The guru had acknowledged his fatigue and was prepared to pause, but could not see the means by which repose might be realized. His pupil's heart was singing, and wholly engrossed in caring for his beloved guru. He leaped toward a likely spot beneath a tree, cleared it, collected some fallen leaves and prepared a pallet. He hung his bow from a branch, stood his quiver against the trunk, and said, "Rest, Guruvar!" As Parshuram hesitated, unwilling to let mere matter win over his mind, Karn gently took his arm and guided him down. When his guru was prone Karn sat crosslegged beside him, gently placed Parshuram's dreadlocked head it on his thigh, and fanned him with a piece of cloth. "Please sleep for a little while, without disquiet."

The guru smiled and said, "It is ever the son who sleeps in his parents' lap – for a role reversal circumstances have to be dire. I am not unwell, and you are not my son… But if ever a student can earn kinship with his teacher you have done so. You have given me much joy – the most and the least I can give you is this right, over me, that a child of my body might have enjoyed. You are as dear to me as any pupil or any son has ever been to his guru or his father…" Parshuram closed his eyes and slept. Karn could say nothing. There was no need to.

All he wanted, all he could think of, was that Guru Parshuram enjoy undisturbed rest. That he had trusted Karn, that he loved him, was precious, so precious that it felt precarious. So Karn thought only about his guru's head on his leg, and remained still, within and without. It was true that Adhirath had never received such devotion – that Karn had never felt such protective adoration for his own father. But what he did feel could only act as intense focus now: he wished simply to prolong his guru's rest, not unlike a mother might wish to for her small, sick son. How could he do anything but everything to preserve it?

A guru sleeping on his pupil's lap – what pupil could earn such felicity? It was an historic moment! Some reward for exceptional action in a previous birth! He would not dishonour such a gift, he would not.

"What happened then?" Duryodhan was getting impatient. "The guru woke satiated, and was pleased with you? He granted you a boon? Some new weapon?"

"He didn't hand you the brahmastr, did he?" asked Ashvatthama.

Karn's joyful radiance was blown like a wick that collapses to ash in the wind. His features contorted in anguish, his eyes brimmed over even as he strained to stop those terrible tears – but he could no more have stayed the collapse than he could an avalanche.

His friends were stunned.

"I did not know this pinnacle of glory was an ephemeral climax – it was the catalyst of disaster."

Duryodhan and Ashvatthama could not speak.

Just as Karn was slipping into full awareness of his bliss, something stung the bottom of his thigh. He wanted to shoot up and slam his hand down at the spot. If he moved, but a muscle, his guru would wake. The thing stung again. It felt as though a blade were cutting, and cutting again, and again cutting up into his flesh. Karn reached his hand carefully down to try and reach it. He could not. His hand came away empty, but soaked and dripping red. The thing was deep within his flesh – was it drinking Karn's blood? There was a pool forming under Parshuram's headrest. The thing sawed on in…

Was this a test? Karn cried inwardly. Perhaps the guru had himself selected this spot. There were hornets here, a wide variety of bees, beetles, wasps, centipedes, crawlers and mantises. The alark drank blood. Perhaps Parshuram had played out his charade of exhaustion just so so he could assess his pupil's loyalty, his devotion… Whether or no, Karn was sorely tested, and must pass the test, come what may. Let the insect devour his thigh whole. He would not budge.

As he sat warding off insufferable pain, sunk in a haze of blood, the guru opened his eyes and sat up. A drop of Karn's blood had stained his cheek. He touched it and smeared his hand. He looked down at Karn's thigh drenched in blood.

"What's this Jnanmitr? Rise. Stand up!"

Karn stood up and reached for the thing that had burrowed into him. A tiny little mite! It had transformed Karn into a wounded warrior, bled him dizzy. He glanced at the guru. Parshuram did not look at all fuddled with sleep. He did not look in the least gentle, with love or pity. He did not look impressed. His eyes were wide with anger. "Who are you, imposter?" He was very harsh.

Karn was puzzled; his wound burned with the full clarity of urgent physical reality. Imposter?

"Brahmins are not long-suffering – and Bhargav brahmins tolerate nothing without vocal protest!" The tidal wave of his fury kept rising – he was angrier with every word. "You are a kshatriy! Answer me! Aren't you a kshatriy? Who possesses such endurance? Who are you?"

Karn thought he understood. Parshuram was sure Karn was one of them – a savage, arrogant, noxious kshatriy. One whose power was an insult, and to whom he would concede no military skill. A kshatriy, he thought, had deceived and cheated, wrested knowledge from him.

Karn fell to his feet, weeping. It was no performance. He was in pain, physical and mental, of a sort not to be borne. The long deception had worn him out – and these last hours had exhausted all reserves of his tremendous fortitude. If there were anyone in the world he could shed tears in front of, anyone he could tell the truth, his Guru Parshuram must be that man. And he did not understand Karn's reality at all – what he thought – that was not it at all…

"I am not a kshatriy, Gurudev! I am Sootputr Vasushen Karn, son of Hastinapur's Adhirath."

The guru was not mollified. "Why did you conceal your identity from me?"

"You would never have accepted me as your pupil!"

"So? If something you desire is not handed over to you immediately you will steal it?" The guru's stern gaze pinned Karn in place. "Is that your code? Would you rob a richer man of wealth, appropriate a woman without her approval, con a king of his kingdom?"

"No, no, I am not a thief! I am not a thief, Gurudev!" Karn cried out in desperation, his forehead at his guru's feet. "Knowledge is no one's patrimony! Learning is not stolen – it cannot, it cannot be private property! Learning is a resource, like water, like light and air – how can such resources be justly reserved for brahmins?"

"Oh, is this academic dissent, Sootputr?" The guru asked with composure. "Very well. No, water, light and air do not belong to any one; but if an individual, community, or kingdom accumulate or safeguard a part, it is theirs. Water belongs to no man or kingdom but a well might, a port might. Knowledge belongs to no man but what I have learned, you may not grab, by force or by fraud." He paused to look at Karn. "You have not just deceived me, you have revealed you will recognise no social law nor abide by any norm against your self-interest. The wish or will of no individual or state has any significance for you, over and above your own. You are selfish, Sootputr."

"No, Gurudev!" Tears from Karn's eyes drenched Parshuram's feet. "No, Gurudev! No! I was being anathematized as a Sootputr! I wanted revenge…"

"With violence?" Parshuram mocked.

"With knowledge! With accomplishment to equal theirs!"

"Listen, Sootputr, I cannot tell you how many times that word was used against you, I cannot say how many times you heard an insult where none was intended and turned your name against yourself. Soot Adhirath is Dhritrashtr's friend. He does not consider his state humiliating. Vidur is the son of a slave, he is a minister in the royal court of Hastinapur. He never attempted to become kshatriys. kshatriy kings touch calloused brahmin feet and abide by brahmin instruction. They don't feel humiliated. Vishvamitr rejected his kshatriy state, not because it is ignominious but because he could foresee growth beyond its scope. He did not pronounce himself a brahmrishi; he produced one through the arduous effort of a lifetime. You proclaimed yourself a Bhargav brahmin; you made no effort to attain the brahmin state. When you chose to tell stories you disparaged application, sustained effort, the work that is a sacred mission. You saw fit to employ dubious means to attain your ends… What are your ends? What do you need the martial arts for? What will you do with all your prowess?"

Karn did not speak.

"Are you in need of the means to defend yourself against violence?"

"No, Gurudev."

"What for, then?" Parshuram paused. "And why are you so interested in the brahmastra?" His eyes glinted, and his voice seemed to burn the air around his pupil. "If you lie to me again…"

"I will not lie, Gurudev!"

"Then tell the truth."

"I am tormented by the triumphs of Kunti's son Arjun," said Karn, as though the words were being torn out of his throat. "I want to be better – the greater archer, the greater warrior."

"I knew it. Your intentions, your outlook, are corrupt," said Parshuram. "You do not want to evolve yourself, you want to extinguish another. You have no creative will; you see yourself as an agent of destruction and ruin. You wanted all this," Parshuram gestured around him, and at himself, "to gratify your pride. Envy and vengefulness will never permit you to distinguish between right and wrong, between dharm and adharm. All this power you have acquired – it will never be used to protect or nurture ordinary, honest courage – rapacious and bloodthirsty brutes will feed off your strength. Dron's refusal – he was right to deny you such power. I have sinned by handing you weapons. I ought to sever your head with my halberd, to prevent the impending abuse of my knowledge," he concluded calmly, "but I find I cannot. My arms will not discharge themselves against my student and my son. But there is no place for you here any longer, in this ashram. Leave, now. Before my heart hardens and I change my mind…"

"So you left?" asked Duryodhan breathlessly.

"Well … no," said Karn hesitantly. "No, I didn't leave so easily. Actually, I saw he was less angry now so I was doubly determined to get my way. I was sure if I begged he'd agree – my training had only just begun. If my secret hadn't come out a few days longer I would have mastered its use… So I thought if he'd just let me continue for a few more days my greatest ambition would be realized…"

"So you disobeyed him too?" Ashwatthama was neither sympathetic nor bothering to conceal his contempt.

"I obeyed him. You can call it anything you wish to," Karn snapped.

Karn joined his hands and prostrated himself. "Don't forsake me at this stage, Guruvar! Let me complete the brahmastr training. I will leave at once."

"That is impossible!" Parshurama said. "Is it not enough that I have not punished you?"

"Gurudev!" Karn sat up. "Is my offence so grave? I adopted my guru's gotr. Are not guru and father kin?"

"Don't make specious statements, Karn!" said Parshuram. "Your guru and your father are alike significant, but the relations are different. You inherit your capacities – your colour, caste and creed – from your father; you guru develops these capacities. This is not about the gravity of your offence. It is about your disposition… There are times we do not reveal our identities. We reveal only a part of who we are, or we present ourselves as one we are not. But we need to consider whether our deception is justifiable, whether it services dharm – our own or otherwise. Your deception was impelled by evil propensities. Your capacities will never benefit society – they will only ever be used to serve your own interests. Your accomplishments do not regard justice or dharm before they are engaged. Truly, vengeance is born of inherent evil… Go away, Karn. In any case you will forget what you have learned of the brahmastr in time, without practice… Go…"

Karn stopped. His absolute unhappiness was evident.

"Never mind, my friend," Duryodhan said with his hand on Karn's shoulder, "Let it go. It isn't exactly imperative that a single cook should prepare your entire meal! What you received from Guru Parshuram, you received – procure the rest elsewhere." He caught hold of Karn's arm and pulled him to sit next to himself on the ground. "Now listen to me carefully. Whatever you've learned is quite enough. It isn't as though you're wielding the brahmastra against a multitudinous enemy force tomorrow." He paused to survey Karn. "I think… You've arrived in the nick of time. I'm rather grateful your secret came out and you were expelled…"

"What?"

"Listen, my friend! All the princes are supposed to showcase their talents in the Hastinapur amphitheatre. You know Yudhishthir – he knows nothing. Bhim and his mace I can smash to smithereens; he probably won't make it out of the arena alive. Nakul and Sahdev are negligible. Which only leaves Arjun, and his bow. Without you here we had no way to contain him. But you're here. You know at least as much as we have been taught. I want you to begrime that inveterate immaculacy of his. At the very least he must not to sail through the day indisputable… Ok?"

Karn nodded fervently. "Yes."

"That's what I meant! What use would the brahmastr have been to you in Mahendragiri, if Arjun had been declared the unconquerable here? What would we do with your brahmastr? Weapons of that class are just ornamental in any case. A warrior parades around as their master in theory, but when are they ever really used. Even if someone does decide to use a thing like that, and is able to overcome his own fear and trembling of consequences, his kith and kin will beg him not to destroy the world, not to go so far… Let Arjun break under the weight of the blasted thing – it isn't as though he will ever be able to use it. Even if you fight a duel with him, he will not be using anything of the kind against you. Hope you get my point?"

Karn laughed. "Oh don't worry, my friend! Arjun will never achieve the royal distinction you are so distressed to imagine!"

As they watched Karn leave, Ashvatthama turned to Duryodhan. "I've never liked this particular friend of yours."

"Why not?"

"He is a walking insult! And I am sure he is against Pitaji," said Ashvatthama. "Also the way he behaved with Guru Parshuram: it was wrong, it was unprincipled in every way. Was it not?"

"Oh, Guruputr," said Duryodhan with exaggerated solicitude, "What you will eventually learn is that morality and ambition are two, equal but different. They each have their place. Think of it this way: I must have my kingdom. If I operate only in accordance with the principles of dharm I will decidedly fail. As it happens, rules are followed by cripples, by incapacitates. The man who can reach out and take what he wants does not make rules about doing it – he does it." He patted Ashvatthama's shoulder. "Karn's strength, his proficiency, and his authority challenge the Pandavs. Karn will and must never be their friend. He is a walking weapon. Why should I deprive myself of it? Why should I not use it? With Karn here, the Pandavs will not survive the day without calumny."

13

Dron's chariot raced towards the construction site of the amphitheater, immortal edifice of his dreams.

In his pre-Hastinapur days, Dron had realized, it was not that he had no ambition; it was simply that his resources were always disproportionately inadequate. Those without ambition were blissfully self-contented; those without attributes were, ironically, always well endowed with means. Natural logic frustrated him sometimes.

He gestured halt at a felicitous vantage point.

A decline in the road, and abruptly his mind too descended from the crest of happiness into gloom. The Aryan brahmin ideal was the self-sufficient rishi, with an established, self-contained ashram where he was approached by pupils and crowned kings paid obeisance to him. They supplied the guru's needs and felt blessed. Here he was, serving at a king's household like an ordinary employee.

Was it a necessary for a man to degrade himself to achieve success? Was it necessary for an individual to barter his conscience for comfort? Was it not feasible for a man to continue with his work, make improvements in his field, and be appreciated for it? Dron had never solicited royal accolades; all he had needed was a cow.

Now he had an entire shed of them, in addition to a royal residence, raiment, and ornaments here at Hastinapur... But he had become an employee... Was the downfall of a rishi necessary to produce an achary?

"No, no!" That amphitheater did not represent degeneration. Warriors trained by him would demonstrate their skills, his name would be exalted not only in Aryavart but across the Jambudip. The royal dynasties would prostrate themselves at his feet for blessings, and so he would train their princes, commanders, and troops

But this delicious lust for attainment and accomplishment… Did it denote a rise or a fall? Did advancement lie in accumulation or abnegation? What would he gain from this amphitheatre, from the success of princes displaying their talents here?

His own accomplishment so far – archery, warfare, his students. What was this?

He reached the amphitheatre gates. Ashvatthama greeted him."I think my own fate is linked with this amphitheatre," he said.

"You say 'my' and not 'our' future, my son! Why?"

"I should have said the future of all of us is linked to this amphitheater; but I am concerned only with my own future."

"This amphitheatre will stand testimony to the efforts of my students, and my own. It is a display of skills learned, evidence of work done… Nothing here will determine our future success or failure."

"Pitaji! Don't you see this amphitheatre will decide the future king of Hastinapur?"

"Really!" Dron feigned astonishment. "Says who?"

"Duryodhan believes so!"

Dron was shocked into gravity. So this was not innocuous gossip. Was it a symptom of conspiracy?

"Why? Will the winner of a contest to be held here be awarded the kingdom?" he asked.

Ashvatthama could not ignore the sarcasm in his father's voice. "You don't think it's true?"

"Why would I?" Dron demanded.

"Duryodhan says the events in the amphitheatre will determine who the best among us is, and establish which is the stronger side – Dhritrashtr's sons or Kunti and Madri's sons."

"So? If Arjun is judged the best warrior, will he become Crown Prince?"

"No!" said Ashvatthama. "If the Pandavs are stronger it will be Yudhishthir; if Dhritrashtr's sons win he will declare his eldest son Duryodhan is Crown Prince."

"But Yudhishthir is older," Dron contended. "And the kingdom is legally his father's."

"So what! Duryodhan says the kingdom belongs to him and no one can grab it."

"But that's politically unethical."

"Duryodhan does not subscribe to that theory. He believes in power."

Dron stared. "And who taught him all this?"

"His matul Shakuni and the master diplomat Kanik," said Ashvatthama in a satisfied voice.

His father was silent for a moment. "Even if the future king of Hastinapur is chosen in the amphitheatre, why should it concern you or me? Both Yudhishthir and Duryodhan are my pupils."

"I did refer to my future, not to ours." said Ashvatthama.

"Your future? Is it separate from mine?"

"Not yet, but it might be, one day. Your favourite pupil is Arjun, and my friend is Duryodhan! Our futures might be both distinct and apart."

Dron was alarmed. This statement was charged with Ashvatthama's juvenility – even if he had no idea what he was saying it did indicate an obstinacy which could lead to action.

He said, "Why must we side with one of them? Can't we be neutral?"

"In politics, it is either our side or the opposition's. There is no neutrality. One who is not on our side is our adversary," parrotted Ashvatthama.

"Duryodhan says so?"

"No! Kanik does."

"So you have gained more knowledge from Kanik and Duryodhan than from me!"

"You teach warfare, not practical politics, Pitaji!"

"Your practical politics seems hinged on bestial force – on might is right – on grabbing and holding. It cannot be beneficent to human beings, or to life at large… And if this 'contest' does come down to force, let me assure you, Arjun will win individually and the Pandavs will beat their cousins hollow…"

Ashvatthama interrupted his father. "You know Karn is back in Hastinapur?"

"So?" Dron was bewildered by the irrelevance of this news, but warning bells immediately sounded in his ears.

"He learned archery from Parshuram. He will challenge Arjun to a duel in the amphitheatre."

"But Guru Parshuram admits only brahmins."

"Karn lied. The point is, he is an expert archer."

"I will not allow him to make a display in my rangshala. This is the exclusive domain of Hastinapur's princes."

"You quit your sacred grove for the sake of my weal, Pitaji!" said Ashwatthama. "Both Ma and Matul claim no one and nothing is dearer to you than me."

"They are right, my son!"

"Then, Pitaji, grant me this wish. You refused to teach Karn, and you received Eklavya's thumb as your fee. You have trained Arjun as your best pupil; you have taught him nearly everything you have taught me. Let him go through this test. Let him compete with Karn, who has trained at your own guru's feet. It will be your test too. And if you deny Karn this chance, I will assume you don't love me."

"And if Arjun emerges the winner? What then? Have you not considered that your own father's best pupil may in fact win?"

"No! It is just that I don't like Arjun. He is too egocentric. Still, I promise that if Arjun wins, I will quit Duryodhan's side and be friends with the Pandavs."

Dron smiled a little, inwardly. He had no objection, really, to permitting the contest. If Arjun won – as Dron expected him to do – his son would be pleased, his pupil would have beaten Parshuram's, and Dron's repute would be at its zenith. If he did not permit the contest, the audience would imagine the worst. If Arjun lost… but Dron's entire being clamoured against such an eventuality.

"Your wish be granted, son!" Dron spoke lowly to Ashvatthama. "I will not prevent a contest between Karn and Arjun."

14

Bhishm was furious. All he had wanted, since the return of Kunti and her sons, was this convocation. One hundred and five Kuru princes would gather together for blessings from gurus and elders, take hold of Hastinapur's reins and, led by the eldest Yudhishthir and counseled by Vidur and Dhritrashr, relieve Bhishm of his responsibilities. The arrived at the rangshala like arrogant ruffians, two rival gangs of them. One hundred, and five. How would they ever defend Hastinapur together, consult each other to safeguard her interests, do any good?

He tried to be pragmatic. His vision had not materialized yet, but perhaps this was a phase. He must endeavour to work out how he could heal this rift.

He surveyed the scene. The Kuru princes had already retreated following the formal salutations, and the curious crowd on the stands awaited their return. The construction was a flat plane on the outskirts of the Hastinapur ramparts. The selection of this plot, its planning and construction, were all accomplished under the personal supervision of Dronchary, Kripachary, and Vidur. It was marvellous how, when people came together to achieve a single objective, wonderful things could be done. What a magnificent amphitheatre these three had created, so each prince would have a chance to display his ability. There was a place for individual performances and adequate provision for group activities. There were separate tracks for horse and chariot races. Yet the rangshala faced imminent threat of becoming a battlefield. Seated in the main spectators' pavilion was Dhritrashtr, flanked by Dron and Krip, Vahlik and Somadatt on one side and Vidur and Bhishm himself on the other. Shakuni and Kanik were seated ahead.

Today, Bhishm was repelled by Dhritrashtr's blindness. When Vidur told him the princes had come to greet him, his only question was whether Duryodhan looked the best. What a curious animal, this King of Hastinapur! He could not see what was going on outside, and people could not see what was going on inside him. He lied and dissimulated in public; in relative privacy he could not even feign impartiality. He had allowed Shakuni and Kanik such proximity that his ears were shut to any other sounds.

Bhishm's gaze roved to the other pavilion, where he could see Gandhari. Bhishm had brought her here, to Hastinapur, as a bride for Dhritrashtr. He did not regret it, exactly, but he did wonder whether it might not have been better for Hastinapur if the kingdom had not been powerful enough to compel Gandhar's acquiescence. She had been so envious of Kunti when Yudhishthir was born while she was still pregnant she had tried to destroy the foetus in her own womb, because the child would never be king. Was she looking forward to the Pandavs' disgrace today? And Kunti! There at least Bhishm felt only joy. Despite all her humiliation at the hands of Gandhari and Hastinapur royalty since her return, she sat beside the queen, reporting all that happened in the stadium. Bhishm marveled at her capacity to endure. Grave, solemn, undeterred, unscathed amidst all adversities. He wondered fleetingly whether Kunti knew only forbearance and forgiveness, or whether she knew too how to strike, at an opportune moment…

The princes, mounted on their chariots with their bows and arrows, entered the stadium. Bhishm basked in the thought that when they embarked on an expedition no army in the world would have the guts to engage them. The chariots retreated, raising clouds of dust. Dron called for swords. Sahdev and Dushasan appeared on horses with their swords drawn. Bhishm sat up. Why Sahdev and Dushasan? Was it an attempt to convert the event into a show of strength between the two groups? Was it a deliberate scheme to see or show which group was stronger? Why couldn't they be one force? Who was bent upon dividing them? Sahdev was a conspicuously better swordsman, but his focus was on displaying his art and agility. He was not sweating to crush his opponent. Dushasan was not a rival he must vanquish; he was only a medium through which Sahdev could put his skill on display. As for Dushasan, defence appeared to be his only endeavour. Either Sahadev was not conceding him any chance to counterattack or Dushasan himself was reluctant. Dronchary called them off and Bhishm was relieved… Perhaps there was no malicious design behind pairing those two. Maybe Bhishm was imagining things.

Next on agenda, a mace fight, and the natural competitors were Bhim and Duryodhan. Bhishm noted that they lacked the exuberance betrayed in such exhibitive events. They were tense and agitated. Duryodhan initiated the offensive stroke. The blow was exceptionally violent; it was no display; it was full-blooded assault. A timely dodge spared Bhim a few bones; he might have been crippled for the contest. He was angry, though, and returned Duryodhan's moves all the more fiercely. Bhishm hoped Dron had not allowed them to wield maces used in a real war. Bhim was the most aggressive of the Pandavs and the usual target of Duryodhan's wrath. Their contest was disintegrating into a furious fight. Bhim was stronger, Duryodhan more agile. He struck Bhim a few times, but this invited so many unhappy returns that Duryodhan had to scamper around in defence. It might be a ploy to tire Bhim, but the outcome was the opposite. Bhim seemed to be gaining momentum.

An abrupt call from Dron stopped the show. Ashvatthama rushed in and positioned himself between the two. "Stop it. This is a stage and not a battlefield where you must kill each other. You are here to exhibit your talent, not commit murder."

Bhishm was pacific again. He was contented too that his observation was vindicated. Others had noticed the malice lurking behind that show. Had their rivalry really reached the point of wishing to spill blood? He also noted that though the first blow had come from Duryodhan, Ashvatthama's protest was primarily directed at Bhim. An answering hush had descended on the stadium. The spectators were both surprised and scared. Was this the beginning of a civil war among the Kurus?

Achary Dron got on his feet and gestured the audience for attention.

"Now I call upon the most charismatic of the Kuru princes, Kunti's son Arjun," he announced. "Though an expert in various weapons, he is fondest of archery. He will not contest anyone as an archer; he will only demonstrate his mastery of the art."

Positioned carefully in the stadium, Arjun seemed to be standing at the very epicenter of celebration. He sought the blessings of his guru, his mother and elders.

Bhishm had always known he was becoming an archer par excellence, but Arjun had accomplished more than his wildest expectations. His exhibition of the diverse dimensions of archery was marvellous! Bhishm was comfortably convinced that with Arjun there, Hastinapur was safe and secure. He need not dread an external enemy. But why did Dhritrashtr and Gandhari look so miserable? It really was unfortunate that Dhritrashtr and Gandhari had not been able to love the Pandavs as they did their sons. They could have rested in the knowledge their kingdom would be safe for another generations, and these five would certainly have cared for them better than their own children were likely to do. Kunti had raised them well.

She looked transcendentally happy. Her sons had blossomed beautifully... She had never discriminated between Madri's sons and her own – she revelled in Nakul and Sahdev's success as fully as she did in Arjun's or Bhim's. Could Gandhari ever have accepted Yuyutsu as her own son? And Bhishm thought of Droncharya. He must be given full credit. Guru Parshuram was not the only one in that line of the great gurus. In Mahendragiri, there was Parshuram, in Ujjayini, there was Sandipani, and in Hastinapur, there was Dronchary.

Even as Arjun basked in his mentors' blessing and acknowledged the deafening applause from the people for the exemplary exhibition of rare talent, a young man in shining armour, with gold in his ears, appeared with his bow and arrows and stood beside him. It was Vasushen Karn.

Bhishm frowned. What was he doing here in the Kaurav amphitheatre? And Dron had not announced him... He was slightly taller than Arjun and six-seven years his senior. He looked powerful and proud. Karn greeted Dhritrashtr by pressing palm to palm, turned to Kripachary and Dronchary to salute them spitefully, and spoke aloud, "Let the audience heed what I am going to say." He said to the hushed crowd, "You watched Arjun's show of archery and appreciated it. I am pleased that you appreciated gallantry and art. But appreciation of art must not discriminate on any grounds but merit. If Prince Arjun deserves praise for his archery, so do other archers..."

"Who is he?" A chorus resonated through the stadium.

"I am Karn," he said. "What Arjun has now performed before you, I can perform better, if you will permit it."

"Show us!" shouted the audience.

And Duryodhan's voice was heard above them all. "Exhibit your excellence, my friend! Show us!"

Bhishm was nonplussed now. What was going on? This was a showcase for the Kuru princes, not an open platform or public contest. This youth could have been granted permission to display his talents by the royal family, but he knew of no such request. Yet Duryodhan seemed to have expected the interruption.

Kunti was annoyed for the first time that day. Who was this insolent boy? He looked like he held a grudge against everyone but the king, and he seemed to be here specifically to challenge Arjun… Throwing challenges around was by no means uncommon among kshatriys, but there was a time and place even for the most outraged protests. Why was this Karn intruding here, why was Duryodhan encouraging him, and most importantly, why was Dronachary not showing him the door? Well, she admitted, Duryodhan would encourage anything that might humiliate her sons – and she was not exactly a stranger to Karn's rancour toward Arjun in particular… But when did this boy gain such currency that he could stride into Arjun's exhibition and demand like treatment? She had never given much thought to the Karn who followed Duryodhan around and mocked her sons – who was he, really?

To her relief, Kripachary stood up.

"Karn! This is not a public platform for people to act out their whims. You are being intrusive and discourteous. Do you have permission from the king and Achary Dron to be here?"

Karn offered no apology, explanation, or salutation. He turned to Dron at once. "Do I have your permission to challenge your prize pupil? Do you trust his talent and teaching?"

The audience seemed to hold its collective breath. Karn's demeanour was so confrontational its current held the entire amphitheatre in its grip. Everyone looked up at Dron: How would he react? Karn had crossed all bounds of decency and decorum. He had challenged not only Arjun but Achary Dron too.

Arjun feared that the Achary would disallow the challenge out of sheer irritation, which might give Duryodhan reason to say both Arjun and his guru were afraid of Karn's valour and skill. This fellow had not been seen or heard from since his expulsion from their class. Arjun had not cared where he went or what he did. He had unearthed himself to challenge Arjun on his day of triumph – well and good. It would have been stranger if the day had ended smoothly. Arjun wished Guru Dron would permit him to expose Karn to the world. Arjun welcomed a duel with anyone, especially him.

Bhim fumed. Duryodhan's attempt to pulverize his bones had energized him, if anything. It took only a moment to switch between exhibition and war: this was Duryodhan, who had tried trip him up for years, had insulted everyone he loved over and over again, had tried to kill him, had killed Chirantan and who knew how many other people. When Dronachary called off the fight Bhim had just been getting started. But of course – rules, regulations, and laws in Hastinapur emerged from where they were buried the moment Duryodhan became a target. Down, Bhim! Now the same treatment was going to be meted out to Kanishth? Karn was going to be allowed to get away with his ridiculous accusations, without Arjun being given a chance to beat him down?

"You have my permission!" called Dron.

Duryodhan and his brothers were applauding wildly, Dhritrashtr was visibly contented, Bhishm looked stunned.

Kripachary was aghast. What was Dron thinking? This man had demanded a thumb off Eklavya because he perceived a threat to Arjun's ascendency, he was supposed to have spent years dampening rivalries among the Kauravs, he had called off Bhim and Duryodhan only moments ago, and now he was going to permit Karn's arbitrary challenge? Of which the outcome might be anything at all?

Kunti looked at Karn appraisingly. He was easily as splendid as any of her sons – and Arjun looked delighted he would have a chance to meet this new challenge. But there was something very wrong with this situation. Pitrivy could not be counted on to protect her sons against their cousins, but she had better hopes from Achary Dron. He was meant to restrain excess and enmity. What was he doing? Did he know for sure that Karn intended only to exhibit his own skill and not to harm her son? If not, why had he just granted a virtual stranger permission to shoot arrows at Arjun?

Karn began.

He was easily Arjun's equal.

Duryodhan and his fellows were shrieking and clapping, Sightless Dhritrashtr was commending the skill of Hastinapur's archers – What about the skills of of its princes? thought Vidur – and Bhishm, sunk in real regret that he ever decided to make Dhritrashtr rather than Vidur Regent, dialogued with his mother's voice in his head.

Karn laid down his bow. "I have performed every feat hitherto attempted by Arjun. I could go on, but real contests require an adversarial mode. I call upon Achary Dron's favourite pupil and Kunti's son, Hastinapur's the greatest archer, Arjun, to a duel..."

The entire stadium was on its feet. Since the day's inauguration there had been more than one occasion for someone or other to point out that this was a rangshala not a yudhkshetr – an exhibition ground not a battlefield – but here was this Karn, standing straight and tall before them all, calling Arjun out for a duel.

Duryodhan hoped he remembered his promise, to not spare Arjun's life on any such occasion.

Arjun took up a position opposite Karn. "Gurudev! May we begin?"

Kunti watched with her heart in her mouth. Karn was as good as Arjun. But she saw no way out.

Bhishm's dejection had given way to rage again. What kind of fool was this boy? Did he think prince's lives were so cheap that they would be sacrificed to the vanity of talented charioteers' talented sons? And did he have any sense at all of the responsibility that was bearing arms? Or was a duel a game too?

"The brave must be allowed to establish their claim to bravery!" Dhritrashtr was crying. "We must find this worthy young man a good position in the Kuru army! Valour and talent must be rewarded!"

"Oh yes, Maharaj," said Vidur in a tight voice, "I completely agree. Even if they end in death, displays of skill are of course of paramount importance. Would you like to call for a continuation of Bhim and Duryodhan's duel too?"

Dhristarashtra was appalled. "Why! Is it policy now to promote fratricide?"

"Certainly not. But we must be consistent. We can also not invite enemies to come pick off our sons. Dronachary did not raise this amphitheatre for charioteers' sons to have a platform for the public assassination of princes."

"Yes!" said Dhritrashtr, suddenly stupid. "But how else do we promote gallantry?"

Fortunately, Duryodhan's clamour interrupted the conversation. "Why is Achary not giving permission?" he shouted.

Bhishm suddenly perceived his life as an extended exercise in futility. Was it for this he brought up these children, and their fathers? So a brother would support an outsider's murderous intent against his own brother? It.was certainly not the kind of adulthood Bhishm had envisaged for Duryodhan.

Duryodhan clamoured for permission to be granted. Arjun pleaded for permission to be granted.

Dron's eyes swept towards Ashvatthama. He seemed to be reminding him of the promise he had made. He did not like the animosity against Arjun that he saw in his son's face. And then his eyes rested on Karn. There was challenge in Karn's eyes – not Karn's but Parshuram's.

"Begin."

Bhishm stood up. His ears were ringing. He would not allow Arjun to be killed before his eyes by this stripling....

"Wait!" It was Kripachary.

Bhishm had not heard Krip speak so authoritatively since Dron had come to Hastinapur.

He approached Arjun and Karn and stood between them.

"Listen Karn," Kripachary said. "This is not a war. Arjun has not humiliated you, so you might demand a duel and expect your demand to be met. There is no swayamvar on to justify your intent. You simply wish to defeat Arjun to gratify your ego. You are taking the easiest route to instant fame, by challenging the ablest warrior in this kingdom. You lose nothing if you lose to him; and if you vanquish him you win exceptional renown. That Arjun accepted your challenge is no mean gain. He is the son of Bharat dynasty's King Pandu and Achary Dron's dearest pupil. By defeating you in the duel he will earn no renown. But if he loses his repute now and in the future will be eclipsed by it. A kshatriy king might demand such an honour, and his right to it might then be debated. Can anyone testify to your lineage?"

Vidur and Bhishm sat back, relieved.

Karn turned tortured eyes toward Duryodhan.

"Achary!" called Duryodhan in a loud voice. "It is not right that you should humiliate such gallantry. Karn's lineage is announced by the splendour of his brow. His caste is manifest in his strength at arms. His credentials are strewn about you, released by his mighty bow."

"Very poetic, Duryodhan!" said Kripachary. "You have recently completed your education and will soon lead armies into battle. I recommend you reserve the rhetoric for encouraging your soldiers, and mind that you do not engage a foot soldier so beneath you in rank and stature his defeat of you sours your command forever."

Duryodhan's mouth turned bitter.

His will could not alter the social norm in a moment. The restrictions that ruled and regulated war and combat in the Aryavart were implacable. How to make the impossible possible? Karn must be allowed to defeat Arjun!

"I declare Karn King of Ang."

Duryodhan's friends at once shouted "Long live the king of Ang! Long live King Karn!"

Bhishm tried not to laugh. Duryodhan's determination to have Arjun slaughtered in full view of Hastinapur really was not funny.

"Duryodhan!" he called across the distance. "You are neither a King, nor a Crown Prince, and not authorised to appoint a king." And he turned to Dhritrashtr, "Why don't you stop him, Maharaj?"

Dhritrashtr, ever the performer, took his time to ponder the question. "Suyodhan is not Crown Prince, but he is my son, Pitrivy! And if a son sees fit to give one of his father's possessions away, how can the father act in contravention of the generous impulse?"

"This is not about generosity, Your Majesty; your son is provoking an external foe against your brother's son. He is disgracing the Kurukul. You son is instigating war."

"Calm down, Pitrivy!" said Dhritrashtr quellingly. "Duryodhan is not starting a war, or even a riot. He is merely honouring valour."

He turned away.

Vidur tried this time. "Ang is disputed territory, Rajan. Jarasandh, King of Magadh, claimed it as part of his empire. He exiled the governor authorised by King Pandu and appointed his own man."

"Then what does it matter? If Ang is ours, Duryodhan can gift it to Karn; if it is not ours, what is the harm if we give it to someone else? When he is not gifting a thing that belongs to us, why should you object?"

Duryodhan turned triumphantly to Krip. "Now Karn can rightfully duel with Arjun, can't he?"

Kripachary laughed. "Because you, Prince Duryodhan of Hastinapur, called Karn King? By all means try and have his subjects recognise him! No, he is not entitled to a duel with Arjun."

Duryodhan stormed out of the amphitheatre, swearing to arrange a coronation then and there. The theatre stood frozen in time. He brought back priests and men of every varn, milk, honey, oils, flowers, rosaries, a jewel-studded crown and a throne....

Kripachary sent Arjun back to the pavilion and his brothers. "Duryodhan is placing a crown on Karn's head. You are not his councilor that you should stay here. When Karn is qualified for a duel, come."

"But to flee the battle field in this manner, Achary...!"

Achary laughed. "This is no battlefield. This is a farce, which you may also watch from your pavilion. Go, my son!"

The rituals and hymns began. The priest poured liquids over Karn's head, threw flowers at him and made offerings to gods and goddesses...

Ashwatthama sat writhing with regret. His matul was angry – this entire adventure was a bad idea... Why hadn't he asked Kripachary before he spoke with his father?

Bhim wriggled in his seat, kicked his feet up and back, clenched and unclenched his fists, muttering.

"What's the matter with you?" asked Yudhishthir.

"I would like to thump both Karn and Duryodhan over their heads with my mace. Once Arjun has beaten this sootputr, I'm going to issue a few challenges myself."

Yudhishthir shook his head. "Can't you see Kripachary trying to prevent bloodshed? Leave well alone; let the gurus handle this. Duryodhan is using Karn – the real players on this field are him and Arjun. Do you want to jump in too, and help him start a civil war in Hastinapur?"

"Then why did Dronachary let all this start at all?"

"I think he may have felt he was obliged to allow his pupil to be tested…" Sahdev laughed, and they all looked at him in surprise. "What's so amusing?" asked Bhim.

"Nothing, of course. But this is so typical of Duryodhan. He needs a scapegoat – he's literally preparing his beast for sacrifice," said Sahdev, gesturing toward the ceremonies taking place in the field. "Even if Karn succeeded in actually killing Kanishth he would probably be ripped apart as the murderer of a prince. How does Duryodhan always manage to find such fools to follow him?" He shook his head, still smiling, though he looked pained and unhappy too.

"Karn is becoming a king!"protested Bhim. "And since this is actually our kingdom, Duryodhan has given what belongs to us to Karn."

Sahadev laughed again. "If you could make kings by seating men on thrones and sprinkling water on them every gallery in Hastinapur would accommodate legions. Duryodhan is an imposter and Karn a nincompoop."

"I still think we need to step up and register our…" Bhim glanced at Yudhishthir… "our dissent."

"Let the elders deal with Duryodhan," said Yudhishtir with finality. "If he manages to circumvent their wishes, or actually defeat them somehow, we will think upon our own strengths."

"Call the father of the Angaraj," the priest was saying. "The king must seek his blessing."

The servants rushed to bring Karn's father.

Karn held the crown to his wet brow, tears mingling with the milk and water on his face. He clasped Duryodhan's hand. "I am grateful to you, O Prince! Obliged for several births. You have not only saved me from disgrace today but given me a life of respect too," he said, his voice shaking. "How will I ever repay this debt?"

"Give me one thing," said Duryodhan, "and the debt will be repaid."

"Anything!"

"Your friendship! Your undying friendship!" Duryodhan extended his arms.

Karn embraced him. "I am your friend," he said solemnly. "I will serve you even against my life."

The servant brought Adhirath, and his name went round like smoke through the crowd. Kunti heard the word spoken, and reached out her arm to grasp the first hand she could. "Adhirath? This man is Adhirath, that king's charioteer? He is Karn's father?"

"Yes," said the man she had accosted, surprised.

She sank back in her chair, dizzy and sinking. Adhirath – that was the name. Adhirath of Hastinapur. The father, the adoptive father, of her son. Her son Karn. Karn was her first born son. Karn, the golden, the challenger of princes, the king of Ang, was her son. He was the eldest Pandav, brother to Yudhishthir and Bhim and Arjun, Nakul and Sahdev… Her son, her son…

She barely heard Duryodhan demand whether Karn and Arjun could resume their duel – barely registered that Krip refused. She was barely aware that Duryodhan and his followers were striding out of the amphitheatre, that the crowd was dispersing… She heard Vidur's voice as though from far away; his concerned face was ablur…

15

Kunti lay in bed and writhed inwardly. The vision of her son pitted against, full of hatred against, her sons was unbearable. And what a horror – that Kripachary and Bhim should heap insults upon him while Duryodhan redeemed him! Kunti wanted so desperately to claim him, to hold him against her chest and tell him how much she had missed him, how often thought about him and felt she was bleeding from an invisible wound, and how proud she was to see him stand there, defiant, competent, vital and powerful. But she did not have that right: Radha and Adhirath had parented him; he was their son, their attainment. Besides, what could she give him, even now? A future of war, of being despised as the other Pandavs were despised – only more because he would also carry the stigma of having been born out of wedlock, and abandoned at birth?

"How are you feeling, Ma?" It was Yudhishthir, accompanied by Vidur and his brothers. All but one.

Kunti sat up. She surveyed the informal assembly, that had in all probability been discussing the wicked ways of Dhritrashtr, Duryodhan, and Shakuni, probably cursing Karn, not knowing Karn was theirs, their own, tossed into the streets from and deprived of home, kin and company.

Karn had befriended a roving pack, unaware that they were unsocialized, recognised no human kindness and would turn and tear him limb from limb if opportunity presented. He was heedless of their contagion.

What should Kunti do? Should she drag her son home from the street? Save her home or her son? Would she disclose Karn's identity to him and to his brothers? She could not. It was too late. He must stay where he was.

"How are you, Bhabhi?"

"I am quite well, I don't know what happened to me. It was a momentary faintness I think." Kunti was at her evasive best.

"The fear of the unknown?" Vidur was amazed at her fortitude.

"The state physician did look me over. What did he say?"

"No physical ailment, which means you are mentally over-burdened..."

"As you know..."

"Yes – and I want you to remember you can share anything with me; don't hide heartache and worry and add to your distress through isolation."

"A woman does not veil herself before her son but she does not bare herself either."

Vidur looked at her face for a moment, and dropped the subject. "We were talking about Dhritrashtr and Pitrivy. The former has lost his grip on decency and the latter is paralysed by this terrible situation unfolding in court and in the streets. I honestly don't know how to present my advice in court so it won't be shouted down and rejected out of hand."

"The only solution is to compel the court to recognise Yudhishthir as Crown Prince." said Kunti simply. "Nothing else, nothing less, will do."

"Even Duryodhan and Shakuni know that. It is the only thing they have thrown the full weight of their opposition against."

"How do they justify it? Yudhishthir has attained majority, completed his education, and proved his competence."

"There are no reasons. There are infinite reasons, each time a different, irrelevant reason that means nothing, but causes one more delay so no decision is made." Vidur's smile was uncharacteristically strained and wan. "Dhritrashtr had his reasons too, for allowing what happened in the stadium to happen."

"What reasons? It was all Dronachary today: he wanted an exhibition of his students – and thus his – achievements."

"And I'm sure he's now enjoying congratulations. But the king does not want Dron's influence to grow – he would never have permitted quite so grand an affair, or one that was as fraught as this, if he had not hoped the events would establish a hierarchy."

"What kind of hierarchy?" asked Kunti.

"Yudhishthir's seniority is not in doubt, so the words 'able' and 'competent' are bandied about. The most 'competent' prince should be crowned heir to the throne. Attempts were made to kill Bhim and Arjun, to provoke a clash between your sons and those of Gandhari. There are more of hers. Unless yours had somehow won a spectacular victory, Duryodhan would by default have been seen as leader to a more powerful group – a fitter 'candidate' to be king."

"But the show is over," said Kunti impatiently. "What prevents Yudhishthir's coronation now?"

"It is not over till both parties cease attack," Vidur answered. "Duryodhan has his brothers, his father, Ashvatthama, and by extension Dron and Kripachary, Shakuni and the kingdom of Gandhara, all furthering his cause. And you ask what prevents Yudhishthir's coronation!"

And once again Kunti felt her entire body erupt with desperate misery – Karn, she could tell Karn, and prevent him from adding to Duryodhan's strength....

Vidur's departing words were directed at Yudhishthir. "This is the crisis, Son. Do not under any circumstances permit a confrontation till it can be a decisive one – do not permit Ḍuryodhan to appear at the head of an army against you. Do not join a combined campaign either – Duryodhan will try to sideline you. And think of a way to distinguish the sons of Pandu, so they become the only reasonable choice."

"As you will, Kaka."

"Father!" said Ashvatthama, hands clasped in veneration, "The princes' training is now over; it's time for the selection of the crown prince."

"Selection? There is a crown prince. He has simply not been crowned." Dron smiled. "As the eldest of Pandu's sons, Yudhishthir is Crown Prince of Hastinapur."

"Age is no criterion here, Pitaji! Shantanu was not the eldest , Bhishm was but was never king, Dhritrashtr was but Pandu was king till his death interrupted his reign."

"Your friend's plea again, eh?"

"Yes, Pitaji, Duryodhan's plea. But it is true."

"If King Pandu's eldest son is not his heir, then the middle or the youngest will be. How does Duryodhan figure into this arithmetic at all? His arguments are a house of cards."

"Dhritrashtr is the King," said Ashwatthama obstinately. "How does Yudhishthir fit in at all?"

Dron laughed. "Dhritrashtr is not King; he is Regent. Attempting a coup."

"Pitaji! This is politics! What you can do is declare Duryodhan abler than Yudhishthir."

"Ask Duryodhan to prove this mighty ability."

"He did, in the stadium!"

"No!" Dron spoke angrily now. "He did not prove himself the ablest warrior or the ablest leader. He proved himself the biggest ruffian and conspirator. Especially under adverse circumstances a leader must keep his cool. I conceded to that catastrophic duel on your request. If I had refused they would have said I was afraid of my pupil's defeat. My honour as well as Arjun's was at stake. But I am infinitely grateful Kripachary did not permit the duel. If Arjun had died I would have been responsible; if Karn had been defeated your friend, Duryodhan would have charged in arms blazing, so would his brothers and supporters, and the rest of us would have had to step in as well. No! I love you dearly, Ashwatthama, my son, but I will not start any wars in Hastinapur today. Instead, go and tell the princes my gurudakshina is Panchalraj Drupad, captive. I will declare the captor my ablest pupil…"

Ashwatthama's face cleared at once. "Excellent!"

16

What were Shakuni and Karn doing in the march toward Panchal? The campaign for Dronachary's gurudakshina was an extraordinary display of Kuru might… but even Dron could not claim it was zeal and devotion that impelled it. He wondered whether Dhritrashtr had had the sense to send Karn for his son's protection when he learned Gandhari's scorpion of a brother was accompanying the princes… Or whether this was another display of the sootputr's loyalty. His ambition. His loyal ambition.

At least Ashwatthama was not here. Of all that he had not foreseen while planning his career in Hastinapur, his son's 'friendship' with Duryodhan, his captivity, his slavery, was the most troubling. Not least because Ashwatthama was binding Dron to one camp despite every effort the achary made to remain neutral, no man's land. His son had not become what he had wanted, and thought he had trained, him to be. Dron was not even sure he had succeeded in shaping the rest of his students. The most accomplished architect of men could not produce an Arjun out of a Duryodhan, or a Duryodhan out of an Arjun. In his darkest and most doubtful moments Dron wondered whether even this were true – or whether he had been deficient, as a teacher. While he was on the subject of doubts… As always, old ones resurfaced, and threatened to deluge him with emotion.Why did he not retaliate the instant he was insulted by Drupad? Why did he leave meekly then, nurse his rage, and wait so long? Why was he using pupils to fight his battle? He had told himself revenge is best served cold, that he was an achary and his best response to insult was his pupils' competence. But ought not his primary impulse be their protection? But they are kshatriys – their best protection is fear of their valour and their skill… But his inner voice would not let him rest. "Yes, you are a venerable achary, it is always veneration or violence. Sometimes veneration, and yet violence. Remember Eklavya? You fear the strength of others, you fear penury and discomfort…"

"I have lived in poverty, and austerity."

"You did not know then what comfort was. You fear, you fear, you fear losing your gurukul, your home, your fine food and your fine clothes…"

"Tarry here, Gurudev!" Duryodhan shouted, with a grand air. "We shall bring and drop Drupad at your feet! Shall I leave some soldiers here to guard you?"

Dron declined Duryodhan's offer and watched him lead the unruly rabble of so–called soldiers rampaging along with wild cries. The five Pandavs were not with him.

Arjun came forward and said politely, "Gurudev, please forgive our audacity."

"What's happened, Arjun?"

"Gurudev! Duryodhan has no regard for discipline and leadership. He does not deserve command. We refuse to fight under his direction and be vanquished, or to win the battle for him to earn report. He refuses to accept Yudhishthir's seniority or leadership. We shall move only under this banner."

Dron was alarmed. He knew the Kauravs would fail without Arjun's participation in the campaign. The Kaurav army without the Pandavs would be weak; it would probably be defeated by Drupad!

"You are uninterested in returning my gurudakshina?" asked Dron.

"We will pay your fee," said Arjun. "Duryodhan will be back shortly with his brothers badly beaten and humiliated, and we five will accomplish this for you."

"You are not five but a hundred and five brothers."

"If Duryodhan had accepted Yudhishthir's leadership we would have remained one hundred and five. But this is not possible under Duryodhan's leadership–it is unsound. We are not being uncooperative, divisive, or disruptive! We do not even begrudge Duryodhan his desire for individual renown. The acharys of ShatShring taught us that we should not hold on to enmity, jealousy, and malice. They pollute the mind."

Dron wondered if that last remark was directed at him. He had been nursing enmity against Drupad for a long time.

"What if Duryodhan brings Drupad back as his prisoner? What dakshina will you give then?"

"That is not possible, Achary," Arjun said.

"He has Karn and Shakuni with him."

"The advantage lies with Drupad nonetheless."

"Neither Dhrishtadyumn nor Shikhandi is in the city. A large portion of the Panchala army is away with Dhrishtadyumn," said Dron.

"Duryodhan cannot defeat Drupad. I do not deny what you say, Achary. But wait and see…"

Drupad was getting ready for the royal court when a panicked group of spies rushed in to inform him about the onslaught of Kuru soldiers. They told the king that the invaders had crashed into Panchala territory and were wreaking havoc in the capital. Their invasion was sudden and swift. They would be at the palace any moment.

Drupad was taken aback. There was no time to reflect, not even upon what had triggered the move.

So he lost no more time, ordered for his chariot and arms. He directed his men to erect barricades at strategic points and direct the citizens to prepare for war and defend the capital.

On his way Drupad ruminated over what could have suddenly spurred the Kauravs' to this insane act. There were no warnings, no emissaries. Though the two kingdoms were usually at daggers drawn there had been no recent provocations. Was it perhaps not a military campaign but banditry? It couldn't be Bhishm. He knew their defences were sound – he also knew a large portion of their forces were away and civilians would make up the difference today. Bhishm was neither cruel nor a coward... Besides, this was certainly the act of an insider.

And then he thought of Dron. He was in Hastinapur now. And Dron was a military strategist – he was no commander, no soldier himself. Certainty took root. In fact, thought Drupad, I should have foreseen this the moment I heard Dron sought shelter with my rivals. Drupad couldn't wait to see who all were supporting Dron in the battlefield... was Bhishm there? Never mind. High time the Kauravs saw how the Panchalas fight.

Drupad's swiftness was enough to halt the Kaurav advance As soon as he faced he realized they were thoroughly inexperienced. They were either ignorant of basic military formations or deemed them unnecessary. They just drove their soldiers like a herd of cattle. They forgot that the rival force could strike too... They came to a standstill and started using different types of weapons arbitrarily.

The Kauravs were overawed by the arrows shot by Drupad and his brothers.

The spies had conveyed news of war through town and conch shells were being blown from every house, which drew more and more Panchala warriors out in support of their king.

Duryodhan's arrows were rendered ineffective by the counter–shower from Drupad's bow. The king's chariot moved so swiftly he seemed to be revolving around

Duryodhan's as rapidly as the surface of a spinning top. Duryodhan would have rather cast away his bow and gotten down on the ground with his mace but Drupad's arrows were travelling so fast even his chariot could not advance; how would he make it on foot?

Duryodhan looked around for Karn who might help him reach Drupad's carriage. But to his dismay and disbelief Karn was outclassed by Drupad; he appeared to be injured badly. Dushasan, Vikaran, and Yuyutsu were all apparently wounded too and had meekly retreated.

Soon another Panchala battalion entered the fray. Their swords pierced the Kauravs' advance guard, which disintegrated whatever structure they had. The Kaurav soldiers started fleeing. An arrow cut through Duryodhan's bow–string; he lost no time in retrieving another bow but this too was undone by Drupad.

Even as Duryodhan stood outwitted, trying frantically to frame his next action, an arrow pierced through his leather glove and into his palm.

Duryodhan directed his charioteer to move close to Karn.

Before the chariot–driver could turn the carriage, though, he saw the severely injured Karn jumping down from his chariot and rushing back. With no option left, his charioteer turned and sped in the opposite direction.

Arjun saw Duryodhan, his accomplices, and his soldiers were nearly finished. He was particularly amazed to find Karn in that awful state. For once, just as he felt like enjoying Karn's damning defeat he could only feel revulsion. Anyone might be in that state on a battlefield. But Drupad was such a warrior! His pride subdued, Arjun wondered over Karn's gallantry, and found himself speculating about why the sootputr had been prevented from confronting the prince at the stadium by Kripachary.

He heard Yudhishthir call out: "Bhim! We are losing. The soldiers of Hastinapur are retreating in defeat… We need to move."

"It's not our defeat, Jyeshth," said Arjun before Bhim could answer. "It is Duryodhan's."

"Is Duryodhan not one of us?"

"If he does not accept you as his leader, he is not one of us."

"What about the honour of Hastinapur, the repute of the Kauravs and Gurudev's dakshina?"

"We shall go and secure them," said Arjun, his words weighty, tremendous. "You shall wait for us here, our king. We four shall go to war. A king fights only when he has no warriors at his side." And he ordered the charioteer to move.

Yudhishthir stood speechless as his four brothers advanced in battle formation toward the town. Bhim led the lot on foot, jogging in his eagerness. The earth shook under his feet because of the heavy mace on his shoulder. He was followed by Arjun, a bow in his hand, quivers at the rear of his vehicle. Nakul and Sahdev followed him on their horses, swords drawn, guarding the wheels of his chariot. Yudhishthir felt unspeakably proud to watch them advance – there was no anger or pride in his splendid brothers' attitude; they behaved like a group of disciplined soldiers. Everything about their movement was planned.

"Yudhishthir! I think your brothers kept a secret from you," said Achary Dron with a smile.

"I think so too, Gurudev! I think they knew I would not have engaged in battle without Suyodhan."

"You still call him Suyodhan!"

"I try, Achary! I want him to remain Suyodhan. I don't approve of unnecessary conflict. Why can't we stay one – what sense is there in division?"

Achary Dron was touched by Yudhishthir's probity,

and impressed. How detached this young man was, how deliberate and generous! He would probably even be willing to relinquish his claim to the throne in Duryodhan's favour. If he did, would it ensure unity among the Kauravs? No. Duryodhan would never recognise the Pandavs' existence, much less their right to continued life or peace. Yudhishthir's nobility did him and his brothers no good.

The Pandavs' entry seemed to cast a spell on Drupad's men, who felt the shield hitherto provided by their king's arrows was no longer present. Drupad's arrows were getting entangled in the net woven by Arjun's. It became difficult for them to defend themselves against Bhim's dangerous blows. Arjun's chariot was a veritable Yamm's trap. Whichever way it went, the soldiers who could not move out of its way faced certain death.

Seeing his older brother in difficulty, Satyajit came forward. He stopped his chariot in front of Arjun to block his way. This diminished the impact of Bhim's blows considerably and the distance between Arjun's and Drupad's chariots increased.

Arjun thought quickly. Satyajit was trying to allow Drupad off the battlefield, and/or waiting for more troops. In the first instance the Pandavs would not be able to give their guru his dakshina – in the second, well, they were not prepared for drawn–out battle. The soldiers fighting for the Panchalraj were untrained. They were ordinary subjects helping out their king with ordinary arms. They were confronting the Pandavs with raw courage. It was the first time Arjun had seen common people fight for their king; if these people had not supported the king, even Duryodhan and Karn would have won their battle. Drupad must be beloved, a just and worthy king. Would the Pandavs and Yudhishthir be able to provide such inspiration?

Arjun could feel no acrimony against these subjects and these soldiers. He wished he could protect rather than harming them. But they were protecting Drupad, and Drupad was Dronachary's dakshina!

Satyajit's arrows had stalled Bhim's advance, which stopped Arjun's chariot. Arjun trained his arrow at Satyajit, and cut off his bowstring. He brought down the pillar of his chariot's canopy. He injured the horses. Satyajit reached for another bow; Arjun destroyed it. Bhim charged forward again Satyajit's position was becoming weak. If he did not force Arjun's retreat, his men would get crushed by Bhim's violent blows. Satyajit picked up a third bow. Arjun cut its string. Bhim picked up his mace and rushed towards Satyajit, and Satyajit's quick thinking charioteer guided the broken chariot back into the safety of his army.

Drupad realized nothing could stop the Pandavs now. In glaring contrast to Duryodhan, Karn, Shakuni, Dushasan, and Vikarn with their 'army', these four had ripped through the Panchala ranks. But this was not the moment to admire them; they would destroy the entire Panchala army.

Drupad stopped his chariot in front of Arjun.

Arjun severed his canopy and his bowstring. Drupad picked up another bow and shot a volley at Arjun; it was countered; the reigns of his chariot were cut.

Drupad smelled imminent defeat. If he did not jump down with a sword or mace for a duel, Arjun's arrow would tear his carriage apart, and his bones would be tested by Bhim's mace.

But Arjun had jumped onto his chariot, the point of his sword pricked Drupad's chest.

"King Drupad! I am not your enemy," he said. "The Kauravs and the Panchalas are kin. I would do you no harm. I am here only because I am bound by my pledge to my guru. I don't want any more innocent blood shed…" He called out to Bhim, "Madhyam! Stop it. The Achary's dakshina is secure. Don't kill men in vain." Bhim abandoned his advance.

Drupad had no wish to cost his men's their lives, when his own life was at the mercy of Arjun and Bhim. As a kshatriy he would have prefered to have gone down fighting, rather than ending up a prisoner of war. But he was a king too, and Arjun did not want bloodshed. He had placed the choice in King Drupad's hands. Drupad climbed on to Arjun's carriage. His soldiers went back, his ministers walked behind him, their hands tied on their backs. They would not forsake their king in such a state, in such a time of misery.

Regard for Drupad revisited Arjun's heart. He was moved by the ministers' devotion to their king, they had surrendered so willingly to captivity to save him the pangs of isolation. How popular a king Drupad was! His subjects, ministers, soldiers, and commanders – all loved him. That love and popularity was neither shallow nor born of fear and expectation. It was an acknowledgement of his just rule… Why did Guru Dron hate such an upright ruler? Why did he seek his arrest and humiliation? Why would an intellectual who loved humanity want to oust a king who is so beloved of his people? Arjun had heard there was personal bitterness between King Drupad and Achary Dron. He had heard that Drupad had insulted the achary. But why? Did he speak lies, did he speak a cruel truth, did he speak an unwise truth cruelly? He would not solve this puzzle today. Today he would offer dakshina to his guru, and that was all. He signalled the charioteer.

"Does the Panchalraj not demand explanations?" he asked Drupad.

"Why!" Drupad laughed, "I already know you are but the blank of aspiration, Prince, serving a proud and unscrupulous achary!"

Bhim felt like a hungry diner who's had to leave his meal midway. Leaving the battlefield without sweeping the rival camp of its champion warriors was unthinkable and unacceptable. He would never have done that of his will. But he could see the logic of Arjun's ceasefire: they coexisted in relative amity with those who actually tried to kill them; why kill men who had done them no harm? Arjun was also right to keep Yudhishthir off the battlefield. Yudhishthir could fight, but he abhorred violence. There was no need for him to fight this battle. Bhim wondered how Yudhishthir would ever win a war, though: he would certainly never allow any atrocities on the field. Bhim, pitied him…He was so unlike a kshatriy. No kshatriy could escape violence. Bhim did not mind it – in fact he had trouble controlling his anger. Arjun himself disapproved of avoidable violence – but he did not hate it as Yudhishthir did… Today Bhim had seen a different Arjun, one who planned everything meticulously. A strategist. Though Arjun was younger than both Yudhishthir and Bhim, he seemed to have grown older today. In hindsight it was surprising that neither older brother had even considered questioning Arjun's wisdom; Bhim was surprised at himself. Though he obeyed Yudhishthir as his older brother, Yudhishthir's patience and pacific nature sometimes turned him off. But he always accepted Arjun's advice. Did Arjun have some mesmeric powers? Or was he extra pragmatic? Bhim concluded that Arjun had simply come of age.

17

Bhishm did not approve of arbitrary invasion and seizure of other people's territories. But he himself was at least partly responsible for this pass: he had not gauged Dron's character correctly, nor anticipated the consequences of appointing him the princes' achary. He had not learned even from the Eklavya incident. An achary ought to be magnanimous, indiscriminate in his dissemination of knowledge, careful of the greater good, of balance in human lives. Dron had only come here for gain: his own, material, and vengeful.

Bhishm should have given thought to whether Dron himself would make Hastinapur more or less powerful. He was an exceptionally erudite military commander, but he had used his position without regard for the state's interests, and by extension, those of his pupil princes. The Kauravs had captured Drupad to satisfy Dron – killing men in the process. Over and above that indignity to the Panchalas, Dron had wrested half Drupad's kingdom – Ahichhatr and the entire adjoining region. What price would Hastinapur always be paying for this incident? Drupad would never forgive Dron, or Hastinapur for harbouring and enabling him; the Panchalas would never accept that Ahichhatr was not theirs, and since the Kauravs had appropriated it, they must continue to defend it. Besides, in all Jambudip, only Jarasandh or Achary Dron would venture to capture a kshatriy king and 'acquire' his kingdom. Vanquished kings were fined; at most they were supplanted by their own son or brother. Drupad would try to get Ahichhatr back, and Hastinapur would hemorrhage men and resources from this day forth.

Neither Dron nor Ashwatthama had entered the fray, of course.

What a game he had played: if the Pandavs had refused to fight, they would have been notorious by now for having refused Dron dakshina. Since they had not refused, Dron was credited with teaching the victors, and now ruled a kingdom without the worry of defending it. Dron had propelled Hastinapur and Kampilya into a state of perpetual war with him as crucial military mediator. He had similarly widened the fissure between the Dhartrashtrs and the Pandavs. Bhishm felt a poisonous tree had been planted in Hastinapur. Now, even if he wanted to get rid of the achary the Kaurav princes would never consent. The Pandavs would venerate their Guru forever. And as far as Duryodhan and Dhritrashtr were concerned Dron had established his military import. Besides, everyone knew Dron had taught Ashvatthama more than he had taught Arjun. And Ashwatthama belonged to Duryodhan.

Bhishm could still see but one ray of hope in this gloom. Yudhishthir.

He seemed to have wakened from long slumber. He should have decided long ago. The eldest son of King Pandu was the rightful heir and successor to the throne of Hastinapur. He was capable, qualified, and deserving. He would face no opposition from the people, or any of Hastinapur's most powerful allies. The Pandavs had declared Yudhishthir their king on the battlefield; they had proved their mettle. It was past time. He rose. "Sentry! Go tell the charioteer to bring in the carriage. I must see Dhritrashtr at once."

"What does Pitrivy say?" demanded Kunti. "Has he too forsaken justice?" Swiftly recollecting herself, she moderated her tone. "Does he not feel my sons' constraints? He at least cannot be partisan…"

Glancing over the five brothers seated silently around his and Kunti's conversation, Vidur said nothing immediately. Surely each had his own view on this family's political bearings, but they rarely interrupted. They listened, and kept their counsel.

"He does see, and feel," he finally offered. "He has brought Yudhishthir's coronation up in court, and spoke at least once about it privately, to Dhritrashtr."

"What did the king say?" asked Kunti at once.

Vidur laughed. "The king is a politician. He listened very seriously, and seriously replied, 'Yes, the coronation of the crown prince is a matter of grave urgency.' He did not say 'Yudhishthir' – he did not say whom he is speaking of Yudhishthir. I cannot dispel my certainty that Dhritrashtr will never crown Yudhishthir of his own volition. He prevaricates so some blessed circumstance will permit him to declare Duryodhan Kuru heir apparent."

"But surely that is no longer possible," murmured Bhim.

"Why?" asked Kunti.

"Duryodhan was never the eldest – he has now failed to prove himself as well. Pressure to crown Yudhishthir is mounting, and they are scrambling to weaponize their household."

"And have they found someone?"

"Yes!"

"Whom?"

"A Kuru elder – Bahlik. But it seems neither he nor his son Somdutt or grandson Bhurishrav are eager to take sides: they have not opposed the king, but neither have they conspired against Bhishm."

"So?"

"So they need an outsider. Who is capable, strong, and eager to settle a score with Pitrivy Bhishm."

Vidur's six auditors looked at him warily.

"They have not settled on a candidate yet, energetic councils progress apace." Vidur smiled to allay the tension. "They intend to settle the domestic disputes via wayfarers on public highways."

Sahdev spoke up: "Who?"

"This is the age of political upheaval, Son! Self–interest, not principle, determines alliances. Caught in a weird vortex of helplessness, even powerful potentates desperately seek allies to consolidate their portion, their position…"

"Whom does Duryodhan seek?" asked Kunti peremptorily.

"I imagine in ordinary circumstances he would have solicited the Panchalraj Drupad's support – would probably have been successful too – it wouldn't really be difficult to convince Drupad he should oppose either Pandu's progeny in general or Arjun in particular, and he's never loved Bhishm… But the Panchalraj and Achary Dron cannot have a common friend… And Duryodhan could never drop the assured support of his friend Ashvatthama's father Achary Dron to seek the Panchalraj's hypothetical allegiance…"

Kunti thought she saw a smile flit across his face. "What in the world do you find amusing in this situation? Or is all this frivolous?"

"No Bhabhi – but yes – I do find Duryodhan's dilemma amusing! I'm told he's heard of Darupadi's beauty and lusts after it just as he does the Panchalas' political support. Yet he can neither quit Dron nor afford to offend Jarasandh."

"Jarasandh?" Yudhishthir was puzzled. "What has he got to do with the Panchalraj?"

"But that's exactly what I've been saying. This situation is positively fantastical." Vidur's smile was less equivocal now.

"No one has anything to do with anyone and everyone has everything to do with everyone." He was speaking directly to Yuddishthir. "Jarasandh created a ring of powerful allies around him – the mightiest was Kans – killed by Vasudev Krishn. He is incensed. Making overtures in every direction. But his friendship implies subordination. What Jarasandh subordinate could sustain fellow feeling with the Yadavs? Drupad is not willing to sacrifice his understanding with Mathura. And Jarasandh's enmity is accompanied by enmity with Bhishmk, Damghosh, Shalv and Dantavaktr… If Duryodhan wants an alliance with the Panchalraj he must accept Jarasandh, Bhishmk, Damghosh, Shalv, Dantvaktr and others as enemies so…"

"So… what?" Kunti's heart was in her mouth.

"So no doubt he'd prefer Jarasandh's 'friendship'."

"Friendship of the Yadavs' foe!" Kunti was incensed. "Friendship of Krishn's foe? Selfishly – and against his pitamah?"

"Yes."

"And does Pitrivy Bhishm know?"

"Probably not. At least, he has never displayed any symptoms of awareness," said Vidur wryly.

"Why don't you tell him?"

"Reasons aplenty, Bhabhi," he said quietly. "But… in the first instance… when it comes to confidential gleanings I don't trust him. Confidential information doesn't remain confidential once it reaches him."

"What are you accusing Pitamah of?" Yudhishthir was polite, but his voice carried steel.

"I am not accusing him of anything. This is my assessment of his personality," Vidur said with a gentle smile, "and I advise you to be careful with your intelligence too. You will remember we did not tell Pitrivy Duryodhan poisoned Bhim."

"I do remember it. And wonder daily whether it was

right that we did not. Is your judgment unbiased? Could you not be wrong?" Yudhishthir asked.

Vidur's smile was supremely and categorically serene, unfazed by Yudhishthir's doubts. "Son, your Pitamah is unreasonably principled."

Everyone looked at him quizzically.

"You know he is scrupulously principled, you know the world he was brought up in was wholly different from ours. From this. His faith in the culture and credo of his time has acquired the proportions of superstition. He believes the principles of his youth are the last word in dharm. He is neither prepared to hear a word against them nor to change them."

"Would you care to give us an example?" Sahdev asked. He did not challenge Vidur either, yet his question too was a warning.

"For example..." Vidur spoke softly, but ultimately without hesitation. "He believes in the maintenance of communal harmony and unity, as he maintained it. Even if one person has to abdicate his rights, as he did. Brother must sacrifice for brother, as he did.

He simply does not comprehend that a brother might betray another. He will not see that Yudhishthir's sacrifice for Bhim, born of reciprocal devotion, would be right, while his sacrifice for Duryodhan would be a farce because Duryodhan would dismiss it as the act of a fool.

Your Pitamah believes one must honour her or his word, come what way, as he has done. He seems oblivious of the injustice of his own bondage. He will treat Maharshi Vedvyas and Dhritrashtr no differently. He will keep his word to either in the same way."

Vidur seemed to be addressing each of them individually now.

"The greatest difficulty is that he persists in regarding societal norms as moral law, as dharm, and is unable to interrogate them." His manner gentled further. "I am not criticizing him. He is himself exemplary, a principled, just, and righteous man; but he does not possess whatever faculty can accurately gauge righteousness. When his chariot of dharm moves, he neither perceives those trampled beneath its wheels nor believes himself responsible for their agony, or their destruction."

"What do we do then, Kaka?" Yudhishthir could not conceal his enervation.

"Why, we safely assume him free of ill–will or malice. This wholesome, benevolent man is nevertheless hobbled by dogma. He is unalterable. He cannot snap the bonds of custom and practice. We honour his integrity, but it is not possible for us to live by his covenant. Sacrifice is an excellent ideal but ceding to someone like Duryodhan is not in the social interest. We will love a brother, but beware a brother like Duryodhan. We will defend Hastinapur, but differentiate between Dhritrashtr and Hastinapur."

Neither Vidur nor the others spoke for a long time. He had left nothing unsaid, and Kunti's clan grappled with the awful truth. The silence grew oppressive, and Kunti spoke.

"Vidur! I believed my sons and I were all but friendless in Hastinapur. We had you, and we had Pitrivy. You say today that Pitrivy is not ours. I have shielded my sons, kept our heads down and our tongues silent, imagining that this tsunami of misfortune would pass overhead and we would rise to reclaim our right… But I see this lapse of time has weakened us. We are not strong but incapacitated, helpless…"

"We are neither incapable nor helpless!" Bhim was outraged. "Look at your sons! Four of us marched and demolished the Panchal force; when it is five? What can we not achieve?"

"He is right, Ma," said Sahdev. "Duryodhan has a hundred brothers and still he needs to purchase the muscle power of Karn, Guru Dron and Ashvatthama; and now he is striving for Jarasandh's support. The five of us have never needed any Karn or Ashvatthama…"

Kunti wished she could have stopped him – "Don't – don't speak of Karn in that way…"

"Your sons are right, Bhabhi!" Vidur was saying. "First, we are not incapacitated; your flock is powerful. Second, it is not as though you no longer enjoy Pitrivy's patronage; we simply have a clearer notion of its limitations. And most importantly, if Duryodhan is looking for allies, Yudhisthir can do the same."

"You want me to adopt Duryodhan's methods?" Yudhishthir sounded mortified.

"Of course not!" replied Vidur. "If you follow Duryodhan's lead where will Hastinapur look, for ethics, or justice, or righteousness, or humanity?" He paused impressively. "I simply propose that for once if vice is assembling, virtue muster too. Evil, impelled by self–interest, gathers armies, strikes blow upon blow, and good women and men neither arm themselves nor those oppressed by their enemies. What I'm trying to say is, we tend to overlook that if Jarasandh is a force, Krishn is a force too…"

"My Krishn!" Kunti exclaimed fondly. "He is only a boy!"

Vidur laughed. "The kids are all grown, Bhabhi! This is their world now. It was Krishn who killed Jarasandh's son in law and ally Kans… And Vasudev is no longer in prison. Neither is he weak. Mathura is dominated by the Yadavs led by Krishn. Ugrasen, Vasudev, Akrur, Krishn, Balram – all are one now. If Shakuni can come from Gandhar to protect his sister in Hastinapur, can't Kunti's brother, from Mathura?"

Yudhishthir immediately interjected, "I have told you, I will not be another Duryodhan! And I do not want my mother to be a Gandhari or my matul a Shakuni. I will not drag outsiders into my family feud!"

"I have not asked you to, son," said Vidur said, "but I do ask that if Krishn has begun a campaign against vicious injustice by dealing with Kans, you continue it. Conspiracies are being hatched in the courts of Bhishmk, Daumghosh, Shalv, and other kings backed by Jarasandh; you must not permit machinations against Krishn in Hastinapur. Even if you do not need him here, Hastinapur must at least remain hospitable to him…"

"Who said we don't want help from Krishn or the Yadavs of Mathura?" Bhim contended. "I do not at all agree with the Jyeshth! If Duryodhan is our brother, so is Krishn!"

"He is," Vidur assented. "But I don't propose help from or to Krishn as a brother. If you are Krishn's cousin, so is Shishupal. But Krishn will never help Shishupal nor seek his aid – Shishupal is iniquitous. You have to seek Krishn's support and endorse him because neither he nor you are. Panchal too will back Krishn only as a matter of principle."

"You are right, Vidur." Kunti said finally, "But I do wonder…"

"What is it?"

"Well… We sit here ruminating on their wherefores and therefores… But do they think of us? Can they help us? Would they care to help if they could, or to seek our help? Do they even need it?"

"We should find out," said Vidur decisively. "Mathura is not far. One of us ought to go to Mathura."

"Shall I?" Arjun spoke at once.

"Me too," said Bhim.

"Anyone could…" – Vidur was suddenly pensive – "but any one of you would be inviting assault… And in your absence… No! I will send a messenger first, or a message through a merchant headed that way." Vidur stood to go, and the others to see him off. His chariot was waiting, sans charioteer; Vidur charioted himself. Kunti had never asked him why: did Dhritrashtr not accord his half-brother this convenience, or did Vidur himself prefer to manage the reins? She and her sons watched the cloud of dust rise and obscure their view. They could see no more of this path than of their lives – impenetrable, oblique, indeterminate.

They stood as the dust subsided. She turned in from the threshold, and paused.

The dust was rising again.

Was he returning? What had happened?

Yudhishthir and his brothers followed their mother's widening gaze to see a chariot – an unknown carriage – emerge slowly from the storm.

Kunti looked again, disbelieving her eyes. The carriage did not sport Kuru insignias. It was emblazoned with the colours of the Yadavs of Mathura.

18

The chariot halted near her and a man got down. Kunti stared at him curiously.The man was in his middle years, a gentleman in formal clothes; he could have been either a royal personage or a rich merchant. But the royal insignia of the Yadavas on that carriage had already announced royalty. Who was he?

He walked up to Kunti and asked: "You are Pritha, are you not?"

Kunti and her sons were alike surprised by the intimate informality of the address.

She nodded. "And you?"

"I knew you won't recognise me. I am Akrur!"

Kunti jumped. Akrur? And she hadn't recognized him! She still couldn't recognize him! "Why, I couldn't!" She clung to him, and suddenly a dam seemed to burst inside her. Kunti sobbed uncontrollably. Tears welled from her eyes, on and on, without any sign of the waters abating, her throat became heavy as she choked on the flood, and went on weeping. She had never felt so happy in her life.

Akrur's mischievous and smiling face became grave, and his eyes became wet. "You are still crazy as you ever were, Pritha. Where is all the dignity and gravity of an empress and queen mother!"

Kunti tried to remind herself: she was, of course, going crazy! Why, her brother had come to her after so many years, and she was crying and crying, without a word of welcome to him. Kunti felt as if she were living in two worlds. In her mind's eye she was the giggling playful girl she had been years ago. She wanted to tease him – "Akrur, brother, whose mustache have you stuck onto your face?" She wanted to pull at his beard and run laughing to the other end of the field. It was the first time someone from her parental home had visited her since her marriage to Pandu. And not just someone. It was the brother with whom she had shared her childhood, who had always insisted on his paltry seniority and that she treat him as an elder, address him as one. The brother whose seniority she could take least seriously, with whom she played and fought and jostled into youth. She tore herself from his reassuring embrace and wiped her tears; she steadied herself and said to her sons, "Pay regards to him, my sons! He is Shivphalle's son Akrur – your matul."

The Pandavs greeted Akrur and Yudhishthir stepped forward to welcome him into their home, apologizing profusely for keeping him standing outside so long due to their failure to recognise him. Kunti drank in the sight. She was proud of the sons she was presenting to her brother, to her father's home! Yudhishthir had quickly and confidently taken charge of the emergent situation. She could relax in faith that it would be handled well. She need not exert herself as the head of the household in this moment of happy shock, need not do everything herself… Her sons would take care of everything. She wondered at the change she felt in herself. She had never been so affected before – not when Pandu started ignoring her after marriage, not when he died, leaving her alone with little children clinging to her breast and she pleaded with every god in turn, wondering what would happen to her and to them. She had never had a chance… the leisure… to weep… Today she had her brother on whose shoulders she could rest her head, and cry her heart out. This man was her kin, one of her own, and yes, capable of helping her. "How are you, Bhaiya?" she eventually asked.

"Thank God you have spoken at last! I could not make out whether you had gone dumb or speechless!" Akrur smiled, "How are you, Pritha?"

Kunti was overwhelmed again: she had a visitor who called her Pritha. She had almost forgotten that she was once Pritha. She could restrain herself no longer. She said, "I am like a doe surrounded by wolves, Bhaiya. My fatherless sons have been denied their right. I can't tell anyone here that these people are not my kin but killers. You all were in trouble. Our father was helpless. Whom could I pour my heart to? Whom could I approach for help?"

Akrur stood up from his place and went closer to Kunti. "Don't worry, Bahin! The crisis is over now Kans is dead. The Yadavs are free now, and powerful. They have endured a lot, Vasudev and Devaki the most. But now we look to a bright future. Led by Krishn and Balram, we have even vanquished Jarasandh."

"But I have heard that Jarasandh is trying to gather forces against the Yadavs," said Kunti.

"Yes. But we are not incapacitated. Krishn exhorts us not to harbour violence and vendettas but organise against the enemies of virtue and justice to shield the helpless…"

"Does Vasudev Bhaiya remember me too?" Kunti said.

Akrur's voice was loud with excitement. "Of course Vasudev remembers you; it was his son who said, 'Kaka! You should go to Hastinapur to see how the Pandavs are. I have received reports they are not happy. How could they be! Dhritrashtr is not just blind he has no integrity. His son Duryodhan is vicious and Dhritrashtr is ruled by him. Go and find out how Bua and her sons are doing. We might be able to do something to make our people happy.'"

"Krishn said so? How does he know all this?"

"All I can say is Krishn seems to know everything. Nothing seems to remain hidden from him."

"Matul," Yudhishthir spoke. "Please forgive my insolence; I am interrupting your conversation."

"No, no, you are not a child. You are the future king of Hastinapur. Speak! Besides, we are used to being led by the young in Mathura. Krishn is younger than you. But we seek his counsel, accept his leadership, even obey him. We find his capacities admirable…"

"You seem almost overwhelmed by Krishn, Matul." Bhim felt encouraged to join the conversation. "Is he that brilliant?"

"He must be. I have never seen anyone meet him and fail to be overwhelmed," said Akrur with a smile. "What were you saying, Yudhishthir?"

"Well, I wonder whether the troubled Yadavs will in fact be able to help us? Kans is sure to have hadsupporters in Mathura, and they will not let Krishn and his allies rest. Then there is Jarasandh, who will not concede defeat. He is already mobilising his allies, isn't he? There have been reports of him connecting with Kalayawan. Likely many will side with Jarasandh to grind their own axes. Duryodhan might in fact be one of them. With such a huge host of hostile powers, will Krishn have the resources to help us, and so make even more enemies? By helping us he will turn Panchal and Gandhar against the Yadavs… may be Sindhur–Sovira too…"

"I'm glad you're thinking about this!" said Akrur. "You have raised not one but many questions. But let me begin with this: yes, Krishn is capable of extending help to all who need it."

"I don't doubt his resolve, Matul! I am only speaking of time and resources."

"Me too," Akrur nodded. "And I do mean Krishn is

inexhaustible. I have no idea how he does it but I have never seen him turn away a comer for lack of time – he makes time. And he has as little troubleassembling, gathering, creating resources."

"How is this possible?" asked Arjun.

"I do not know," said Akrur slowly. "For Krishn, it seems nothing in the world is impossible... We have only to act in keeping with the logic of the world..." He smiled reminiscently. "As it happens, I think, Krishn seems to understand it... And the fruit of every action is inevitable."

"The fruit of every action is inevitable!" Bhim exclaimed. "But we never got any fruits for our actions! I always feel that others invariably enjoy the fruits of our actions."

Akrur laughed. "When you meet Krishn you must ask him who eats the fruit of your labour," he suggested. "I couldn't possibly clear all your doubts or explain him to you. To him nature is anything but haphazard. It operates in accordance with clear laws, actions beget reactions in accordance with them, and if we misunderstand them we misunderstand too the reactions our actions will generate. What looks like the injustice or unfairness of nature to me does because I am either ignorant of vital facts or my analysis is faulty."

"Does Krishn say this?" said Kunti. "Such faith in such faithless times?"

"Yes, Pritha. Krishn is a great believer in action. Right now, he says, if Jarasandh can gather forces, we shall do the same."

"How are they different, then – Jarasandh and Krishn?" asked Yudhishthir. "I have never thought ways open to Duryodhan are open to me too..."

"I am glad, again, Yudhishthir – you are cautious! Even of Krishn, as you should be."

Yudhishthir looked distressed, but Kunti was sure he

would say nothing, would carry whatever had upset him all alone… "What is it?" she asked.

"Nothing, Ma!" He paused, then said in a rush, "I am sorry – I was unclear – or perhaps my words are ill–chosen. I have no qualms about Krishn, and no reservations about his leadership, none. He is not only our kin, he is the only person to have asked after us. He has proven his mettle, his ingenuity, and his generosity. I would accept his leadership regardless of kinship, as the leadership of my superior."

"I did not misunderstand you!" said Akrur with a pat of Yudhishthir's shoulder. "Even if I had I would enjoy working out in words how Krishn and Jarasandh are different – it would be refreshing to convince the unconvinced! In Mathura everyone is already a convert." He was quiet for a moment. "Look! Kans patterned himself on Jarasandh, his father in law. Under him the Yadavs had no friends, only foes. Even Kans's friends were Yadavs' foes, for Kans himself was an enemy of the Yadavs. We were his people – he was our soverign – but we all felt like prisoners – prisoners of atrocious laws, despotic subjects of a despot. We were not free to laugh, to weep, to love, or to hate. When even people like Ugrasen and Vasudev were imprisoned, who could remain free?"

"But you were!" said Bhim with a laugh with careless criticism. "You were free! You stayed at the palace, visited the royal courts, enjoyed all the amenities due to a royal personage… I marvel at your luck, Matul! You were Kans's representative, and now you are Krishn's. Very few retain their positions even after a regime change."

Kunti had tried to restrain Bhim silently, but under his expression of amuselment he was thrumming with thinly disguised contempt.

"Well said!" said Akrus with a small smile. "Now I know what others think of me…This too I've learned from watching Krishn: how to listen to accusations with attention. It does help us correct our behaviours, as well as our presentation… If you are admiring my luck, I will say only that it did not feel like a gift – to watch people I loved get slaughtered, maimed, imprisoned and feel I could do nothing. I stayed on the council because I thought I might occasionally do some good, restrain some of Kans's excesses once in a while, inform people who were going to become his victims… Your Kaka Vidur is in a similar position. He enjoys royal amenities as a minister. When Yudhishthir is crowned will you dismiss Vidur? Or consider his craft as a statesman, or even as a politician, valuable to your court and appoint him Prime Minister?"

"Pardon me, Matul! Kaka Vidur has come to your rescue." Bhim laughed again, but in apology, and at his own folly.

"Pritha, your sons are very earnest!" Akrur laughed a little too, ruefully. "I felt that if Vasudev was a prisoner at Kans's prison I was one in his courts. He was at least not compelled to obey Kans. It is true – there are things I felt at the time I must do that I cannot now forgive. I knew Kans had learned Krishn and Balram were Vasudev's sons and he intended to murder them. Yet I brought them from Vrindavan to Mathura… Krishn liberated not only Vasudev and Devaki but us all. He cut our bonds – physical and mental. We acknowledged our past. We stopped feeling servility as our destiny, and learned to plan a future of freedom and responsibility. Kans captured his father to usurp his kingdom; Krishn who vanquished and killed this king neither occupied the throne himself nor enthroned his father! Yudhishthir, my son, do you see? The difference between a man like Jarasandh, or Kans, and a man like Krishn?"

"I do."

"You know," said Akrur, "these so-called allies of Jarasandh – Damghosh, Bhishmak, Shalv, Dantavaktr –

Jarasandh allows none of them individual liberty. They are not his friends but his subordinates – his slaves, in fact. They can't even arrange marriages for their children without Jarasandh's sanction. He is their ruler, not their friend. To Krishn individual liberty is supreme – individual freedom to facilitate, in accordance with individual dharm, social wellbeing, and social dharm… He harbours no ambition," laughed Akrur, "but that all torture everywhere, and suppression of the weak in all its forms, should end. And that man should live happily and comfortably in harmony with nature. Just that! So he has struck an alliance with King Drupad of Panchal, King Virat of Matsya… and now he extends a hand of friendship to you, the Pandavs of Hastinapur. These kings will rule their respective kingdoms without intereference – those are the only terms possible with Krishn. Krishn is the most exemplary karmayogi I have ever met."

"I fully agree with you, Matul," Yudhishthir said. "But if Krishn perceives that by siding with us he will antagonise several powerful kings against the Yadavs, will he still care to do so? Won't he weigh the consequences of his actions?"

Akrur did not say anything. Would Krishn have sent him to this place if he was ignorant of the possible outcomes?

"Only Krishn can actually answer that question. And he is not here now. I can only try to explain it from my perspective. I think Krishn believes that an action has to be motivated not by the self but by dharm, and when an action is motivated by dharm, we don't have to worry about its consequences in isolation. As long as your action is motivated by dharm and not individual desire…"

"What is action sans desire?" asked Sahadev.

"You can ask Krishn himself! Krishn saw that Kans had made arrangements to kill him, he decided that his immediate action must be self-defence, for which he must destroy all instruments of death and whoever controlled them. He proceeded to do just that, calmly, methodically, and without being overcome by fear, without recoiling from all the blood he did not wish to shed… If Krishn had thought that destroying Kans completely would annoy his friends, or would cause trouble for Krishn and his kinfolk, he would not have succeeded. What I mean is that pain and greed and fear should not be considered obstacles in work inspired by dharam. I think if Krishn has resolved that dharm does not permit him to let his virtuous brothers and Bua suffer in Hastinapur, he will not be deterred by fear of creating another set of foes…I even think that those treading a sinful path cannot be Krishn's friends at all, and the righteous cannot really be his foes." Akrur laughed. "But that is how much I love him. What is more important just now is that he says truth will never be destroyed and the untruth does not exist! So, don't remain tangled in maybes, act!"

Vidur received Akrur respectfully into his home and asked him, "Are you in Hastinapur as kin of the Pandavs or as an emissary from Mathura?"

Vidur's posture perplexed Akrur: not only did it give nothing away, but he seemed to be at once hospitable and hostile. Akrur wished to reassure him, as well as to remain in himself implacable.

"I am an emissary from Mathura, of course, and do not roam aimlessly. I am also not here on a public relations exercise. I am here to submit the Yadav foreign relations policy to Hastinapur's royal assembly…"

Vidur smiled. "And pray what is this policy, which you would announce to Hastinapur's royal assembly and not to Mathura's? Hastinapur is an autonomous independent kingdom. We do not generally entertain announcements of foreign policies."

"Of course not." Akrur's voice was neither intimate nor conciliatory. "And yet we feel it important to declare that the Yadavs have no ambitions to establish an empire. We do not aspire to subjugate or dominate any independent rulers, nor do we desire to meddle in their domestic affairs, though also do not wish to deny that where impropriety prevails, political conspiracies are hatched and alien forces do interfere. We urge Hastinapur to take this into account and formally declare our common son Yudhishthir Crown Prince without further delay, so our enemies are discouraged from anchoring their forces in neighbouring lands and creating problems for us…"

"And?"

"And we have no reservations about admitting that the Pandavs are our kin and may rest assured of our political and personal support."

Akrur looked at Vidur with half a challenge. There was none in the Prime Minister's smiling face.

"You have come at the most opportune moment possible, noble Akrur. You are are the most welcome of solutions to a huge problem!" Vidur exclaimed. "Our king has propelled himself beyond all considerations of conscience. He purports to support noble policies but does not think it necessary to translate them to action. He wants to preserve the status quo. He entertains all debate but evades conclusion. He wants to retain the throne and encourage rivalry between Yudhishthir and Duryodhan. He does not oppose Yudhishthir's right to the post, but does not declare him Crown Prince. He says work must be done but neither does any nor commands others to do it. He knows that nobody can or will force him. So please, tell him if the king will not accomplish what needs to be accomplished, some other hand will."

"Excellent," said Akrur. "Krishn sent me to do just that…"

"Vasudev Krishn?"

"Yes. Our leader."

"He's not your king?"

"No! That is Ugrasen."

"Then how is Krishn your leader?"

"He was not appointed. He confronts our perils, is trusted, followed, and obeyed by our people. He is talented, capable, and energetic. That is all. He holds no formal post."

"The Kauravs have unfortunately produced no Krishn! Pitrivy Bhishm was always bound by his attachments and is now powerless before the throne." Vidur said, "But that statement of yours, by itself, is going to be a problem."

"What? Why?"

"If we agree that the formal post is occupied by chance, if Krishn has voluntarily refused the throne to use his talent more directly for good, for the people, we might need to answer why Yudhishthir cannot permit Dhritrashtr to continue – and Duryodhan after him. Why Yudhishthir and his brothers cannot do good work beyond the royal palace and prerogative."

"If, like King Ugrasen, Dhritrashtr will heed the demands of justice and virtue, follow sound advice, recognise the sentiments of his people, take pains and energetically accomplish their best interest, he must be indeed be allowed to retain the throne. Yudhishthir and his brothers may apply their talents to the public benefit. A king must spend a lot of time in worthless administrative tasks; if Dhritrashtr is willing and able to perform them, he must be permitted to do so. But if the king is like Kans, who was vicious himself and followed Jarasandh's vicious advice, who would neither let a virtuous woman or man act rightly nor let talent grow, he must be deposed. If political leaders stifle worth and social structures stifle the development of individuals and their relations with others, it is the dharm of a people to overthrow their government and install a new one. Krishn does not want political power because his interests run across states. He wishes to facilitate the rule of dharm in all kingdoms – not one. You, and your people, must decide whether Yudhishthir or Dhritrashtr, controlled by Duryodhan, is the better choice. Of course Krishn believes Yudhishthir is. By far."

"And it has nothing to do with Krishn and Yudhishthir being cousins, kin by blood?

"No!" said Akrur with a smile. "Krishn's relations, friendship, and love are not determined by relations of blood. Shishupal and Kans both claim a close blood bond with Krishn. Followers of dharm, protectors of justice, and proponents of truth, are Krishn's kin."

"I have heard a lot about your Krishn," said Vidur a little wistfully. "He always sounds eminently lovable. Worthy of reverence."

"I am not at all surprised." said Akrur, smiling too. "Krishn is like that, people adore him. And he does feel familiar, always."

"Those close to him are fortunate," said Vidur.

"We are all close to him, if we agree with what he has taken a stand for."

"You are right," Vidur conceded, but a taste of bitterness had drawn more lines across his face. "When I am in the Kuru assembly, at best I feel stifled. You know the person sitting from across you is wicked, unjust, selfish, violent, and yet you must extend every courtesy. It is a hard, brutal environment. To see the corrupt and the cruel – it is difficult to sustain any kind of faith. It feels too outrageous for truth to survive in."

"Did you never think of resigning from the Kaurav assembly?" Akrur asked.

"I think of it daily. But they will be glad. Who will even bring up Pandav interests in the council then? Will you be here till Yudhishthir is appointed?"

"No," said Akrur. "Krishn and Balram will personally grace that occasion. But I would like to stay till I can send back confirmation about Yudhishthir's coronation."

"Would you like to meet Dhritrashtr and Bhishm?"

"I will see Dhritrashtr at the council as a representative of the Yadavas; it will not be a personal meeting. And Bhishm, I will visit, in his home."

"Come, Akrur! You are welcome to the house of this old Kaurav," Bhishm greeted Akrur with open arms. "Though this one is nothing like any you may have visited, all that while back."

"No two residences are identical, Pitrivy," said Akrur, a little puzzled "All houses reflect their master's personality."

"Is it true, Akrur, what some people are saying?"

"What have you heard, Ary?"

"People are saying you are here for a show of Yadav strength? Though I fail to see show in the five or seven chariots you have brought.. But I heard the Yadavs have finally noticed Duryodhan's matul tilting the political balance of Hastinapur in his nephew's favour, and you have come here to balance scales. Is it true?"

Akrur paused before answering.

"It is true I am here about Pritha and her sons."

"I am afraid I take the idea that Kunti and her sons are unhappy here as a personal affront. Her relatives have every right to support her and look to her wellbeing, but I cannot accept accusations from the representatives of another soverign state."

Akrur kept himself from rolling his eyes with difficulty. "Do you yourself feel that Pritha and her sons have received their due in Hastinapur, Pitrivy? That they have had a just return to their forbearance, that they have a share in the comforts enjoyed by Duryodhan and his brothers?"

"I know they have not," said Bhishm with visible

agony. “But which household treats all its sons equally? When do some not sacrifice for the sake of equilibrium? Some children are more demanding and obstinate than others and their wishes are fulfilled even at the cost of their gentler siblings. Have you not seen mothers give a crying child her sister’s share of sweet, promising her other child she will have twice the number later?”

“Yes. This often happens in families.”

“In this family Dhritrashtr is the demanding, invalid child. I keep thinking he must calm down some time, enough to make him understand… ”

“So you agree that injustice is being done?” Akrur asked.

“I refuse to call this justice or injustice. If we start doing that outsiders will immediately begin playing the Pandavs against the Dhartrashtrs. The kingdom belongs to Yudhishthir, and that is where it will go at last. But not through the intervention of others.”

He looked at Akrur and continued. “I know Duryodhan is becoming difficult to restrain. But Yudhishthir and his brothers are tolerant. Kunti is sensible. They will wait. And I have taken responsibility for Yudhishthir’s succession to the throne; I have told Dhritrashtr as much.”

“Then there is nothing else to be said. There is no greater surety than your word.”

Bhishm calmed down a little. “I know it’s not just to persuade a contented and obedient child to sacrifice under pressure from the persistantly obstinate one. But I am not a judge, nor is this a tribunal – nor have Yudhishthir and Duryodhan appeared before me as rivals. This is our family; we must think only of the concerted good of this family. I will not have the whole household devastated to ensure justice to one individual…”

“Neither would I, Pitamah!” Akrur said. “A weakened Hastinapur will debilitate us too.”

"Now you speak like an emissary, Akrur," Bhishm laughed. "Well, tell me about your Krishn. Is he planning to establish an empire, after killing Kans and subjugating Jarasandh? Will he vanquish other kings to become Emperor?"

"Krishn needs no kingdom," said Akrur said. "No one could have prevented him from sitting on Mathura's throne – and ordinary Yadavs would have showered him with rose petals – many do consider him their king."

"It is possible he installed Ugrasen to prevent unrest after Kans was killed – perhaps he was waiting for an opportune moment for another coup. From what you say of his popularity, it can't be too difficult?"

"No, Pitrivy. Krishn's mind is genuinely free of attachment, to this kingdom or that, to power. He always emphasises love. Attachment binds, love frees, him as well as those he loves." Akrur said again, "Krishn needs no kingdom to rule."

"Here, at least, every passing pedestrian needs a kingdom of their own, to rule."

"Krishn's aim is much broader than any single kingdom or state, much greater and more ambitious."

"What is his aim?"

"The establishment of dharm. To get individual kingdoms to institute virtue, justice, and detachment."

"Does he even understand dharm?" demanded Bhishm impatiently. "Killing Kans, was that a dharmic act? Does Krishn know the essence of dharm at all? How old is he?"

Was Bhishm just curious or was he feeling insulted by this upstart spouting dharm? For generations now, Bhishm had been the final word on dharmic action across this and all neighbouring territories… Did the venerable and grandfatherly stalwart of dharm feel threatened?

"Just about your Arjun's age," Akrur answered. "It is

love he lays out in large swathes, Pitamah. Love for friends and love for foes, love for all beings…"

"This is beyond me!" said Bhishm. "If he loved Kans too, why did he kill him?"

"Killing Kans was an act of mercy. According to Krishn's philosophy Kans was suffering; pride viciousness, folly, selfishness that breeds only violence and pain… He says it is short-sighted to think of individuals apart from, divorced from and distinct from the communities they live among and the roles they play in them. Damage is damage – singular or plural – and it spreads, damaging further. We must consider creation as one organic whole. To advance one community, we must not damage the other. To advance mankind, we must not destroy the creation. Mankind's advance is based on the advancement of creation; the cattle's wellbeing is in the cowherds' interest; and the farmers' in the cowherds'."

"This Krishn, your Krishn, appears to be a seer," Bhishm observed. "No warrior would think like this."

"Who knows what he is? All we know is that he is our Krishn," Akrur answered.

"I would like to speak with him about dharm with him. Invite him to Hastinapur for Yudhishthir's ceremony on my behalf."

"He will be here in any case, to see his Bua and her sons. And he would never miss a chance to return you regards. And now that you have called him, he will certainly come."

Akrur stood up to leave.

Bhishm too stood. "Akrur, I have spoken to you in fear as well as love. Do not imagine I other you, or any of Kunti's family, my son."

"I understand, Pitamah."

Akrur touched Bhishm's feet, and left.

Dhritrashtr stood to welcome Akrur to the royal council. Akrur greeted him and took his seat.

"Akrur!" Dhritrashtr said. "I am told you are here to ask after your sister Kunti and her sons. I hope you are satisfied?"

Akrur was taken aback by the direct question. It would be politically incorrect of Akrur to give an honest answer. For all that it wore a mantle of simplicity and ignorance, the question bit, slyly.

The truth would exacerbate the family feud, and spark civil war. And the court would stand behind its king.

"My nephews have completed their education, Rajan! Pitrivy Bhishm has informed me that you are planning Yudhishthir's coronation as we speak," said Akrur with an easy smile. "That leaves no room for discontentment... But I would not have asked to be at this council for Pritha alone!"

"Your presence has a political purpose, of course. I am all ears."

"Rajan! As you are no doubt aware, the Yadavs of Mathura are well rid of the atrocious Kans and have reinstated King Ugrasen. Instead of a wayward, oppressive and cruel rule, the Yadavs have ushered in popular and beneficent rule. They are no longer a suppressed, downtrodden, and hapless populace but an independent and competent citizenry. They know they have to defend themselves, their welfare, their rights, their freedom, and their happiness. They are thus engaged in crafting a just and equitable society."

"Naturally, no people would wish a repeat of suffering," said Dhritrashtr.

"But the world does not run in accordance with our wishes," Akrur continued. "The kings who colluded with Kans are unlikely to tolerate an independent and capable Yadav kingdom. Jarasandh intended to usurp the Yadavs' land and subsume it in the Magadh Empire. For him the Yadavas were a resource – a renewable storehouse of amenities, necessities, and luxuries for the residents of Magadh. He wanted them to sacrifice their lives as his soldiers, produce grains for his troops, work as his servants and attendants, and rear animals to provide meat for him and his courtiers. How could he possibly tolerate their present lives, of freedom, prosperity, and honour?"

"Do, the Yadavs solicit our help to fight Jarasandh?" asked Dhritrashtr.

"No! The Yadavs have no wish to fight wars and shed blood unnecessarily! We solicit no military support. Your kinship is quite enough. What I wish to submit, however, is that power equations are about to change quite drastically in this Jambudip. A pact is brewing even between the Magadhas and the Panchalas…"

"I see no grounds for such a pact," said Dhritrashtr, too quickly.

"Jarasandh is mobilising his allies to invade Mathura and Drupad is looking for a powerful ally to help settle his score with Hastinapur." Akrur pointed out. "If – when – Magadh and Panchal unite, the Panchalraj will surely attack Hastinapur in revenge for Ahichhatr."

"You think the Kauravs are afraid of them? We can foil even a united assault by the Panchalas and the Magadhas!"

"You misunderstand me, Maharaj!" Akrur replied courteously. "We only warn Hastinapur to be on the alert, and ready. We wish you a strong and indomitable regime. I am here to announce that Hastinapur will never be alone. In any such crisis, the entire Yadav army under Krishn and Balram will be in Hastinapur to support Yudhishthir."

Dhritrashtr as well as his Kaurav councillors were stunned into silence. To support Yudhishthir? Not Dhritrashtr, not Duryodhan? Dhritrashtr briefly considered declining goodwill with strings attached – declaring that

Hastinapur would need to assistance while Bhishm, Dron, Krip, Karn, Ashwatthama, Duryodhan were their force of arms – but it was the Pandavs who brought Drupad down…

"Suppose the Panchalas and the Magadhas fail to strike a deal?" Dhritrashtr asked instead.

"Then Jarasandh will seek an alliance with Hastinapur…And because we will never countenance Jarasandh's presence this close to Mathura the Yadav troops will assault Jarasandh." He continued, "We have no wish for Hastinapur to be crushed between Jarsandh's and our own armies – but if it happens here the Panchalas will also send the Yadavs help…"

"If Hastinapur avoids pact with the Magadhas?" asked Dhritrashtr.

"Then Jarasandh will invade Hastinapur. But in that scenario too, Krishn and the Yadav troops will be here under Krishn's banner, to support Yudhishthir."

Again, Yudhishthir! Dhritrashtr was doubly rattled. This was the second time Akrur had mentioned the Yadav army coming to aid Yudhishthir – in the guise of friendship he was handing out ultimatums. Pitrivy Bhishm and Vidur both maintained a shocking silence over these muffled threats. Suddenly fear gripped Dhritrashtr's heart. What if Duryodhan intervened at this moment? If Dhritrashtr did not speak himself, something terrible would happen.

"We are pleased, Akrur, that we will not be alone in such an hour of crisis. I appreciate Krishn's and the Yadavs' good wishes and goodwill.. I am pleased Krishn is eager to see us. Do extend him our invitation to visit Hastinapur."

"He will be here for his cousin Yudhishthir's coronation," said Akrur. "You only have to declare a date; Krishn will be here."

Vidur wanted to stand up and applaud this master of diplomacy. Akrur had established amity and alliance, issued an ultimatum framed in kinship, love and concern, and had made it impossible for Dhritrashtr's delays to appear anything other than obstinate, childish procrastination. It was marvelous.

"Shall we settle on Sharad Purnima, Akrur?"

Bhishm rejoiced, incredulous. Had he after so many years of ditherings, just heard a date?

"I will relate your decision in Mathura. The Yadavs will be here." Akrur bowed to Dhritrashtr, just as Duryodhan stood up too, and walked out, followed by a veritable battalion of minions.

Gandhari demanded an explanation.

"Duryodhan says he will kill himself the day Yudhishthir is crowned."

"Which is preferable to being killed by another man," said Dhritrashtr.

"What do you mean?"

"I have said only what time has been whispering to me. I have only internal eyes; I do see far, you know."

"What? What do you see?"

"Powerful political forces are emerging all around us. There will be a savage war – I am sure there will, no matter how many alliances are made. Panchal, Yadav, Magadh, and Hastinapur are expected to be strong and powerful. If the king himself is blind and old, the crown prince is beyond reproach, and mighty."

"Duryodhan is far mightier than Yudhishthir."

"That is your perception," said Dhritrashtr coolly. "What I know and everyone else remembers is that Duryodhan, with his friends and supporters, was beaten hollow by Drupad on the battlefield. Yudhishthir and his paltry four brothers took on his army, captured him alive, and surrendered his person and his kingdom to Achary Dron… Which cousin is mightier?"

"Even if the veracity of this story is beyond doubt,

shall we surrender our kingdom to Yudhishthir before we lose it to some other force?" asked Gandhari.

"I haven't surrendered it to anyone, my queen! I have simply appointed a crown prince to fight the coming war… If the Panchalas and the Magadhas come together, the combined forces of Drupad and Jarasandh will invade Hastinapur, and Crown Prince Yudhishthir will march out with his brothers to fight them…"

"And Duryodhan won't?" Gandhari asked in disbelief.

"Why should he? When Duryodhan fought against Drupad, was he supported by the Pandavs? No! Duryodhan ought to pay them back in kind. Krishn and the Yadavs will be there, standing beside Yudhishthir. I wish them all the best of him. When they have worn themselves and each other out, Duryodhan can pick his partners, and take back what is his."

Gandhari was silent for a moment, calculating the possibilities of war, of alliances and opportunities. Finally she asked Dhritrashtr, "What if there is no war?"

"Has that ever happened?" laughed Dhritrashtr. "So many brave kshatriys have gotten together. They are brandishing their shining weapons. They are all proud of their bravery. War is inevitable, my dear queen!"

"And if Yudhishthir emerges victorious?"

"The only person with any strength left after a war is the one who did not fight. Even if Yudhishthir and his brothers come out of it alive, they will be weak… Victorious or no. And Duryodhan will be strong."

19

Drupad raged.

Dron! His childhood friend-turned-foe! What was Drupad's fault? Only that he spoke the truth? It was true – friendship between a palace and gurukul was impossible – they were contrastive entities! Was Dron so ashamed of being an achary that he needed the friendship of a king to validate himself? For this perceived insult Dron had dispatched his students to make war on Drupad, had him bound and brought before him, mocked and humiliated Drupad in front of an eager audience, and then taken half his kingdom. In the Aryavart not even for the gravest offences were kings treated thus. Drupad wanted more than anything to engage Dron in battle. The coward who had set out deliberately to train students up for this single cruel act… But he despaired both of the possibility that he would have the opportunity, and that he could by himself afford to launch a full assault. To Hastinapur's many gurus and accharys, one hundred and five trained princes, not to mention Ashwatthama and Karn and Bhishm, Drupad only had Shikhandi, Dhrishtadyumn, and Satyajit. Yet Drupad must accomplish his revenge and regain his kingdom, or he would lose all the respect he commanded among Kings of Aryavart. And his subjects…How could the subjects of a cowardly and weak king hold their head high? What would happen to the pride of Somak Kings? He wished for a kshatriy death. That was all.

"Why are you being so cruel with yourself, Pitaji?" said his daughter Krishna. "Do you think any of us can eat and rest, when you do not?"

"If I were a brahmin I would try and forgive him," said Drupad. "But I am kshtriy. Even if forgiveness came naturally to me, I am required by the precepts of my varn to resist consolation at this pass. I must burn."

"Then don't burn alone. We are kshatriys too, Ma and Bhaiya and I. If we are to burn let us burn like a yajn fire, with purpose, rather than spreading ruin like wild fires. Arrange for an initiation – let us pledge and prepare ourselves to avenge what has been taken from us!"

"You know a sacrificial fire purges all life's sublime joys – pleasure, kindness, grandeur, and replaces them with vengeance?"

Krishna thought of Krishn, and the conversation she had had vith Shailaja only days ago. "I am his sakhi," she had insisted. "Yes," she said to her father.

"Will Dhristadyumn agree?" Drupad asked.

"Bhaiya is your son, Pitaji! He wants nothing so much as he does to retrieve Ahichhatr and destroy Dron."

"Then do it," said Drupad.

The Kampily palace was abuzz with celebration.

Drupad had cast off his depression as he would worn-out attire. He looked rejuvenated and stern. A yajn was to be performed in the chamber adjoining the throne hall. A group of brahmins were seated in their prescribed places. Prominent royal staff, but no outsiders.

A conch shell was blown, Drupad and his consort entered. Dhrishtadyumn followed in warriors' gear; Krishna stepped out as a bride. The royal priest igniting the sacrificial fire sang preliminary hymns of thanksgiving and pronounced: "Anger is man's shield. If man commits not anger, he will not be inspired to self-defence. Therefore, anger is man's dharm, his sacred duty… Anger is used against a tyrant to end his tyranny… We pray to be inspired to anger against our enemy, to hate and to oppose him; to empower us to slay him…Agni! Heed King Drupad of Panchal's prayer! Grant him his wish."

Drupad offered his oblation and prayed: "O Fire! I give my natural offspring over to you. Give me in their stead offspring of fire; who shall slay my enemy Dron and exterminate his protectors the Kuru clan. Give me victory in war!"

The priest addressed Dhrishtdyumn: "O Prince! Now you exist anew, from the pit of fire. You emerge with your arms and shield, and your chariot. Your arms are from the other world and cannot be destroyed. Your vehicle cannot be broken or burnt. You are invincible; and you are born to kill Dron. The Dhrishtadyumn whose guru Dronchary was is no more. You will kill Dron and help destroy his protectors, the Kurus."

Dhrishtadyumna was received by Drupad. "Come, O Son! You who are gifted by fire! Destroy my enemies!"

The priest addressed Krishna, "O Princess! You have offered all your existence so far to the fire, your thoughts, your passions and attachments. Henceforth you exist anew. Heretofore you are consecrated in fire. You are not born of your mother's womb but from the sacred pit of fire. You have taken existence to kill Dron and exterminate the Kuru dynasty. This is your singular mission in this life. You will do that. Arise! On behalf of Agni, I give you over to King Drupad."

Draupadi got up and was received by Drupad.

Drupad dreamed. He tries in vain to lift his bow. When he does manage to pick it up, he finds the bowstring broken. When he ties the bowstring, he finds his quiver has no arrows. In desperation, Drupad calls out to Dhrishtadyumn but finds no voice comes from his throat. And the Kaurav army comes marching on. The army is led by Arjun. Arjun showers arrows and keeps on advancing. Nobody can stop him. He goes through anyone in his way as if there were no solid obstruction in front of him, only air. As he gets closer to Drupad, he is transformed into a thick rope, which curls like a snake, entwining around him. Drupad lies helpless, an inanimate object. Dron puts his right foot on Drupad's chest; Arjun pranams to his guru and is blessed. Drupad's entire body was bathed in sweat. He stirred himself back to wakefulness but fragments of the nightmare curled about his mind like miasma. In an effort to shrug it off, Drupad wove the future.

He finds himself standing near a huge sacrificial pit praying to Agni. Fom the pit a splendid chariot emerges, with horses made of flame. The chariot is driven by Dhrishtadyumn, wearing armour too of fire and armed to the teeth. Dhrishtadyumn's chariot does not run on the earth or fly in the air like a bird but swims through it like fish. It moves ahead by cutting through troops like a sharp sword. Dhrishtadyumn's eyes are blood red. They do not recognise anyone. Whereever they look, they cause a rain of blood. Slowly Dhrishtadyumn inches towards Arjun, who shoots arrows at him, but they vanish in air. Dhrishtadyumn's eyes fall on Arjun, who is soaked in blood. Dhrishtadyumn cuts Arjun in two with his long sword... Drupad wakes up with a scream.

"What have you done, Dhrishtadyumn! What have you done!" he wails.

"Why, Pitaji!" Dhrishtadyumn looks up, his blood red eyes fixed on his father, "Is it unfair and unrighteous to kill your enemy?"

"But when was he our enemy?" Drupad protests, his voice choking his throat. "Don't you know what he said when Bhim was demolishing the Panchala troops in battle?"

"What did he say, Pitaji?"

"He said, 'We are not the Panchalas' enemy. We are here only to pay off the guru's dakshina.' Have you ever seen a warrior who fights but does not hate his enemy? Who accomplishes but his duty?"

Tears appeared in Drupad's eyes.

20

A week or so ahead of the ceremony Uddhav arrived in Hastinapur. Krishn was not far behind.

Kunti couldn't stop tell her sons stories about her childhood and maiden youth. They too were infinitely curious – their mother had never spoken of her parental home; the present and Pandu's Hastinapur, had always been too urgent a topic of talk and for thought. Their affection and respect for the Yadavs and for Krishn grew apace, and the novel feeling of having family that did not mean to kill or at least displace them felt luxurious, genuinely good.

The people of Hastinapur too had been hearing stories about Krishn – they lined the streets to see him enter their city, to catch a glimpse of the celebrity. Though greeted formally at the Vardhman gate by Duryodhan, Krishn avoided the palace and opted to stay with his bua and her sons.

Kunti received Krishn at her doorstep, and as he bent down in reverence to her feet, held him up to exclaim, "So you are the one who emancipated my brother and sister-in-law! My son! You sent Bhaiya Akrur and now stand here yourself to see my son crowned! Unexceptionable redeemer!"

Tears filled her eyes and Krishn rested her head on his shoulder. He said gently, "My mother. To live in the shadow of death is not any less tortuous than facing the physical thing. But your worries are over now. You have five incomparable sons, and we two are here, and the Yadavs stand behind you. The seven of us will establish dharm in the world and demolish all despotic rule."

"My son, Krishn!" said Kunti, "I have faith in your every success! Stay with me, with your brothers here. I would not lose you even to Mathura for the world."

"No bonds, Bua!" Krishn smiled. "We succeed by snapping bonds, not by tightening them."

"But love is strength, though it does bind, my son! Look! I am bound by my love of my sons, and they are bound by love for me – I would, I would do the same with you."

"No, Bua!" Krishn smiled again. "You have set them free with your love, given them the will to do what they will. Those we love, we liberate. We do not restrain them, we expand ourselves."

Kunti laughed. "They were right! You are no common charmer; you are charm personified!"

"Krishn!" Bhim would not sleep nor let anyone else sleep till his curiosity was satisfied. "Matul Akrur said you said the fruit of any action is certain?

"Yes."

"Then tell me – we have always been good to Duryodhan, what fruit did we get? Did he ever do us any good in return? If it were upto him, he would kill us all."

Krishn was silent for a moment, and then said, "Madhyam, does a ball counce back from a wall?"

"Yes of course."

"Think of every action like it is throwing a ball. The fruit is the ball's return. Simple? Now analyse closer. Does a ball of iron bounce back from a wall?"

"Of course not," said Bhim, startled by the sudden vision of an iron ball tearing through a wall.

"Will a ball bounce back from a sandheap?"

"No!"

"Will a ball made of wood bounce back with greater force or a ball of wool?"

"Wood!"

"If you toss a ball into a slag heap, will you not not only lose your ball but also get splashed with slag?"

"Yes – I get it. Duryodhan is a slag heap. We should never have bothered to throw balls at him."

"Exactly!" Krishn smiled. "And we have to remember that the ball, the wall, the sand, the mass of iron, slag – nothing in itself is good or bad. All these things conform to the laws of nature and act in accordance with them. Suppose you caress a thorn and your finger gets pricked – would you blame and curse the thorn? To do so would only be a fruitless attempt to impose your will onto nature's laws. Got it?"

But Bhim was already snoring.

"Bhaiya Krishn," laughed Sahdev, "Madhyam has got his answer. He is not interested in any philosophization."

Krishn smiled and said, "I can see that."

"I have a question, though. Why did our teachers not teach us to throw only wooden balls at wall, to touch only flowers, not thorns?"

"What they taught you was ethics," said Krishn. "Not everyone thinks carefully before she or he acts; ethics is abstracted conclusions to regulate conduct."

"What I want to know," said Arjun, "is what punishment Duryodhan has received for his crimes against us or atrocities perpetrated on his subjects. His entitlement and his comfort has grown steadily. He stands only to gain from his villainy."

"Nature awards no punishment, no prizes. Only human society prescribes those. There is only action and reaction. When a farmer sows seeds well, takes good care of his crop and foresees problems, makes arrangements to deal with them, the yield is good and we say nature rewarded him.

When a farmer doesn't do all that or cannot, we say nature punished him. Neither conclusion is true. And, human reactions – rewards and punishments – are instantaneous. Nature takes her time."

"Are you saying we need not reward or punish – we should let nature take its course?"

"No! What I am saying is that punishment is always coming for those who have acted in unsound ways."

"What about Duryodhan's punishment?" Yudhishthir spoke for the first time.

"A person who has a serene pond of potable water begins to fill it up with mud because he wants more land instead, and nobody stops him, the pond will cease to exist. Then, when he is thirsty, or the people around him are thirsty, they will either die of thirst or dig the pond up again. Duryodhan is that man. If the Kurus don't stop him, they will die."

"What does that mean? That the entire clan must inevitably be punished for the deeds of one evil man?" Yudhishthir asked.

"Those who stay silent are implicated in his crimes. Every one of them will face reactions to their actions – or to their inactions." Krishn paused, and looked away. "In any case I don't believe Duryodhan's entitlements and comforts are worth much – he is consumed with envy, malice, and violence. He cannot be a happy man…"

Kunti looked around the door, an annoyed look on her face. "Will you all go to sleep? It will be morning in a moment!"

In the morning Krishn and Balram visited Bhishm.

Though he was years older Bhishm could not help feel an incongruous calm descend on the room as Krishn walked in, smiling, at ease, and uninhibited Bhishm had expected a subtle politician, serious and self-centred. But

Krishn's charm was spontaneous, generous, indiscriminate.

"I have heard only praise of you. Akrur told me you not only freed the Yadavs from tyranny, you also gave them the strength to defend themselves and new purpose."

"Kaka takes pleasure in praising me," Krishn laughed. "The only praises I hear – have been hearing all my life – are yours. All Aryavart regards you as a resolute Himalaya!"

"He does not know that the mind of this Himalaya is slurry with doubts and questions."Bhishm looked at Krishn carefully. "Ever since Akrur told me I have been incessantly comparing myself with you… Not in some puerile competitive way – I haven't been able to help thinking, before I act, what you would do in a situation…"

Krishn laughed again. "But I am! I am in competition with you!"

"Why…?"

"The young are always in competition with the old, simply because they are old. To become old is the attainment we race toward…" He continued more seriously, "But your firmness and integrity are legendary – the story of your vow… Aryavrat sings its praises."

Bhishm instantly became cautious. He had never found flattery particularly seductive… But Krishn's levity was affectionate and playful; he did not appear either frivolous or insincere, or exude the arrogance and airs of a man bestowing praise as patronage. He seemed to feel at home with Bhishm, as everywhere. He seemed to convey honest veneration, as well as a kind of reassurance, a capacity and a readiness to offer support and strength.

"In what way were you comparing yourself with me, Pitamah?"

Bhishm had never spoken openly with anyone about his doubts or uncertainties before. To whom could he speak? Everyone was younger than him; all respected and depended upon him.

Inexplicably, Krishn was an equal. "Akrur told me you don't want to rule," Bhishm said. "That started me off. I forfeited my own entitlement years ago, but the kingdom has not forfeited me! I wonder sometimes why I have not been able to leave it behind…"

"Oh but how can Hastinapur release its savior?" laughed Krishn. "Spies hunt through forest ashrams for your equivalent at the behest of kings and ministers; commanders vie to emulate you, and patriarchs despair at the thought of how unequal they are to you!" No one had made Bhishm's status in Hastinapur the subject of a joke before – certainly never to his face… "It is the magnet which releases – or refuses to release – the iron."

"Sycophancy doesn't suit you!" said Bhishm, with as little gravitas as his interlocutor. "But in all seriousness, I have been waiting a long, long, time, for an able descendent of Shantanu to take the reins so I may leave for the riverbank and be free of politics."

"The object of renunciation is never the physical world, Pitamah, it is your attachment to it."

Bhishm looked at Krishn sharply. Is he suggesting I not worry about Hastinapur? If it is unprotected, so be it. If chaos comes, let it? "I am not attached to the kingdom as a geopolitical entity, but yes, I am attached to my clan… I cannot see the kingdom of my forebears divided and defeated, because I do not wish the Kurus to be."

"So you have no will to territorial expansion, but you do wish to preserve it as it is," said Krishn.

"That is why I am looking forward to the investiture of Yudhishthir. I have faith in his ability to maintain the Kurukul," said Bhishm.

"Do you?" asked Krishn. "It will be a long time before the crown prince can establish any kind of peace, Pitamah! As far as I can see Duryodhan will not let Yudhishthir settle any time soon."

"That's the problem," Bhishm said. "I tried everything to convince Duryodhan to let go his grievances… I love them both – that is why I have never been able to punish their misdemeanors…"

Krishn smiled. "Love is not attachment, Pitamah! Attachment only ever breeds delusion; love makes us keener sighted. We do not let the ones we love take the wrong road, make wrong turns. And neither silence nor ignorance has ever done any real good – nor would it here. Neither you, nor Duryodhan, nor Hastinapur."

"My real problem is that when it was time to choose a king I decided against the sightless Dhritrashtr."

"Do you regret that decision?"

"No, I do not regret it. My problem is not regret, my son. My problem is the navigation of conflict past my decision. I believe what I did was my dharm to do. But Pandu died, the kingdom ended up in Dhritarastr's hands, and despite all odds governance has not stalled… which means Dhritrashtr's sightlessness was not an impediment at all, and he had the right to occupy the throne. So was I unjust? If Pandu's kingship was unjust, the fault should be remidied. Dhritrashtr should be recognised as the rightful king of Hastinapur and his son Duryodhan be invested as the crown prince…"

Bhishm paused to observe Krishn, who was listening attentively but in silence, without interruption or the slightest impatience. In fact he appeared almost aloof, neither agitated by the past nor dreading the future. Fully present.

"But the state of the subjects and of the royal assembly does not escape me. The Kuru assembly has lost its magnanimity, its decency and probity. The likes of Kanik and Purochan have gained importance at the helm of state affairs. Chivalry, nobility? Duryodhan, Dushasan, their confidants Karn and Ashvatthama, have no appreciation even of ordinary etiquette. Dhritrashtr attaches excessive importance to what Shakuni says… It's all cunning and deceit. I wonder how Vidur has stayed on through such chicanery… Dhritrashtr seems incapable of seeing as well as of feeling. No, I do not regret my decision," said Bhishm again, with renewed certainty in his voice. "He did not deserve the throne. If I blundered it was in granting him the regency. Yudhishthir should be crowned at once."

"And tomorrow, when this is done, will you be satisfied?" Krishn asked.

"I fear Dhritrashtr will not vacate the throne and Duryodhan will not accept Yudhishthir even when he does."

"Why don't you assume faith instead of doubt?"

"That is precisely what I find in you!"

"Well, why haven't you cultivated trust in yourself, Pitamah. Why should you distrust yourself?"

"We slide into doubt and distrust over time – I lost faith and trust in my decisions – I am trying to regain them. Tell me what you think: who has the right to rule? Dhritrashtr? Yudhishthir? Duryodhan?"

Krishn laughed. "Oh, I? I think contrariwise, Pitamah! In my view, no man has the right to rule over another."

Bhishm looked at Krishn in amazement. What was this innocuous-looking youth an anarchist? No king, no government, no one to protect the weak?

"But men have to be safe and live ordered lives for mankind to grow and develop itself. To think about and battle its evil tendencies, think about and sustain what is good."

Krishn smiled and continued. "We have any right only over ourselves. We also have the capacity to stretch our 'self', which knows no limits. The head of a family 'rules' over it because she cares for the family as she does for her self – her family has become her 'self'. The teacher has right over her student. Husbands and wives have rights over one another. A person might expand her self to include a city, a state, a society, a caste, or all of entire creation. You have no right to rule anyone you don't love as much as you love yourself."

Dhritrashtr loving creation? He barely loved Duryodhan – by Krishn's standards even his love for his son was mere attachment.

"All I see around me is the contraction of 'self'," said Bhishm. "There is no expansion of the kind you speak of in sight."

"You are right, Pitamah," Krishn responded. "Men do not recognize themselves in the things and people around them. It is a self-imposed limitation of vision. They keep on reducing the circumference of kinship and keep pushing what and whom they should love out of their self-circumference. It is only the man who does not consider the mango tree in a public garden part of his 'self' who can chop it down and use it for kindling. And he feels so proud of his achievement! Uncaring that he has diminished himself irredeemably, has diminished mankind irredeemably. It is of course the greatest irony of nature that the fool always considers himself the wisest man in any room."

Krishn looked at Bhishm for a moment, and continued. "I feel the creation of divisions and fissures among peoples is a crime against humanity – whether it be a person who create them, an organisation, or an idea, a system of thought. The truly great demolish walls artificially erected among men. They are the real humans, prototypes of creation, and immense, like the creation they serve."

Bhishm had lost track of time – but Krishn seemed suddenly to remember. "Do forgive my presumption, Pitamah. I came here only to pay my respects! When I start talking about all this I forget even who I am talking to – that I am speaking with our grandfather – himself a fount of knowledge, and the one who has done more than anyone to keep this dynasty together……" He got up to go, and Balram stood as silently as he had sat. "I will leave now. Will come another day, though, with your permission and according to your convenience…" Both saluted Bhishm respectfully before leaving.

With the neighing of the horses and the whirring chariot's wheels, Bhishm seemed to wake from a trance.

He had asked Krishn a question! Krishn had got him entangled in some other discussion – about humanity and dharm – and the small question about his family had been lost…

But had it? Hadn't Krishn answered it, and very directly? We have the right to rule only over ourselves. Over those we are able to love as we love ourselves. Dhritrashtr… did not rule even over those he purported to love; they ruled over him. He had no authority even over his own physical self – he was ruled by his desires. Attachment bred delusion, desire bred delusion, and made Dhritrashtr willfully blind. The willfully blind, the self-limiting limited self, cannot love. Its capacity does not rise above attachment.

If Dhritrashtr stayed on the throne of Hastinapur, the entire orchard would become a storehouse for fuel. Ah, what an answer Krishn had given his Pitamah.

21

An informer from Mathura briefed Krishn on the banks of Ganga. "Jarasandh has launched his campaign. His force has marched out in small contingents to install posts along the way. He has invited his allies to the war, including King Drupad of Panchal, with whom he intends to discuss a pact, and also to request a passage for his troops through his territory… which is apparently a ploy. He has dispatched an emissary to Kalayavan as well…"

"So Jarasandh is trying to include the savage rakshases in his alliance?"

He dispatched the informer disguised as an anchorite back to Mathura with categorical instructions to keep developments under wraps and allow no public revelations.

"Let everything go on as usual. The Yadavs shall continue with their war exercises. The security measures in and around Mathura shall be tightened. Warships shall be kept ready. The chariot races shall continue. The stock of food grains shall be increased. The cattle shall not be sent far," Krishn told him.

To Uddhav he said, laughing, "Nothing to worry about, just keep in mind that immediately after the coronation ceremony our chariots should rush off to Mathura. But there should be no indication of any expedition, here or there."

"Pitaji," Duryodhan stood before Dhritrashtr as he was readied for the assembly before the ceremony.

"What is it, Son?" Dhritrashtr detected anger in his son's voice.

"Why didn't you allow a duel between Karn and Arjun at the stadium?"

"Kripacharay stopped it, not I," Dhritrashtr reminded him.

"But you could have overridden Kripachary's ruling."

"That would not have been appropriate."

"Then please permit a duel today."

"What do you mean, son?"

That was his cue to wail, "I cannot see Yudhishthir as Crown Prince.

"So?

"I want you to permit us to kill the Pandavs before they arrive at the venue."

"So you and your friends are killed at once as well?"

"What do you mean, killed? Don't we have weapons? Don't our hands have strength, and power? We will finish them off in no time."

"I sincerely wish this was possible. But it is not. My son, they have Krishn, Balram, Satyaki, Uddhav, all on their side. Together they would kill you in no time and nobody would blame them because you attacked first. And," he said as an afterthought, "you can't kill your kin in this manner."

"They are not our kin; they are our foes."

"The world recognises them as your kin; they are my brother's sons," said Dhritrashtr.

"They are not Pandu's sons." Duryodhan was losing his temper. "They are Kunti and Madri's sons. They are not the descendents of King Vichitraviry."

"Careful!" Dhritrashtr cried, trembling with anger. "Never ever let those words cross your lips again! Never let them be voiced in your hearing! In fact, crush that idea out of existence, and forget it ever came into being!"

Duryodhan was stunned at his father's reaction. "Why? Isn't it true?"

"If that is your logic, I am also not Vichitraviry's son either – I am Ambika's! You yourself are not related to King Vichitraviry at all!"

Duryodhan's fury vanished. He was so frightened tears came into his eyes. "What should I do? What should I do?" he cried.

Dhritrashtr wanted to calm his son but was himself too agitated to try. He stared into space with blank eyes. And then he spoke.

"I am still alive. I am the king of Hastinapur. I wield absolute power. There is no need for you to be disappointed enough to kill yourself...."

"Then allow me to exile myself," Duryodhan said at once.

"No! You are coming to the assembly with me and we'll see who is exiled from Hastinapur!"

The royal assembly wore a festive look, guests dressed with all the magnificence each could afford were packed into the magnificent, bedecked throne room.

At an auspicious moment priests presided over by Kripachary started chanting hymns. Yudhishthir's head was consecrated with water from several rivers and holy places. Dhritrashtr crowned him and he did homage to his office and to the assembled gurus before taking his seat on a throne beside the king.

An elated Vidur asked him to "take the oath before royalty and the people's representatives, so your subjects rest assured."

Yudhishthir's gaze found Krishn in the crowd, and he spoke directly to him. "I shall ever aim to establish dharm across Kuru governence. Our policy will be non-violence and equality irrespective of varn, caste, and class. If any subject suffers injustice or oppression during my reign, may I may suffer an eternity in hell."

The assembly applauded and cheered.

Dhritrashtr stood up and raised his right hand. "With the princes' arms-training over, I call upon Achary Dron to take up another mantle: I appoint him supreme commander of the Kuru troops and commanders."

Bhishm, Vidur, Vahlik, Somdutt, even Dron himself was amazed. That was Bhishm's prerogative – had been for decades! Was this an attempt to elevate the Achary's stature, or to curtail Bhishm's rights, disable him and thus render Yudhishthir virtually powerless?

"What's going on, Krishn?" whispered Arjun.

"That much talked about foresight of a sightless man!" Krishn smiled. "Probably a ploy to ensure the Achary's allegiance. The son used Karn against you; the father will try to use Dronachary in the same way."

"I am happy that Hastinapur has a crown prince after so long." Dhritrashtr resumed, "and I firmly believe he will continue each proud Kuru tradition to its exaltation."

The assembly dispersed, and Yudhishthir headed straight to Bhishm's home to seek his blessing.

Bhishm greeted him gladly.

"Today your right has been returned to you. It is a just and right return for all you have borne with grace and integrity. You are a beacon for the Kurukul, and for the people of Hastinapur. I am proud of you, my son." His eyes were moist, and he placed his hand on Yudhishthir's head. "But Yudhishthir," he could not help saying, "it is difficult, it is difficult, to wield and to hold on to power, my son."

Yudhishthir was painfully aware of just how difficult the task before him was likely to be. It was comforting to hear Pitamah acknowledge it, however.

"There are many who want to or wrest authority from whoever has it, many always in the room solely for personal gain… And your right amounts to a moral obligation. Even by itself, no easy one to meet sincerely," said Bhishm. "I have complete faith in you," he continued, in a more encouraging voice. "Adversaries – yours and those of the people – will always try to obstruct you. And they will attack you together, always try and overwhelm you through force of numbers – that is all they have, since the right is never on their side… But I have faith in your abilities, in your integrity."

"I will try my best, Pitamah, to be true and fair to protect my subjects, to ensure their wellbeing always, and never to exploit them," Yudhishthir vowed.

"May God realize your words!" said Bhishm, and placed his hands on Yudhishthir's head again, in blessing.

He saw Yudhishthir leave with as much trepidation as ever. In the distance, Krishn turned toward Mathura.

Translator's Note

English translations of Sanskrit and Hindi names usually append an 'a' at the end: Krishna, Duryodhana, Bhishma are all pronounced Krishn, Duryodhan, and Bhishm in Sanskrit and Hindi. Owing to the scrupulousness of early Western scholars who were attempting to pronounce the consonants with due emphasis (as they are indeed pronounced, in Sanskrit), we find ourselves unable to recognise the difference in pronouncitation between the name of the blue god (Krishn, krish-nuh, (male) dark one) and the Draupadi (Krishna, krish-naa, (female) dark one). Neither 'Draupadi' nor 'Kunti' are names of course; they are designations. The daughter of Drupad and the daughter of Kuntibhoj are named Krishna and Pritha respectively. The vowel sound in both names is long: Krishnaa, Prithaa.

Similarly, words we would recognize as 'Dharma' and 'Karma' are pronounced without the long vowel sound that is usally appended to them by readers in English (and by extension and via translation, speakers of other languages globally). An attempt has been made in this edition to correct this tendency, by dropping the problematic 'a'. The attempt may lead to some confusion in words like 'Achary/Achary' and 'Arya/Ary' given that while 'y' is a consonant, it also denotes the long vowel sound otherwise denotable as 'ee'. 'Achary' is not 'Aa-char-ee'. The 'y' at the end of 'Acharyy' and 'Aryy' should be pronounced like 'y' in yummy.

It is also important to note that stories from the

Mahabharat are not traceable to a single origin or a single geographical location, cultural frame, or linguistic paradigm. In Bengal 'Duryodhan' is 'Duryodhon'; in Tamil Nadu 'Krishn' is indeed 'Krishna'. Since this book is a translation, I have followed Narendra Kohli's Hindi. In Hindi, Bhim is a Pandav, Dushasan a Kaurav.

Glossary

Modes of Address

Bahin: sister
Bhabhi: sister in law
Bhadre: sister, female friend
Bhai: brother
Bhaiya: elder bother
Jeth: brother in law
Jethani: sister in law
Ma: mother
Pitaji: father
Pitamaha: grandfather
Pitrivy: patriarch
Didi: elder sister
Devar: husband's brother
Matul: mother's brother
Kaka: father's brother
Kaki: father's sister

Among the Pandav Brothers:

Jyeshth: eldest brother (Yudhishthir)
Madhyam: middle brother (Bhim)
Kanishth: youngest brother (Arjun)
Anuj: little brother (Nakul and Sahdev)

Formal Modes of Address

Achary: teacher

Ary: Aryan (as opposed to Dravidian, tribal, or other non-Aryan)

Arye: female Aryan

Guru, Guruji, Gurudev, Guruvar: teacher

Maharaj: king

Maharani: queen

Putr: son

Putri: daughter

Rajan: king

Rajmata: queen mother

Samrat: emperor

Yuvraj: crown prince

Disparaging/Satirical/Playful Modes of Address:

Sootputr: son of a charioteer. The designation 'soot' also refers to stable-hands, storytellers, tailers, and ropers (Vasushen Karn)

Dharmraj: one with command over dharm (Yudhishthir)

Dharmavtar: incarnation of the god Dharm (Duryodhan)

General Glossary:

Arre: exclamation of exasperation

Aryavart: land/authority of AryansBasti: colony or collective habitation that shares characteristics of cohesiveness and sovereignty with a housing society, a township, or a slum

Dharm: ethical code, both an objective or shared differentiator of good/evil, right/wrong, appropriate/ inappropriate, and a subjective conceptualization of one's own 'ought'

Gotr: clan

Gurudakshina: literally, donation to guru. Euphemism for fees

Karmyogi: one who acts, consistently and diligently, in accordance with dharm and without reference to fear or favour

Kul: clan or centre (Gurukul = school; Kurukul = the Kuru clan)

Laddoo: sweets

Pattal: leaf platter

Pranam: salute by joining hands, sometimes accompanied with a bow

Sakhi: literally, friend. Krishn's sakhis are his lovers too, in both spiritual and physical senses

Sharad Purnima: harvest festival on a full moon night at the end of Ashvin, the lunar month covering September to October

Swayamvar: contest for the hand of a prospective bride

Varn: caste

Yajn: ritual, sacrifician fire – an offering and prayer to gods

Yudhshala: military seminary